THE ST. AUGUSTINE TRILOGY: BOOK ONE

Sliding Beneath the Surface

Doug Dillon

Old St. Augustine Publications

Altamonte Springs, Florida

Published by

Old St. Augustine Publications
Altamonte Springs, Florida
www.oldstaugustinepublications.com

www.dougdillon.com
or
www.oldstaugustinepublications.com

Library of Congress Control Number 2011905857
ISBN 978-0-9833684-1-0

Edition: August 2013

To all young people who find themselves in very confusing and difficult situations.

Contents

Prologue

St. Augustine, Florida
January 15

The thing is, I can't get what happened a couple of weeks ago out of my head no matter how hard I try. Sometimes when those memories flood my brain, I even start sweating, and my hands shake. Like this morning when I went to Carla's house so we could walk to the bus stop together. As soon as she opened the door, I had this flashback of how she looked on a day near the end of December—exhausted, dirty, pine needles in her hair, and blood all over her. Oh man, it gives me chills just saying those words. You see, we both came so close to …

Wait. Wait a minute. I'm moving too quickly here. Carla would say, "Jeff Golden, you're always getting ahead of yourself." She'd be right too, so let me back up here.

Look, it all began with a vivid nightmare I had for three nights in a row starting on Christmas Eve. I'm telling you, that nasty dream definitely freaked me out. After not sleeping well for three nights, my butt was really dragging. My head and even my eyes ached. It was December 27, a date that would have a lot of meaning for Carla and me, but we sure didn't know it at the time. On that morning, while I made myself some breakfast, mom left for work early and in a rush as usual. I'd been up since 3:00 a.m. drinking coffee after nightmare number three so I wouldn't have to go back to sleep. Did I tell mom about the dreams? No, no way. Why? What can I tell you? Let's just say my mom's focus hasn't included me for a very long time, so why waste the effort?

Anyway, I finished my breakfast, ignored the housework I was supposed to do and instead watched a James Bond marathon on TV. It kept my mind busy, you know, not thinking about that dumb ass dream. Well, at least not as much.

Somewhere in the middle of Goldfinger, Carla called, inviting me to lunch. I almost didn't go, knowing I wouldn't be very good company. In the end, she talked me into it. Being with Carla while she had some extra time over her winter vacation and shoveling down one of her grandma's great meals were too much to resist.

Oh, I forgot, you don't know Carla. Well, Carla Rodriguez is fifteen, like me, and we both go to St. Augustine High. Unlike me, she's one of the real academic types—Advanced Placement and all that stuff. She and her grandma keep pushing going to church with them, but I'm not religious. Even though we're so very different in more ways than I can count, Carla and I are … well … pretty close, I guess you might say. I'm not talking about romance exactly, but because of what happened back in late December, we, ah, are connected in ways I could never have imagined before that time.

How did I meet Carla? Ha! Maybe I'll tell you about it later. Kind of embarrassing, actually.

Soon after I arrived at her house for lunch, both she and Grandma figured out I wasn't doing very well. It didn't take a pair of geniuses to figure that out. I realized I must have looked and sounded like crap. Oh, I tried hard to appear alert and cheerful. So much for my ability to cover up how I'm feeling. I'm sure my jittery coffee nerves gave me away as much as anything else.

Right as I walked in the door, the questions started, but I refused to say anything at first. I mean, as I said before, I didn't even want to think about what had been going on with me, no less talk about it. I did eventually tell them though—after lunch. Carla has this way of opening me up like nobody else can. Even so, it took her a while.

When I finally explained the details of my wild, repeating night-mares, some of the same terror I felt at those times seeped back into my mind. You might think a stupid dream shouldn't scare a big guy like me, but size has nothing to do with fear. After I finished giving them all the gory details, except for how much those dreams really scared me, Carla and Grandma didn't say anything at first. Instead, they stared at each other for a few seconds. After Grandma nodded to her ever so slightly, Carla looked back at me and said, "Jeff, maybe we can get you some help. We have a friend, someone who understands, well, a lot about dreams and things like that. You should meet him and see what he can tell you."

What she meant by "things like that," I didn't know, but think-ing back, I was just too involved in my own thoughts to care. Oh, believe me, I eventually found out. After a half hour or so, those two ladies eventually did talk me into seeing this next door neighbor of theirs, a man named Lobo. Did I really want to go? No, but I was so tired, headachy, and still a little freaked out, I figured anything that might get me a night of good, undisturbed sleep was worth a try. Makes sense, right?

Tell you what. I had no idea how much I was letting myself in for. Really. But if I hadn't gone to see old Lobo … Wait, wait. There I go again. All of this is too complicated for me to explain in a few words.

Listen. What happened after Carla and I walked over to Lobo's place continued into that next morning of December 28. See why I can't spit this out in a few short sentences? Besides, there's so much more to all this than just the actual time involved. I mean, in less than twenty-four hours things went on that, when I look back on them, feel like they took days or even weeks.

I know, I know. What I've said to you so far probably sounds crazy, but hang in there with me, and I'll tell you everything I can remember.

PART ONE

The Awakening

1

Bad Dogs

The sign attached to the front of Mr. Lobo's big old aluminum gate in front of us on that unusually cold and cloudy Florida day said, "No trespassing! Beware of BAD DOGS!" Not a very welcoming entrance, right? *Time to go home*, I said to myself. Instead of acting on that thought, I studied the beat-up old mailbox behind Carla and wondered what the "R" stood for in the name, "R. Lobo."

Even though I had ridden past that warning sign a million times on my bike, for some reason on the afternoon of December 27, I had trouble taking my eyes off the words, "BAD DOGS." The more I looked at those big, bold letters, the more my recurring dream poked its way into my mind. I'm not afraid of dogs, and I've been known to ignore no trespassing signs once in a while, but for a few seconds there, I didn't want to go anywhere near that gate. At the time, I thought lack of sleep caused my reaction. How wrong I was.

The sandy driveway where Carla and I stood went under the gate and then curved back out of sight through a thick stand of bamboo—the skinny kind—about ten, twelve feet tall or so. I already knew the driveway ended on a tree covered peninsula that stuck out into Matanzas Bay. Since Carla lives next door, you can see that point of land from her back yard.

She stared at me with one eyebrow raised. With her, that could mean a lot of different things, but I figured this time she was definitely losing patience with my stalling.

"What?" I asked, trying hard to sound innocent.

"Jeffrey Golden," she replied with her hands on her hips, "are you going with me to see Lobo or not?"

When Carla uses my full name, I get the message that she's, well, less than happy. Before I could say anything, her Black Lab, Spock, barked and wagged his tail. The poor dog had been waiting to go for a nice long walk. I guess he thought the time had come.

I sucked in a big breath and let it out slowly. How, I wondered, can I possibly go share something so personal as a really bad dream with a perfect stranger who warns people away from his property with a sign about his vicious dogs? You can see why I hesitated, can't you? Behind us on Water Street, a tow truck pulling a racecar splashed across puddles left from rain earlier in the day.

"OK, OK, I'm ready," I finally replied to Carla's question. "If we're going to do this, then let's get on with it." Was I sure of that decision? No, but my throbbing head told me I had to do something.

"About time," Carla said. Flashing me one of her brilliant smiles, she pulled her key ring out of her coat pocket with its attached silver oval dangling beneath her fingers and selected one of the keys. In seconds, she had the gate unlocked and open far enough for us to enter the property. To my questioning look, she jangled her keys at me and said, "Lobo's like family."

"That's convenient."

"Um hmm," she replied while stuffing the all silver key ring and oval back into her pocket.

Silver. That girl loves the stuff. No, really. She's a silver freak if there ever was one. Right then, for example, she wore dangly silver earrings, several silver bracelets and a couple of silver rings. Against her light brown skin though, all that shiny metal looked good. Well, it always does, and so does she.

"What about the 'BAD DOGS?' " I pointed back at the sign after we walked through the gate and Carla had locked it again.

After giving me one of her *you worry too much* looks, she came over, reached up with an *I know something you don't* grin, and ruffled my hair with her fingers. "What's the matter Golden Boy, afraid of a few little puppies?"

God, how I hated that nickname in school. Kids started calling me Golden Boy when I was little because of my blond hair and my last name, Golden. When Carla says it though, somehow I don't really mind very much. Of course, she says it sort of like a compliment, so I really can't complain.

"Puppies?" I was sure she couldn't be describing Mr. Lobo's BAD DOGS.

"Stay close to me and you'll be OK." She said that as she flipped her long black hair out of her face and gave me a confident looking wink. "Besides, do you believe everything you read?"

"Of course not but—"

"Just leave those silly critters to me," she said as if she was bored with any possible danger. "I'll protect you." Carla likes to use the word, "critters," for some reason. "Where's Jeff the adventurer I used to know who would go anywhere?"

"Oh, so now you're the great warrior princess, huh?" I rubbed my left temple, trying to massage away that nasty headache without Carla seeing. Even though I really was more worried about talking to this Lobo guy than getting past the dogs, it was good to hear that the "critters" wouldn't be a problem.

With her relaxed attitude, I wondered if Carla's friend had his dogs tied up or maybe they weren't actually so *BAD* after all. As I thought about how many times I had ridden past that gate, or looked at Mr. Lobo's peninsula from Carla's back yard, I realized I had never actually seen any *critters* or heard any barking.

The driveway was still a little mushy in places from the rain, so

we had to watch where we stepped. My shoes sank into the soft-
ness, especially where tires had pushed lots of sand, dirt and leaves
into big, wet clumps. Before we walked very far, Carla unhooked
Spock's leash, but he stayed pretty close to her. Again, I wondered
about Mr. Lobo's dogs—if there really were any and if so, how
Spock got along with them. Spock. Oh yeah, that's quite a name for
a dog. No doubt about it. Carla calls him that because, like me, she's
wild about all those old Star Trek programs and movies.

Anyway, Carla's use of my old nickname, Golden Boy, reminded
me that the following week I had to start school. I say, "start school"
because after mom and I moved here right before Thanksgiving, I
talked her into letting me put off registering for a while. Actually
she agreed to let me begin classes after the first of the year if I did
all the housework up until then and promised to work hard in my
classes. That gave me over a month off school and the house all to
myself during the day while Mom got settled into her new job. Not
a bad deal, actually.

Why did we move to St. Augustine? Ohhh, it was, ah, mostly
because of financial trouble after … after my dad died. My grandfather's house here in the city had been vacant since his death a couple of years ago, so we just moved in. For Mom it was like starting
life over. Me? I hated the idea of moving away from Orlando and
my friends, you know? Besides, the thought of having to live in a
small town jammed with tons of tourists all the time didn't exactly
make my day. Yeah, we had tourists in Orlando, but at places like
Disney World, not right outside our neighborhood like it is here.

"So tell me about this Lobo guy," I asked while we followed the
winding driveway deep into the bamboo forest. What a dark little
jungle it looked like on that cloudy day, I swear. It even smelled like
it, or at least how I imagine a jungle would smell—wet and moldy.

Carla twisted her face like she wasn't sure how she wanted to
reply to my question about her friend. Finally, she said, "Lobo?
Well, he's a Native American and he ah … is a very … different *type*

of person, I guess you might say."

Her hesitation and emphasis on the word "type" made me wonder what she was hiding.

"Lobo is probably in his sixties or so. I'll warn you now, he can be very grumpy."

I would have never guessed by looking at the warning sign on his gate.

"To make a living, he does wood carvings. His work is quite beautiful really, and it's for sale in art galleries here in St. Augustine as well as in Savannah."

"So, he's an Indian. What tribe?"

"Jeff!" she said in her *I can't believe you're saying that* voice. Carla proceeded to give me some instruction on the proper use of words, and how Indians got that name—something every kid hears in elementary school. She only uses the term Native American and hates the word Indian. Anyway, all that time, I'm thinking, who cares if Columbus got it wrong and named the natives of America after where he thought he was, India, the Indies, or wherever?

"And as for Lobo's tribe," she said, responding to my question, "I have no idea. All he says is he no longer has one. I don't understand exactly what he means by that, but he won't say anything more."

At about that time, the driveway turned slightly to the right, and the bamboo ended. From there on, big old oak trees dripping Spanish Moss lined each side of the mushy road and merged on top, making the whole area in front of us look like a tunnel. Near the end of that tunnel, and the peninsula, I saw the back of a two-story house. It looked a lot like other old buildings in St. Augustine's Historic District where we live, only not very well maintained.

While looking at that place though, I had a strong urge to turn around and run like hell. I mean, it was this almost overpowering need to be anywhere else—sort of an instant flash of panic. Really strange. Never had anything like that happen before in my life.

Besides, there was no reason for such a strong, negative feeling like that to suddenly take hold of me. It didn't make any sense. All I was doing was looking at an old house. Just as quickly as the feeling exploded into my head, it evaporated, leaving me a little spooked, to say the least.

My mind seemed to be running away with itself. When I put that panicky feeling together with my weird obsession with the BAD DOGS sign, and my crazy dreams, I knew I had better get some rest, and soon. Little did I know that I wouldn't actually be sleeping until mid morning of the next day.

The first floor walls of Mr. R. Lobo's house might have been white at some time, but the two I could see looked more like a dirty grey color. Streaks of mold and stains dripped downward as if the place cried from lack of care. I don't think paint had ever touched the wooden upper story. A huge pile of firewood sat near the back door. To be perfectly honest, the condition of the place reminded me of where I live.

Carla stopped before we actually passed the last of the bamboo, pointed at the house and said, "There's where we're going. Isn't it gorgeous?"

"Gorgeous? You've gotta be kidding." I had to laugh, but I should have known better. Me and my big mouth. The look on Carla's face told me I was in for it.

"Haven't any of my explanations about the architecture in this city gotten through to you?" I knew she didn't really want me to answer her question. Instead, it sounded like I was in for one more of her St. Augustine lectures. You see, that girl loves history, St. Augustine and archaeology—bad combination, because she can go on and on, forever. Her parents had been archaeology professors so I guess she comes by it naturally.

"You've got to look beyond the dirt, grime, and needed repairs," she said in a very exasperated voice. "That house is one of the oldest still standing in St. Augustine. Parts of the bottom floor date from the first Spanish period, probably 1745 or so. Underneath the messy looking plaster are thick blocks of coquina. The top floor was added during the short time the English controlled Florida."

Oh, here we go, I said to myself. She loves the history of the city so much she even likes to see tourists flood our town—America's oldest city and all, founded in 1565, etc., etc. "Yeah," I told her once, laughing, "what do they do, your tourists? They come here and spend good money on things like those stupid ghost tours we have all over the place." She got real quiet after that so I figured I had gone too far.

Anyway, with my head aching the way it was, I had no patience to listen to another one of her history lessons right at that moment. I had to do something. Even though we'd only known each other about a month, experience had taught me to try and short-circuit her train of thought at times like those.

"The walls are made of coquina, huh?" I said, doing my best to grab hold of the conversation and divert it at least in a direction of something interesting. "What is it anyway? A coral rock of some kind?"

Carla rolled her eyes as if every six-year-old should know the answer, and said, "It's like limestone, in a way, made up mostly of small seashells compressed over time. The Spanish used to mine it over on Anastasia Island and bring it here to the mainland by boat so they could build the Castillo." She pointed to our right in the direction of the old Spanish fort not far from our neighborhood. While she spoke, I gave Mr. Lobo's property a quick scan.

Just beyond the house and to the left about fifty feet, sat a small-er, one-story wooden building—unpainted. It had large windows across the front, right next to a door. Parked between the house and the smaller building, a battered old pickup truck seemed to stand guard over the whole area. From that distance, I couldn't tell where the red color left off and the rust began.

Beyond the trees, buildings, and truck, a small dock jutted out towards grass covered islands in the dull gray water of Matanzas Bay. Next to the dock sat a blue canoe, bottom up, resting on one side. As I looked at the bay, just for a second, it turned hazy. Then it wasn't. Weird. I blinked my eyes several times, but then everything looked normal. Once more, that need to turn and run away slid through my mind and quickly out again. "By boat?" I asked, taking a step forward. Instead of thinking about my warped vision and that strange feeling, I chose to refocus on Spanish coquina transportation.

Before Carla could answer, a deep growl came from somewhere to our left. In seconds, the growl built into vicious, rapid barking, and it was coming our way. You know how a big dog sounds when he's angry and doesn't like you messing with his territory? That was exactly what I heard.

Oh crap! My stomach did a flip-flop as the words BAD DOGS flashed into my mind. Once more, I felt a panicky urge to run away but with good reason this time.

Carla stared at me with a startled and scared look. I barely had enough time to wonder what happened to her promise of, "Oh, leave those silly critters to me," when the sound of other dogs back in the bamboo on our right joined the original dog noises to our left in an explosion of snarling, growling, and yapping.

I couldn't see them yet, but the sounds were rapidly growing louder. I knew they would be on us any second.

2

Lobo

Automatically balling up my fists, I braced for the attack. Karate kicks a friend taught me flashed through my mind as that dog noise rang in my ears. Glancing down at Spock, I reminded myself he was good-sized, and I hoped he might jump in to help us.

Spock? In that split second as I looked at him, I realized something was not quite what it was supposed to be, but I didn't know what. Then it hit me. Old Spock was doing nothing but standing there calmly at Carla's feet, as if nothing was happening. Obviously, the possibility of being ripped apart didn't concern him at all.

Startled, I looked at Carla and saw her trying to stifle a giggle as she pointed towards the edge of the bamboo forest. Amazed at how she could find anything funny about our situation, I frantically tried to find what she wanted me to see. "Son of a ..." I really wanted to add the word "bitch" in there, but I stopped myself even though I felt very justified. You see, Carla doesn't like what she calls "foul language," and I had been really trying hard to change my ways in that area of my life. Actually, even now as I'm talking to you, I'm watching what I say, believe it or not, sort of practicing. What did I find that stimulated such a reaction? A huge speaker hidden in the branches of a large oak tree.

When I looked back at Carla, she chuckled and pointed out a tall platform back in the bamboo. Uh huh, another stupid speaker.

I had no idea what type of sensor I had activated, nor did I care.

After the snarling, growling, and yapping dog sounds stopped completely a few seconds later, she burst into laughter. I usually love it when she laughs, deep and rich sounding, but not at that moment. I mean, I couldn't believe she had tricked me. The headache I had been fighting the past couple of days throbbed even more. I hadn't told Carla about it. "Thanks a lot," I shouted at her. I was really embarrassed she had seen me so scared for no good reason.

"No, no, no." She wagged her finger at me with a more or less serious face. Her almond shaped eyes were wide with determination, even as she continued trying to stifle another burst of laughter. "Don't you go venting that famous Jeffrey anger on this girl. Look, I'm sorry, really I am. I was just about to warn you when you walked ahead of me and triggered the system before I could say anything. With what's going on inside your head today, you didn't need a scare like that."

"Oh," I said. As quickly as it arrived, my hot temper drained away. No matter what, I couldn't stay mad at Carla for long. "Apology accepted, but if you're so sorry, how come you're still laughing?"

"I'm trying hard not to, but I wish you could have seen your face when the dogs sounds started." Then she lost it, and laughed her way through her next sentence so hard she could barely say the words. "Really … for a white boy … I swear … you got … ten shades lighter."

With a final laugh, Carla coughed, caught her breath, and said, "That alarm system is Lobo's way of scaring off unwanted visitors without actually having to use real dogs. So, are you finally ready to meet him?"

"Anything to get away from you letting me get attacked by wild dogs," I said, trying to sound serious, even though I realized I probably had looked pretty silly.

"Oh poor baby," Carla said with one of her sly, sexy smiles.

God she looks so good when she smiles. I mean she looks good all the time, but her smiles are something else, like a flash of warm sunshine. Ruining the moment, the screech of a power saw sliced the air for a short time and stopped. It sounded like it came from the small, unpainted building. I remembered hearing that saw noise from Carla's back yard.

"He's in his workshop," she said. "Not good. He doesn't like being interrupted when he's concentrating on his carvings. He might even be a little grumpier than usual, so try not to be offended."

"Great, can't wait." I groaned, massaging my left temple with the tips of my fingers when Carla turned away. "Sounds like so much freakin' fun." The idea of facing some bad tempered old man was not really how I wanted to end my day, you know? Bad dream or no bad dream. By then though, we were approaching Mr. Lobo's beat-up truck. To the left of the truck, light shown between the blinds of the two large windows in the workshop, but I couldn't really see anything inside.

"Being sarcastic isn't going to make things any better," Carla said. "We're not here to have fun, we're here to get you some help, OK?" She sounded like a mother taking her child to see the doctor for the first time.

"Yes, momma," I kidded, using a squeaky child's voice, "I promise I'll be good."

Carla rolled her eyes, shook her head and punched me in the arm. "You are absolutely hopeless sometimes." When I say punch, I mean *punch*! For a small person, she packs a wallop.

As we walked past Lobo's battered truck, I stopped, stuck a finger in one of its many rusty holes and felt the rough, crumbling metal give way when I pressed down. It didn't seem possible something so old could possibly run. Inside, I saw pure mess. There was stuff everywhere—Styrofoam cups, bags from fast food places, stained rags, notebooks, what looked like balled up clothes, and all kinds of tools.

"Come on," Carla called. She and Spock were already standing in front of the workshop door.

"Well, at least he's not a neat freak." I whispered those words, jerking a thumb back towards the truck as I joined her at the door. "Anybody that messy can't be all bad."

"Wonderful," she whispered back, smiling and putting her hand on the doorknob. "You both have something in common. Isn't that nice?"

Ignoring her question and hint of sarcasm, I tried looking through the partially opened blinds. All I could see were long, thin slices of equipment, wood, carvings and someone moving around.

Again, the high-pitched whine of an electric saw shattered the silence making poor Spock tremble. Carla gave him a hand signal to stay where he was, and then waved for me to follow as she entered the workshop. Once we stepped inside, that piercing noise blasted us full in the face causing us to cover our ears. With each step, wood shavings on the concrete floor crunched beneath my feet. The air smelled strongly of sawdust Mr. R. Lobo was creating. He stood opposite the front door close to the building's back wall, bent over. He had his back to us, his bare, muscular arms moving forward ever so slightly. Even so, I could tell the guy was big, way bigger than me, and I'm close to six feet tall.

A workbench covered with tools sat against the wall to our right. Stacked up on the floor to our left were wood blocks and tree trunk sections of varying sizes. A large table in front of all those dead tree parts held carvings of people and animals. One of them, a large head of a realistic looking eagle, stared at me from its tree trunk base. Carla's friend had talent all right.

The guy wore a dark blue, sleeveless shirt and faded black jeans. Both his belt and badly scuffed work boots looked like they might have been brown at one point in time. A thin strip of leather kept his long steel grey hair pulled together at the base of his neck, creating a thick strand that ran down between his shoulders.

When I took another crunching step, he straightened, flipped a switch on the table saw in front of him, and pulled a rag out of his back jeans pocket to wipe his hands. There was no way he could have heard that one footstep, but it sure seemed like it. A wonderful silence slowly filled the workshop as the saw motor ground to a halt.

"Lobo," Carla said before the man could turn around, "this is my friend Jeff Golden and he—"

"You know better than that!" The man scolded. What a voice. A deep one, like a big old Harley cranking up. While using the rag to wipe sawdust off his hands and arms, he turned around and faced us. "Nobody comes here unless they're invited by me personally, especially this boy who has problems buzzing around him like angry yellow jackets."

Angry yellow jackets? The guy's attitude reminded me of a crappy teacher I had last year. Hated the man. Not a good beginning.

Lobo didn't have a big belly like a lot of older guys. A broad chest matched his big shoulders, but the man's face is what really made me stare. It looked like the front of a ship, as if it could cut through water. A large thin nose stuck out above a small mouth with full lips that puckered just a little. From those lips on each side, a permanent frown sliced down to a sharp chin. Other deep lines across the rest of his face and neck showed the man did have some age on him, like Carla said.

His eyes though, are what really caught my attention. Deep set under thick, bushy brows the color of his hair, the pupils looked completely black. Even so, they glittered as if a tiny powerful light inside each one kept trying to get out. I swear, when he looked at me, I thought for a second I was seeing twin lasers rapidly firing in my direction. Talk about weird.

Carla walked over to him, placed her hands on her hips and slowly raised her head so that Mr. Lobo couldn't help but look at her. I tell you what, all five foot four inches of Miss Carla Rodriguez was poised like a little snake ready to strike. I wanted to smile, knowing Lobo was in for it, but I didn't. The guy deserved it.

"You Lobo are my friend," she said in a level but firm voice. "Jeff is also my friend. I help my friends and I expect them to do the same for each other and me. You worked with me when I had a special problem at my house and now Jeff needs some help. Maybe you can even get rid of those yellow jackets you mentioned for him. Now how about it?"

For at least ten seconds, Carla and Lobo stood staring at each other before the man shifted his gaze back in my direction. This time, he not only looked directly into my eyes, he also looked all around me—like he was scanning the air or something. Really strange. Then he threw the rag in his hands onto the table saw behind him causing a little soft sounding eruption of sawdust.

"Take him up to the house," he finally said, still staring down at Carla. "Pull some drinks out of the fridge for us when you get there. I'll clean up and be with you shortly, but we do this on my terms, got it?"

"Of course," Carla agreed with the sweet little smile she gives people when she gets her way. Without waiting for any more discussion, she grabbed me by the arm, and in no time, we were on the way to Lobo's house. I didn't say a word until we were outside.

3

Weapons and Poltergeists

You're something else," I said to Carla as we neared Lobo's house. "I can't believe how quickly you turned that old guy around."

She just shrugged her shoulders and said, "A girl's got to do what a girl's got to do. Besides, underneath all that big bad gruffness, he's really pretty soft."

"Uh huh, right." Carla sometimes tends to make excuses for people, as you can see. "The problem is he doesn't like me."

Carla snorted. "Lobo rarely shows he likes anybody. Out there," she said, changing the subject, and pointing at the dock about fifty feet from where we stood, "is where I go fishing when I come here to—"

Before she could finish her sentence, a huge flapping of wings made us both look back towards the workshop. I ducked as a big crow swooped down and dove at my head. The stupid bird came so close I felt air fanning down from its wings. Flying past us, it landed on the balcony over Lobo's front porch facing the bay.

"Caaa," the thing said as it balanced somehow on a single leg. He didn't seem to have two. Yeah, I know. Animals can't say anything, but I felt like that crazy bird had said, "No Trespassing."

"Meet Edgar." Carla laughed. "He's Lobo's one and only pet." The crow stared at me with its little black eyes. The thing looked like it was defending the house or something.

"Yeah, well, Edgar was aiming for my head."

"I noticed. Sorry, but he's about as hospitable to new people at first as Lobo is."

"No kidding."

"He named him after Edgar Allen Poe," she said, changing the subject.

"So that's a raven and not a crow?" I asked, trying to show Carla I at least knew about "The Raven." That was the only one of Poe's writings I had read.

"No, he's a crow. Lobo found him late one night on his porch after a bad storm, half-dead. Poor bird lost a leg that night."

Edgar moved his head side-to-side. I figured he was getting a good look at me with each of his dark eyes in order to plan a more accurate attack.

"So you fish, huh?" I asked, doing my best to ignore Edgar. "I never knew that."

"Catch 'em, and release 'em." She flashed one of her great smiles as we stepped onto Lobo's wood porch under Edgar's watchful gaze. "What about you?"

"What, me fish? Nah, I'm a city kid all the way through."

"Well, Golden Boy, I'll have to teach you one of these days."

In front of us, most of Mr. Lobo's front door looked a lot like a church window. An oval stained glass picture, taking up about half the space, showed a wolf on a cliff at night, howling under a full moon with the Orion constellation in the background. Surrounding that was a strip of individual mirrors and around those, another strip of clear glass. An oval inside an oval, inside an oval.

"Nice door." I caught a glimpse of our multiple reflections in the mirrored pieces. There was small, slender Carla in her short, black leather coat and big old chunky me in my orange and blue Florida Gator jacket. My shaggy blond mop on a square head versus Carla's perfect oval face peeking out from long, shiny black hair.

Another oval to fit with the stained glass door.

It seemed like I could see Carla's light brown eyes and my blue ones in those mirrors, but it was probably more my imagination. Those reflections weren't really big enough to show such detail unless maybe you got up real close. The only thing similar about us, really, was that we both wore the same washed out color of blue jeans. The two of us. What a contrast. Not as much of a contrast though, as watching Carla standing toe-to-toe with big old Lobo.

"That glass door panel is not only nice," Carla corrected "it's an original Tiffany. Very valuable."

"A what?" *Valuable? In that old house?*

"A Tiffany. Stained glass designed by Louis Comfort Tiffany from New York sometime near the end of the nineteenth century or the beginning of the twentieth. It was his company that did all the stained glass in both the old Ponce de Leon and Alcazar Hotels here in town. Lobo says a rich friend gave it to him as well as three Tiffany stained glass lamps in his house."

"It must be nice to have rich friends." At times like that, Carla's understanding of history and architecture really overwhelms me. "Why would your friend want a wolf on his front door?" I asked, pointing at it, glad I could at least say something, if only to ask a question.

"You just said it. His name," she replied as if I should understand. I must have given her one of my blank stares. "Lobo means wolf in Spanish." She followed this explanation by another sentence, also in Spanish.

"Which means?" I asked, only recognizing a few of the words. Yes, I knew what the word lobo meant wolf, but I hadn't made the connection, nor did I know what else she had said to me.

"I told you to be more observant of the world around you and you'll learn a lot." With a wink and a grin, she tapped the wolf on the stained glass door with a fingernail.

"Showoff," I said, looking through the clear outer oval of the door into the house. Couldn't really see much in there except an archway to the left and a dark hall in line with the door. On the other side of that archway, it looked like a living room in there.

As if I hadn't spoken at all, Carla grabbed my arm, opened the door, and pulled me into the house. "When I teach you to fish, I'm also going to give you some Spanish lessons." That's what you get for having a friend who's lived in Mexico. And who's father was Puerto Rican.

Being with her some more sounded great, but not the lessons part. "What would I ever do without your guidance?" I asked as she shut the door once Spock joined us inside.

"Oh Lord, you might fall apart into little tiny pieces," she teased.

The house smelled musty. Large hand-cut beams and wood planks made up the ceiling. The floor? Nothing but smooth, but old looking, cement. No carpets or rugs anywhere. The dark hall I had seen before went past stairs leading to the second floor and ran straight to the back of the house with rooms on each side. Through the archway on the left, I could see furniture, including a couple of stained glass lamps like Carla said. Instead of going in there, we took a quick right turn into a tiny kitchen. There we raided the fridge, grabbed some drinks, and then walked across the hall into the room with the furniture.

When we entered, Carla flipped a switch turning on the two stained glass lamps I had seen before, and one other—all old-fashioned things, like you would see in a museum or something. Expensive, maybe, but not very impressive. To our left, a picture window showed a nice view of Matanzas Bay.

In front of the picture window sat a small dining room table—dark wood of some kind. Over it, hung one of the stained glass lamps. On the floor to the right of the window, a large alligator curled around itself—one of Lobo's realistic carvings, I figured. The thing looked like it might whip its tail around at any minute, smashing anything in its way.

The rest of that room though, made me think of museums again, and even libraries, places like that. It was clean too, not like the man's truck and workshop. Except for a huge fireplace made out of bare, grey coquina opposite the arched doorway, dark wood paneling covered the walls. On those walls were book and display cases painted white. The three display cases surrounded the unlighted fireplace, a circular one above it and two long rectangular ones on each side.

"How cool," I said, walking over to the case to the left of the fireplace. It contained old weapons. I mean there were old-time revolvers, muskets, rifles, spears, knives, bayonets and even bullets. "How cool," I kept saying until I realized what an idiot I must sound like. But when I touched the case, an icy chill ran its way up my spine and my head started throbbing even more. I jerked my hand away as if I the case had burned me. *What the hell?*

"Boys and their toys," Carla called from somewhere behind me as if she hadn't seen what happened. "And you keep saying you could care less about history." I heard her pop the top of her Coke can.

"Uh, well, there's ... some fascinating stuff here all right." As I stepped back from the case and turned around, my headache eased a little.

"There you go, Jeff. You and Lobo really do share some interests."

"Yeah, sure," I replied vaguely, trying to shake off the effect of that spike in my headache and those chills in order to focus on what Carla had said to me. "With your buddy's attitude, I'm sure we'll end up the best of friends."

Carla just laughed. Seated on the light brown leather couch facing the fireplace, she still wore her coat. The house was a little chilly, but tolerable, so I took my jacket off and flipped it over my shoulder. Cold doesn't bother me as much as it does Carla. I wondered if Mr. Lobo would light the fire for her when he arrived.

In front of where Carla sat, stood a low, rectangular, wood coffee table, almost the same color as the couch. Dead center on its high gloss top rested a white ball about six inches across set on a small, cup-shaped holder. It, the ball, had holes and designs carved all over its surface. The thing looked familiar, but I didn't bother trying to figure out where I'd seen one like it before.

Facing each other on opposite sides of the coffee table were two matching black leather recliners . On the floor near Carla's feet, Spock had somehow wedged himself between the couch and the coffee table. Carla, I noticed, had placed her friend's bottle of water on the coffee table in front of the recliner to her left.

"Carla," I asked, after opening my own Coke and taking a swallow. "Back there in the workshop you reminded Lobo that he helped you with a problem once. What kind of problem?"

"Oh, that," she answered and looked down at her drink. "Let's talk about it later," she suggested.

"Aw, come on," I pushed. "Your pal's not here yet. We have time."

Closing her eyes for a few seconds and then nodding, Carla began her story. "Well, it was soon after my parents died a couple of years ago. That's when I started living with Grandma full time. We both got freaked out when ... well, things started happening." Her eyes kept darting back and forth between her Coke and me. I had never seen Carla that uncertain about what to say.

"Things started happening like what?" I prompted.

"Well ... objects ... moved around without me or Grandma touching them. Not only that, but we'd get up in the morning and find furniture all over the house had shifted out of place. Then books, dishes, all kinds of things, started crashing to the floor, sometimes even flying through the air." While she talked, Carla hugged herself, like she was getting colder. "We could even sit there and watch that all happen. It was really scary."

"So, somebody was playing tricks on you, right?" This wasn't sounding like the Carla I knew.

She looked up at me with this dead serious expression. "No, no tricks. Some people said we were haunted. They called it poltergeists. That's German for 'noisy ghosts.' "

"Yeah, OK, but you don't mean like on those old poltergeist movies on TV do you? A family fighting evil spirits and things like that?"

"You're talking about Hollywood fiction." She spoke in a firm, but quiet voice. "What happened to us was very real. It got so bad my grandma even thought about having a priest come in and bless the house."

"Really?" I had seen that done on TV shows for houses being haunted and all, but I didn't think good old logical, history-loving Carla could accept such a thing. "So did you? Have the priest come in?"

"No, somehow, Lobo showed up at our place before that could happen. The three of us talked for the longest time."

"So what did he say?"

"To make a really long story short, he told us we weren't being haunted. Instead, he said all of those things moved because of me."

"You? No way. How could that be?"

"He said everybody and everything are ... connected in ways you really can't see. For some people in the world, like me, that connection is so strong at certain times in their lives they can ... well, make things move sort of like remote control."

"Come on Carla," I said, "you didn't believe him did you?" Her story had gotten a little too weird for me. Wouldn't you have thought the same thing? Anyway, after what she said, I started getting nervous. At that moment, talking to this Lobo guy about my dream didn't seem like such a good idea, and my head responded by again aching a little more.

"No, I didn't believe him at first," she replied. "To me, his words made no sense. He went on to explain though, that when some teenagers with this ability get upset about something, they can move things without touching them at times and not really understanding what's going on. It also has to do with hormones and certain types of energy levels, he said. In my case, he told me I had a lot of anger and sorrow about my parents' death all bottled up inside. My moving things was just my mind and spirit's way to, well, let those feelings out in the last place I saw my parents."

At that point, I absolutely didn't know what to say. Instead, I chugged a couple of cold swallows of Coke. As Carla continued talking, she looked like she was going to cry. Her eyes glistened and when she spoke again, her voice sounded soft and small. Quite a contrast to her usual way of expressing herself.

"When Lobo talked about the feelings I had for my parents, I, well … burst into tears. He had it right. I was super angry and sad because of losing them, but I needed to stay strong for my grandma. You know, keep my feelings to myself and all. I had lost a mother and a father, but she had also lost a daughter and a son-in-law she loved a lot."

After saying all that, Carla took a deep breath, wiped her eyes with her fingers and said in a stronger voice, "My crying made me feel better. Lobo told us my inner healing had already begun and things should start getting back to normal if grandma would talk to me more about my feelings."

"So, did they? Get back to normal?"

"Yup," she replied with a little smile, "but slowly. After Lobo's visit, I started coming over here more often. We fished and talked a lot. He worked with me on controlling my ability to move things without touching them. Finally, after about a month or so, no more weird happenings in Grandma's house."

Before I could say anything, I heard heavy footsteps on the porch that made us both turn and look towards the hallway. I could see Lobo approaching through all that clear and stained glass in his front door.

Quickly, Carla looked back at me and said, "Look, I got you in here, but now it's up to you to work with the man. From here on, you're pretty much on your own."

As I watched the front door open, I started feeling like I had just stepped into some very deep water.

4

Rules

When Mr. Lobo entered the room, his weird-looking eyes instantly locked with mine.

Without shifting that laser-like gaze, he lumbered over to the recliner opposite me on the other side of the coffee table and sat down. Even when he picked up the bottle of water Carla left for him, he kept up that intense stare. Man, I felt like a germ under a powerful microscope—a germ still fighting a headache.

No one spoke, and the silence around us seemed to get heavier somehow, thick like clear syrup or something. I tried not squirming in my chair, but it was hard. I mean all that silence got really uncomfortable, you know? Instead of looking at Carla's friend directly, I stared at the Tiffany floor lamp next to his chair. It's glass bowl pointing downward showed little green leaves against an light orange background. What can I say, looking at the thing kept my mind busy.

And another thing. It wasn't freezing in the house, but it sure wasn't warm—no heating going on that I could tell. Carla had her coat on and I wore a heavy long-sleeved shirt, but old Lobo sat there in that same sleeveless shirt he wore in his workshop. The guy seemed not to notice the room's coldness at all.

The snapping sound when he opened his bottled water broke the spell, but only when the man chugged a couple of deep swallows did he look away. What a relief not to have those eyes slicing through me for even a short time. In seconds though, he was staring at me again, hard as ever. Still no one spoke. At that point, I figured if nobody else was going to say something, I would—anything, to get things moving. Yeah, I wanted the guy's help but sitting there facing him in complete silence, especially with Carla watching, wasn't working for me. "Ah, Mr. Lobo," I did my best to smile, "Carla thinks that maybe you can—"

"Save it" His deep voice filled the room. "First rule, don't call me Mr. The name's Lobo, nothing more."

"Uh, OK." I tried to look and sound as relaxed as possible. Actually, I was starting to get irritated.

"Rule number two, *Mr.* Golden," he lectured, like I thought he might. "If you want my help, you do things my way. Got that?"

When he said, Mr. Golden, with the emphasis on the word "mister," I could feel the tension building in the pit of my stomach—the edge of anger. The man didn't want me to call him mister, but he was saying it to me just to be sarcastic. I knew, because something like that had happened to me before. You see, I had this woman teacher once who used to do the same kind of thing, saying *"Mister"* all the time to the guys and *"Miss"* to the girls. On the surface, it sounded respectful, but the *way* she said those words made people want to smack her. So, there was Lobo doing the same thing, acting the dictator and all. I felt like I was back in school, but instead of saying anything to the old guy, I stole a quick glance at Carla.

She shook her head ever so slightly, warning me to keep my cool. Then she winked and gave me a nice little encouraging smile. That melted at least a little of the resentment I felt.

Before I looked back at Lobo, I took a long, deliberate swallow of Coke instead of responding to him right away. OK, I tried not to show that remaining resentment, anger, or whatever you want to call it, but I also wanted him to know he couldn't intimidate me.

"Yeah, I got it," I nodded. *You old fart!* At least I wasn't going to let him control my thoughts, right?

Lobo took a sip of water and then studied the air all around me like he did when I first saw him. What he was doing, I had no idea.

"Jeff Golden!" He spit my name out as if he was getting rid of a bad taste in his mouth. "Rule number three!" he barked like a drill sergeant. "If you want help from me, stop feeling sorry for yourself so much and worrying things to death. Instead, pay attention. If you paid more attention to your life, you wouldn't end up angry all the time and thinking the whole world is against you."

Right after he said all that, I started feeling cold, like I wanted to put my jacket on or something. I tried to be angry about how aggressive and mean-spirited he sounded, but I think I was too surprised by my body's reaction to what he apparently knew about me. It was really weird, you know? I mean, other people in my past had told me the same thing, but they knew me pretty well and old Lobo didn't. On top of all that, the man had said what he did in front of Carla. Before I could sort out my thoughts and feelings any further, Lobo jumped on me again.

"Listen up, young man. If you had been paying attention the right way back in Orlando, you wouldn't have made yourself so miserable. 'Poor me,' you said deep inside your mind over and over again. 'My teachers are unfair,' you told yourself. 'Lots of kids don't like me because I'm pretty smart and I have a near photographic memory,' you wailed inwardly. Then down deep, you whimpered, 'Woe is me. I spent most of my life around adults and don't really know how to relate to most teenagers.' You griped that your mom didn't really care about you. You continually moaned and groaned about not having the nice life style you used to have before your parents went bankrupt. Worst of all, you convinced yourself you were the cause of your father's suicide. None of that has changed, has it?"

I couldn't reply. No words came to mind. My stomach twisted and did flip-flops. My head pounded even more than before. I tried to think of ways Lobo could have gotten all of that information about me. Even Carla didn't know those things, especially about my dad's suicide. All I could do was stare at the man with what I'm sure must have been the most idiotic blank look in the world.

"Lobo, come on," Carla pleaded, "you're going way too far."

"The answer is obvious." Lobo ignored Carla and continued to stare at me. "You're still sitting on that same little pity potty you've been on for a long time now. It's always somebody else's fault, isn't it, huh? Instead of working on your problems, you fight them in silly ways. You even gave your teachers grief because they pushed you to do better and you thought you were being picked on."

"Lobo! Stop it! What's the matter with you?" Carla sprang to her feet, and as she did, Spock also jumped up, letting loose a huge bark. I had never heard Carla shout at anybody before and it really startled me.

"Remember rule number two?" Lobo growled, looking first at me and then at Carla. "It goes for both of you. Do things my way or leave. Your choice."

"Fine!" Carla yelled back at him. "Jeff, I'm so sorry. I had no idea this would happen. Come on, let's go." She had embarrassment and hurt written all over her face.

I tried to collect my swirling, confused thoughts. Too much had happened too quickly. At that point, part of me wanted to tell Lobo where he could stick his damned rules and then run out of there with Carla as fast as possible. I was embarrassed, scared and angry, but I had agreed to do things his way if I wanted help with my dream. Sleeplessness and the dread of that nightmare coming back even one more time finally overcame my reactions to the man's terrible, controlling ways.

"Uh, well ... that's OK, really," I whispered. Yeah, part of me wanted to shove Lobo's water bottle down his throat, but a bigger, more exhausted and fearful part of me sensed the guy might really be able to help. With a look of absolute surprise, Carla slowly sat back down, looking at me as if I had lost my mind. I have to admit that I even startled myself.

"Well, well, well," Lobo said in his rumbling voice. "You have some potential for self control after all."

"Just get on with it." I tried sounding tough, as if I could care less. Besides, I didn't need his empty compliment. Yeah, some of the anger seeped out even though I tried not to give in to it.

"Oh, I'll get on with it all right." Lobo's eyes blazed even more brightly than before.

Crap. Not the thing to say. "Sorry," I replied, trying not to get things even more stirred up. "That sort of slipped out." I knew how to play the "keep-the-adult-happy" game until I got what I wanted.

"Uh huh," Lobo replied in a less intense voice but with an even deeper frown than usual. "Happened all the time back in Orlando, didn't it? Exactly as you conducted yourself with me seconds ago, you gave a smart mouth to your teachers and other adults to try and keep them off your back. If that didn't work, you played word games and manipulated as many of them as you could until you got to do things your way.

"With your friends, you covered up your intelligence, used the worst language you could think of, drank beer and got into trouble to show how cool you are. Oh, you ended up with friends all right but what kind were they, huh? I'll tell you what kind—the dropouts, the deadheads, and the juvenile detention crowd, that's who. Have I got it right so far?"

I didn't say a word. Instead, I shrugged and looked down at the white carved ball on the coffee table. Anything was better than looking into those flashing eyes. What he had said was too impossibly close to the truth to deny, but I had no intention of agreeing with him.

Lobo shook his head, downed the rest of his water and then stabbed a big, old finger at me. "As far as your parents are concerned, you try to wipe them out of your mind most of the time, don't you? It's easier that way isn't it? If you don't think, you don't have to feel. Well, I'll tell you one thing, that fight between you and your father had nothing to do with his death. He planned on killing himself long before you argued with him."

Man, I'm telling you, I felt like I was drowning in all of Lobo's words. The guy somehow knew my history and had gotten deep inside my head where nobody else was supposed to be. As scary as all that felt, what he said about my dad's death ... well ... it choked me up a little. Talk about embarrassing. I hadn't been teary-eyed since my dad died a couple of years before. As much as I hated what gambling did to him, his death hit me like a runaway car.

There was absolutely no way Lobo could have found out about that problem between my dad and me, and nobody in this world could have known what Dad was planning. As logical as that seemed, when Lobo said what he did, this strange wave of relief swept through me. I really did blame myself for my dad's death, but I never told anybody.

"I'm going for more water." Lobo abruptly got up from his chair and left the room, his voice less harsh than it had been. His absence reminded me of how it feels when a sudden severe thunderstorm finally goes away.

5

28

With her friend gone, Carla came over to where I sat, squatted next to my chair and put her hand on my arm. "I guess this wasn't a very good idea," she said softly. "Lobo can be rough, but I've never seen him like this before. Sure you don't want to get out of here?"

"You warned me about him." I chugged some Coke, blinking my watery eyes rapidly. The last thing I needed was for Carla to see how deeply Lobo had gotten to me.

"What Lobo said to you about your dad, it—"

"Yeah, well ... my dad ... my dad did kill himself like Lobo said. He deliberately drove his car into an overpass on I-4 near Orlando." I thought it would be hard to say those words, but for whatever reason they just tumbled out of my mouth and I kept on going. Instead of keeping eye contact with Carla while I continued speaking, I kept scanning the Tiffany lamp sitting on an end table next to the couch on my left. I didn't want to look into Carla's eyes when I explained everything. Old fashioned or not, that lamp seemed a little prettier the more I looked at it. With an upside-down bowl made up of light blue pieces of glass, it looked a little like flowing water. At the edge of the bowl, dragonflies with yellow bodies and blue-green wings pointed their heads downward. Bright blue eyes seemed to stare all around searching for a way out of the room. Sort of like how I felt, in a way.

"That argument Lobo talked about? It was all over $20 I caught my father stealing out of my dresser. You see, Dad … well … he pretty much wiped out our family finances because of his gambling addiction. He always needed money. Even though he left a note apologizing for what he was going to do because of being in so much debt, I blamed myself for his death because of that fight we had. Guess I still do to some degree. That incident in my room was the last time I saw him alive."

Carla was silent for a few seconds and then said, "I am so sorry. I had no idea."

"No … of course not. It's not something I talk about." My mind kept going back to Lobo's knowledge about so much of my past. "How did he do that, pick up on so much information about me?" Not giving Carla time to answer, I fired another question at her. "And how could he possibly know what my dad was planning?"

Looking uncomfortable, Carla shrugged her shoulders. "Ah, well, you see," she began, but then hesitated.

A split second later, Lobo appeared in the arched doorway without making a sound. In his hand was a fresh bottle of water. "How I know what I know isn't important right now."

I wondered if the man heard what I said, or had possibly tuned in to my thoughts. My head still ached, but I somehow felt more relaxed than I had in a long time. Carla looked up at me, smiled, rubbed my arm for a few seconds and went back to her seat on the couch. I was sorry to see her go.

"So tell me about this dream," Lobo said to me in his rumbling voice as he sat back down in his chair.

"Dream?" Neither Carla nor I had mentioned my dream yet. If anybody else had brought me there besides Carla, I would have sworn that person had already talked to Lobo about my problem.

"Am I not speaking clearly enough for you?" The man replied with this sour look on his face. "Yes, your dream."

"Uh … OK. My dream. Well, for the past three nights I've been waking up with a horrible pain in my chest like something has stuck me hard while I'm sleeping. When I sit up and look down, my bed is glowing and there's something long and pointy coming up out of the mattress trying to get me. Blood is everywhere, all over my chest, my stomach, my sheets and on the pointy thing. It's all so real, like it's actually happening. Then when I jump out of bed and turn the ceiling light on, it all goes away, but my chest still hurts. I still feel like I've just been stabbed. I'm telling you, it scares the crap out of me." I hadn't planned on saying that last part. It just popped out.

Lobo grunted and looked all around me in his weird way, his unblinking gaze all fiery.

Everybody blinks, right? Not him. I'm telling you, it felt really odd to be talking to somebody who keeps his eyes constantly open. Shifting his attention away from me, he put his water bottle down on the coffee table, got up and went to the display case I had touched earlier, the one with all the weapons. As I watched him, for the first time I noticed the circular display case over the fireplace held a huge collection of arrowheads, spearheads and stone knives. I wondered if they were Seminole. "Come over here," he said, his words a rumbling command. I could feel my stomach twist the way it does when adults try to boss me around, but I resisted the temptation to say something back.

When I got to the case, he asked, "That something sharp coming out of your mattress look like any of the objects in here?" He squinted as if he somehow wanted to see the answer within me as much as hear it. I guess by then I was a little paranoid about the possibility of him being able to get inside my head. After what I had experienced while standing there before, I wasn't sure I wanted to look, but I did. As I searched, my headache intensified, making me wince, but even so, my eyes stayed glued to this one item.

Without saying another word, Lobo unhooked the door, opened

it up, pulled out the bayonet I still stared at and handed it to me. Somehow, the guy knew exactly which thing to grab.

The weapon I held felt really cold and heavy. Again, an intense chill radiated across my body. This time though, I chalked up the sensation to having touched something with a much lower temperature than mine. The base of the thing was round and hollow with a cut out space I figured had to be where it attached to the end of a rifle or musket. Man, that blade! So slender and skinny sharp at the end. It was triangular in shape and about a foot and a half long. I always thought for some reason bayonets were flat, like a sword, but not the one in my hands. I'm telling you, after running my thumb over the stabbing end of the thing, I could sure see how it might do some serious damage. I didn't want to imagine what it felt like going through the insides of a person, but I did wonder if that particular bayonet had ever killed anyone.

I shuddered as I imagined it coming up through my mattress and sheet. A dull ache in my chest accompanied the throbbing in my head.

"That's the one," I told Lobo. As I started to give the man back his bayonet, it started warming up and then quickly got so hot I couldn't keep hold. It slipped from my fingers and clattered on the cement floor, barely missing Lobo's feet and mine. The old guy didn't flinch, move, or of course, blink—at least from what I could see. Me, I jumped out of the way.

"Your friend is dangerous," Lobo said, looking at Carla and shaking his head.

"It, ah, got too hot to handle," I explained. How the thing could heat up like that, I had no idea. Only then did I realize the pain in my chest was gone.

"Hot, eh?" Lobo asked, his voice full of curiosity. He bent down, scooped the bayonet up in one hand, and held it for a few seconds before putting it back into the case. "It's not hot now."

"It was," I said. "Really."

Lobo didn't reply at first. Instead, he walked back to his chair and sat down, leaving me standing near the display case. "There's something more going on here than just a dream," he said, again squinting like he had done before. "Think about it, carefully. What else in your life seems odd besides your dream and what happened seconds ago with the bayonet?"

I knew the guy had asked me a question, but I kept thinking about the bayonet's change in temperature and how holding it seemed to make my chest feel all tight for a second, almost like I couldn't breathe.

"What about it?" Lobo demanded.

I tried to think. "Well, there's this one, really dumb kind of thing I've noticed." I hesitated, unsure if it was what he wanted.

"Spit it out!" he ordered. "We'll be here all night at the rate you're going."

You turd! The man's pushy attitude was really starting to irritate me, but I didn't call him on it out loud.

"Mind your thoughts and anger young man," Lobo growled.

His statement stopped me cold. Had he actually seen those words flickering through my brain, or did he simply know how to read expressions? When I stole a quick glance at Carla, she looked down as if she knew exactly what had happened, and it had embarrassed her.

"Now," Lobo asked in an unusually even voice, "what's this one, 'really dumb thing' that's been going on with you?"

Instead of answering him right away, I walked slowly back to my chair and sat down. It gave me time to think, organize my swirling thoughts and memories. Taking a deep breath, I said, "It's probably nothing, but everywhere I go these days, I run into the number twenty-eight."

"Twenty-eight?" Carla asked as I sat down, again facing Lobo. I knew she couldn't keep out of the conversation for very long. "What do you mean?" Lobo didn't object to her question.

That was cool. I could talk to her instead of directly to Lobo. "Well, when I turn on the TV or radio, it seems like somebody is always mentioning number twenty-eight. Mom left me food money for the week this morning and it was $28. I don't remember her ever doing that before. There are also these kids who have been writing on the sidewalk with chalk near my house. Yesterday they wrote twenty-eights everywhere. And car license plates—so many I see have twenty-eights as part of their numbers."

Carla stared at me like I had lost my mind.

"OK, remember when we were standing at Lobo's gate a while ago," I asked her. "A pickup truck went by pulling a race car? It had a twenty-eight on the door."

This time, Carla's eyes widened in surprise. "You're right. It did."

"Got any change on you?" Lobo asked, boring holes in me with his eyes.

I reached in my jeans pocket and pulled out a quarter and three pennies. That about blew me away. Carla arched both eyebrows and old Lobo nodded like the twenty-eight cents in my pocket was the most natural thing in the world.

"Now we're getting someplace." After he spoke, Lobo rapidly scanned the air all around me. "The Jeff Golden puzzle is starting to take shape. There are still a lot of missing pieces, but Carla is one of them. Not just *a* missing piece, an important one." Here he looked long and hard at her for a few seconds before turning his attention back to me. "Something happened when you and Carla were together that you've never told anybody, even her. What is it? Start from the beginning and leave nothing out."

Carla? Then it hit me. *The accident.* My bike accident. I never had told Carla what I saw on that day. While I worked on putting the pieces of that event together in my mind, a cat silently jumped onto the back of the couch where Carla sat. A pretty thing I guess, if you like cats—an orange color with patches of black, and some white here and there. Carla didn't seem to notice as the thing stared at me with its yellow eyes, but I watched Lobo glance in that direction.

From his place at Carla's feet, Spock looked up. Both animals stared at each other for a few seconds and then they both looked away. Lobo continued to watch as the cat silently walked across the back of the couch behind Carla's head and then jump down onto the cushion next to her. Still without Carla noticing, the thing curled up and went to sleep.

"Pay attention to the conversation," Lobo said to me, jerking my thoughts back to the accident. To be honest, I didn't want to talk about it. What happened was so embarrassing and weird that I had tried to forget the whole thing, but I couldn't get out of describing it. Then again, I figured, I had been embarrassed so much already, I could handle a little more.

"OK, OK," I said to Lobo, but I actually spoke to Carla. "You remember when we first met?"

"Remember?" she said with a little laugh. "You really made quite an unusual impression."

Just hearing her talk and laugh made trying to explain what I had never shared with anyone before a lot easier. "When I first met Carla," I said, without looking at Lobo, "we were both in the parking lot of the county library. We, well, started talking to each other, you know?"

"No I don't know," Lobo grumbled. "If I did know, you wouldn't have to explain anything. Regardless of my ability to perceive things you think I shouldn't be able to, you do need to fill in blanks. Besides, using the words 'you know' is a lazy speaking pattern and tiresome for the listener."

Oh man, talk about tiresome. The guy was worse than a whole bunch of my teachers put together. But he had admitted, in a way, that he could sense at least a part of what I was thinking. Trying hard to ignore the idea of Lobo's mind probing into my brain, I went on with my story, this time looking directly at the old guy.

"As I was saying about the library. When Carla's grandma arrived to pick her up, well ... I decided to see if I could impress her, Carla I mean, not her grandma. So, as they were leaving the parking lot, I raced ahead of them and tried to do a really simple bike trick. Problem was I hit sand, went over backwards and cracked my head open."

"Oh did you ever," Carla groaned. To Lobo she said, "He knocked himself out for a minute or two and there was a pool of blood on the driveway under his head. Scared Grandma and me to death. The paramedics came and carted him off to the hospital. It turned out he only had a little concussion, but that's how we met."

"A few days after I got out of the hospital, I ran into Carla here in the neighborhood and figured out we lived down the street from each other. That's how we became friends."

"And," Lobo questioned, "what is it you haven't told us?"

"Ah, yeah, that. It's ... hard to explain. "You see, at the same time I was knocked out ... I could ... well ... see myself."

"See yourself?" Carla asked. "You were out cold. You couldn't have seen *anything*.

"That's the thing. I was awake somehow, really wide awake, but looking down at my body lying there in the blood. Carla, as crazy as it sounds, there was two of me, one on the ground and one looking down from maybe ten feet above. I watched you and your grandma jump out of the car and rush over to me, my body that is. Other people came around too. I remember seeing a little girl, a toddler, looking up at me floating there in the air and waving while everybody else looked at, well, my body. Then you yelled for someone to contact 911 and a redheaded woman opened her purse, pulled out her phone and made the call. None of what happened upset me. I just ... watched."

Carla sat there with her eyebrows raised and her mouth hanging slightly open.

"After that lady made the call, I wondered how I could be in two places at one time, and as I did, I ... started rising into the air even more. You, your grandma, my body, the crowd of people and the library kept getting smaller and smaller. Pretty soon, I could see all of St. Augustine below me. I remember thinking how weird it looked to see the Castillo from so far up. Its design from that high up looked like a huge star. And Matanzas Bay out there," I pointed to the water beyond Lobo's window, "looked so sparkly and beautiful in the sun, like, like a million little mirrors were flashing up at me. After that, it's real blurry except for waking up in the hospital."

"Hmmm," Lobo said. "There's even more to your experience than what you've told us, but right now, I have an appointment in the bathroom." Without any more conversation, he exited the room and headed down the hall.

At the sound of the bathroom door shutting, Lobo's cat looked around, stood up and stretched. Taking its time, the thing jumped off the cushion onto the floor next to Spock and scooted out of sight behind the couch with its tail straight up in the air.

"Why didn't you ever tell me all that?" Carla asked, hurt clearly showing in her voice and on her face.

"It was too wild, Carla," I explained. "I felt stupid enough after having that accident in front of you and your grandmother, you know?"

"I guess," she replied, still not very happy. "You're right about one thing. That was ... quite a story."

"I don't blame you for not believing me."

"I didn't say that."

"Well anyway, now you know. Hey, I thought you said old Edgar the crow was Lobo's only pet?"

"He is, why?"

"So who owns the cat I saw in here a few seconds ago?"

"Cat? Jeff, what are you talking about? There was no cat in this room."

6

Cat Got Your Tongue?

"Wait ... waaaait just one minute," I said. "You can't be serious. How could you not see it? That thing sat right next to you!" I know my voice must have sounded beyond nervous. That stupid headache again hammered away at my temples and behind my eyes, not helping the situation at all.

"For real? You saw a cat?"

It was obvious Carla hadn't seen anything, so I didn't reply at first. I was beginning to wonder if maybe I had been hallucinating or something. Down the hall, I could hear a toilet flush.

"I'm not crazy!" I took a deep breath and sat on the edge of my chair.

"I didn't say you were but—"

"Lover's quarrel?" Lobo walked back into the room and once more took his seat.

That question of his made me want to sink through the floor and out of sight.

"Lobo!" Carla screeched. "Cut it out. We're just friends."

Without saying it, I applauded Carla challenging the man, but part of me felt a little disappointed. Her statement about us being "just friends" came out a little too strong. Not what I wanted to hear.

"My, my, my." Lobo looked at us both. "Aren't we sensitive.

Well it's time to get over it. So tell me. What's this disagreement I heard coming up the hall?"

Carla sat there with folded arms staring at Lobo like she wanted to wring his neck. As unhappy with the man as I was, I really wanted to find out about the cat. "Look, Lobo," I said, "ah, when you were in here before, I saw a cat, but Carla thinks I was seeing things."

"That's not what I said," Carla interrupted. "You're twisting my words."

"Well, that's what it sounded like. You don't understand, I also watched Lobo and Spock look at that cat. I wasn't the only one watching it."

"Did you see this little feline creature or not?" Lobo asked Carla in an even voice.

"No. There was definitely no cat in here unless it was behind me, but that's not what Jeff is saying."

"Well now!" Lobo said to her, his voice a rising rumble. "How wonderfully interesting. Discrepancies in perception. In this case, however, your friend Carla over there is right."

"What?"

"He did indeed see a cat, as did I and Spock."

Carla looked at him like he had to be kidding, but he continued talking, this time, to me.

"So, explain to the young lady, if you will, what this cat looked like and what it did."

For a few seconds, I didn't know what to say. Surprisingly, old Lobo appeared to be agreeing with me. I mean the guy had told Carla and me I wasn't hallucinating. Man, what a relief! But how she didn't see what Lobo, Spock, and I did, flat didn't make sense.

Doing as I was asked, I slumped back into my chair and explained to Carla all about my cat sighting. As I talked, she had a squinty-eyed look, the one that says people aren't believing a word of what you're saying. But when I described the cat's orange, black and white coloring, her eyes widened and to Lobo, she asked a one-word question. "Seloy?"

"Seloy it was," Lobo agreed, and Carla's mouth dropped open.

"What's going on?" I asked. My head continued to ache, but I didn't want to ask Lobo if he had anything for the pain.

"My cat Seloy," Lobo replied. "You, Spock and I saw my cute little kitty, so why on earth didn't Carla see her?"

"Why are you asking me?" I replied. "That's what I want to know."

"OK, Mr. Golden, it's time for you to put your big boy pants on and really pay attention here. By now, it's clear to you I have the ability to find things out about people in ways you don't understand, right?"

I couldn't argue with the guy on that point. By then, for some reason, even the "big boy pants" comment didn't bother me very much. I needed to find out what was going on.

"You've seen for yourself," he explained, "that there are people in the world who definitely have extremely unusual sensitivities and even abilities of various kinds. The child in the crowd of people around your body when you had the bike wreck for instance. She looked up and saw you hovering overhead when no one else did. That child is such a person, a person very much like you."

"Me? Come on Lobo," I said, starting to get extremely uncomfortable, and my shaky voice showed exactly that.

"For a smart kid, you really don't get it do you? You obviously have the ability to see something Carla could not, don't you?"

Lobo asked the question, but he went on talking. "Your dream is an example of what I'm saying. A bayonet actually did come up through your mattress in a manner of speaking, but only you could see it. In ways you do not yet comprehend, it was as real as the one you held in here just a while ago. And when my bayonet got so hot in your hand, that meant you had somehow touched on a part of the truth—the truth about what's happening to you."

I knew the man couldn't possibly believe what he said, but my insides still felt like they had turned over somehow. I didn't understand how the conversation had gone so far away from seeing that stupid cat to talking about me having unusual sensitivities, abilities, or whatever.

"Down deep inside," Lobo said, speaking to my unsaid thoughts, "you actually do understand. It's your conscious mind that continues to block that awareness. We need to do something to help break through your mental barrier."

Rapidly switching his attention from me to Carla, he said, "In this case, when I say 'we,' I mean you as well."

"Me?" She looked at him as if he'd lost his mind.

"Don't let her kid you," Lobo said to me while still looking at Carla. "She knows a lot more than you think. Miss Carla here has her own, well, shall we say, special talents."

"Lobo, come on. I don't want to go there," Carla pleaded.

"I've got to use you as an example. This boy is in danger."

"Danger?" Carla and I both said at the same time. Again, my insides did a little dance.

"I didn't see it clearly at first," Lobo replied, "but now, as your puzzle begins to fit together, some dangerous patterns are definitely emerging."

Again, Carla and I spoke at once, peppering the man with all kinds of questions. Finally, he stood up and bellowed, "Now you two hold it!" Man, the volume of the guy's voice was not what my headache needed. In the silence, Lobo looked back and forth between us to see if he had made his point. Satisfied we would wait for him to explain, he said, "To figure out exactly what's going on, we need to start with some basic education here." To Carla, he then spoke in a very soothing voice I didn't know he had. "Carla, I need you to give a little demonstration."

"Oh no. No way, Lobo! I won't do it." Saying she looked upset barely describes the emotions I saw flowing across her face.

"Besides, what does that have to do with Jeff being in danger?"

"To get at the danger, this boy needs a crash course in believing what's happening to him. A little help from you will truly begin that process."

Carla held his gaze for a few seconds, looked over at me and closed her eyes. "OK," she said nodding after a few seconds, "OK."

"Good. Now, finish your drink," Lobo said, nailing me with those laser-like eyes.

"Finish my drink?" I asked, looking at the Coke can in my hand.

"Did I not speak clearly? Or perhaps you simply don't know what the words 'finish your drink' mean when put together in a sentence?"

Smartass. I didn't care if he could truly read my thoughts or not. Glaring at the man, I chugged the last few swallows of my Coke, and shook the can from side to side to show it was empty.

"Now," Lobo ordered, "hold out one hand, palm up, and stand the can on it, bottom down."

I did exactly as he asked.

"Carla," he ordered looking at the can as if she would know what to do.

Poor Carla seemed even more uncomfortable than before. She shifted her position on the couch. He eyes darted all around for a few seconds but eventually came to rest on the can. After focusing on it for a few seconds, she took a couple of deep breaths and closed her eyes. Nothing happened for maybe ten or fifteen seconds until ... well ... the damn can slowly lifted off my palm without anybody touching it. I'm not kidding. The thing moved straight up about three inches and just sat there in mid air.

Yeah, yeah I know how that sounds, but believe me it happened. Before I could react, I heard this crackling sound, and watched as the can started crumpling. No lie! The can sort of ... imploded, slowly at first and then with a snap, it completely flattened as if somebody had stomped the thing—but in mid air. God it was eerie.

The smashed can slowly floated back onto the palm of my hand.

"Holy crap," I whispered, staring at the red, white and aluminum colored mess. My mind whirled, trying to figure out how Carla had crushed it, but no answers popped into my head. When she finally opened her eyes, she looked at me kind of apologetically. In return, I stared at her in astonishment. Sure she had told me about her unconscious ability to move things. That was hard enough to swallow, but to actually see her levitate my Coke can and crush it?

"What's the matter," Lobo asked me, "cat got your tongue?"

Real funny, old man. Grasping the crushed can with my other hand, I looked at it, for a few seconds. "No way," I said, shaking my head and finding it impossible to believe what I had just seen. "It's a magic trick," I said with a halfhearted laugh. "Yeah, that's it, magic." Even as I spoke, I didn't fully believe my own words. I think I wanted to believe the two of them had pulled a smoke and mirrors type thing on me, because to consider anything else was way too wild.

Without saying another word, Carla and Lobo stared at me, causing another chill to race its way up and down my spine. In that moment, it was as if I was looking at the two of them from across a very deep, dark canyon only they understood and knew how to cross.

7

Worlds-within-Worlds-within-Worlds

No trick, really," Carla said with this super serious face. When she spoke, her voice came out almost in a whisper.

Oh man, that did it. I mean Carla doesn't lie, stretch the truth, or anything like that. "Remember when I told you about Lobo helping me to control my unconscious ability to move things without touching them?" she asked, her voice a little stronger.

"Uh, sure." I sat there looking at her in awe.

"You see, Lobo ... well, has also been educating me so that I can now touch things with my conscious mind—to do so by thinking about it. An aluminum can is light and soft, so we use them in my training."

"Do we have your full attention now?" Lobo asked, as I struggled to accept Carla's explanation.

"Oh yeah," I said, stressing each word in order to leave no doubt in the man's mind. Even so, I still couldn't get over Carla having such an amazing ability. As I wondered how she could do something like that, I put the crumpled aluminum on the coffee table in front of me.

"Good," Lobo replied. "Now we can proceed." After getting out of his chair, he grabbed the carved white ball sitting on the coffee table, and suddenly tossed it in my direction—underhanded and high in the air. Without thinking, I grabbed the thing as it came down with both hands, and was surprised it felt so light. When the ball hit my hands, there was a clicking sound.

"Have you ever seen anything like that?" Lobo asked after sitting back down.

"Yeah, I just remembered. There's one like it at the Ripley's Believe It or Not Museum." I held it in one hand and brushed my other hand over the intricate designs and holes carved into the surface. Gradually it became clear to me that the ridges under my fingers tips were actually dragons curling around the openings. "What's it made of?"

"Mammoth ivory," Carla replied. "Lobo has it shipped in and then he does carvings."

"A piece of mammoth tusk?" I said in wonder, studying it even more intently. Inside all the holes cut out of the surface, I could see another, completely movable, but smaller ball. Carved into it were odd shaped stars and more holes leading to yet another ball farther down. Beyond that, another ball, and so on. All of the balls I could see or touch with my index finger moved. That's why the thing was so light, it had been carved out on the inside, layer-by-layer.

"How many balls are in there all together?" Lobo asked, not answering my question.

"Um, looks like five or six maybe."

"Not even close." He reached into a drawer in the side of the coffee table, pulled out a slender, brass letter opener, and handed it to me. Feeling the thing in my hand made me think of the bayonet over in the display case, even though it was a different color. "Use the sharp end as your probe to see how many you can find."

"What's this all about?" As beautifully intricate as the man's ball was, I didn't understand how it related to my dream, or much of anything else for that matter.

"Just do it," he ordered, "and you'll find out."

"OK, OK, don't get all bent out of shape." I did as he asked until I had trouble putting the blade into the twelfth hole. That meant there were at least eleven balls inside the big one. I found it hard to believe Lobo or anybody could get tools in there so deep and do all that tiny carving. When I got ready to tell the man how many balls I found, something happened. It was so quick I was sure it had to be my imagination, but my whole body jerked. As I released the letter opener and left it sticking in the ball, I saw that both of my hands were shaking.

"Explain what you just experienced," Lobo said.

"I ... don't ... know. I'm not sure."

"Don't be so certain. Look at your hands again. Your body is telling you something. Give yourself a chance and then tell us what you can remember."

My hands still shook, but not quite as much as before. As I stared at them, bits and pieces of memory floated into my brain. Slowly, I pieced together what I could of my experience and explained it to Lobo and Carla. "When I finished counting the balls ... it was as if I sort of ... well ... dived into all those holes and into the central part of all the balls. At first, I thought it was interesting—seeing the edge of each ball's holes as I flew by. But when I got to that last ball, it wasn't ... ivory. Instead, I entered a ... thick ... blackness. That's it." I shrugged, not understanding what my memory was telling me.

"Put the ball back on its stand," the man directed, "and leave the opener sticking inside."

When I did as he asked, Lobo got up from his chair, walked over to the display case where the bayonet hung and stared at it for a while. After a short pause, he turned around to face me, his eyes glittering.

"People call things like that one on my coffee table, Chinese Puzzle Balls," he said. "Carla calls it my 'Ball of Realities.' I realize that doesn't have a lot of meaning for you yet, but you had better hope it will, and soon. Think of all those separate yet connected spheres as the different levels of awareness and existence."

My face must have shown that I had no idea what he was talking about, because he put one big hand palm outward in my direction as if he was asking me to forget my confusion for a minute.

"Get up, reach over and touch the surface of the ball one more time," he asked.

I wasn't sure I really wanted to, but after looking at Carla and seeing her nod, I did what Lobo wanted and sat back down.

"What you just touched is like the surface part of life everybody generally agrees upon—things like people, animals, stars, air, dirt and the wood we use in the construction of our homes." As he said the word, "homes," he slapped the mantelpiece over his fireplace loudly with the flat of his hand. Carla, Spock and I all jumped at the same time.

"The problem is, there's more to it than that. Beneath the surface of life that most of us agree upon lies so much more. Carla showed this to you when she changed the molecular structure of your Coke can with her mind. Magic didn't lift and smash the can, but Carla's mental and spiritual connection to other worlds beyond our own did.

"Scientists see into some of these worlds as they probe into the very essence of the universe. People who believe in a spiritual world beyond this one connect with it through prayer and meditation. Most of all, people like the three of us, understand this because we experience it as you have here today, and as you did when you saw yourself after your accident. Your separation from your body, my ability to see into your mind, and Carla's power to affect things at a distance are all examples of what lies beneath the surface of all our lives."

The more the man talked, the more I felt like I was getting lost in some kind of weird Star Trek episode.

"My Ball of Realities there on the table, is a symbolic way to show there are unseen worlds-within-worlds-within-worlds. They are all around and even within us. The opener sticking through all those holes shows you how we as human beings connect to all those worlds even when we don't consciously know it is happening. People like you, Carla and me happen to be able to perceive those connections more than most."

"Wait. Wait just a freakin' minute. What do you mean people like you, me and Carla? You keep saying that."

"And you don't listen, because you don't want to accept the reality of who you are down deep. Moments ago you were sliding beneath the surface of many realities. A deeper portion of yourself showed you those multiple levels. Carla and I both have similar abilities.

"Unfortunately, the blackness you found at the end is the danger I sensed before. Make no mistake, your inner self gave you very clear evidence of what I'm saying. When your body jumped, it was the wordless realization of what you had discovered."

I sort of understood what he meant, but it was too much to take in all at once, especially with that headache of mine. I definitely remember saying to myself I needed time to think it all over.

Right as that thought entered my mind though, Lobo looked at me hard and said, "You don't have time to think it over."

What he meant by that, I had no idea, but it certainly didn't sound good. Before I could ask him about it, he turned his attention to Carla.

"Tell your friend here about my cat." Without waiting for her to respond, he got up and walked out of the room again. The guy sure seemed to make a lot of rapid exits and entrances.

"OK, what about the cat?" I asked.

Carla didn't answer right away. "I'm not sure how to tell you this," she said, "but what you evidently saw was Lobo's calico, Seloy."

"I kinda got that figured out already."

"Kinda is right. Seloy died over a year ago. She's buried behind Lobo's workshop."

8

Conjuring

"No freakin' way!" I said, shaking my head. "If Lobo's cat died, then its twin was here, walked all over the couch, and even laid down next to you."

"Jeff, I told you, I didn't see a thing."

"So, I saw what? A ghost cat? Is that what you and Lobo are both trying to tell me by talking about different realities and all?"

Before she could answer, Lobo came back into the room carrying a bulging cloth sack about a foot long and six inches wide. After laying it on the dining room table, he looked right at Carla. "Answer his question."

"No," she replied. I guess she had had enough of Lobo telling her what to do. She folded her arms and arched an eyebrow as she looked at him very coolly. "Lobo, this is your show, not mine. I can't tell him for sure what he saw, only you can."

"You underestimate yourself," he fired back at her and turned his attention to me.

"What Carla means to say is that, yes, indeed you saw the ghost, spirit, apparition, however you want to label it, of my long lost cat, Seloy."

"You can't be serious. There's no such thing as ghosts."

"Worlds-within worlds-within-worlds," he replied, pointing to his Chinese Puzzle Ball and the skinny letter opener sticking out of it. "Get this straight and get it straight now. When people and animals die on this planet, it's only their bodies that are gone, not the deep essence of who or what they are. You saw Seloy because she still exists in a way only a few people like you can see. Like it or not, understand it or not, you are one of those people.

"Carla knows what I just told you is true because she was able to look into that world beyond death on one occasion. Now, Carla," he said, rapidly shifting his focus to her. "If you would be so kind, I would like for you to tell this hard to convince young man about your experience relating to the topic at hand."

"Me? Why me?" Carla asked with a sharp edge to her voice.

"Because he's your *friend*," Lobo barked, "remember? He needs your *help*. You're the one who brought him here and now you don't want to do everything you can to assist him?"

As soon as he finished talking, Carla's face softened. The old guy had pushed her emotional buttons just right.

"That's not fair," she replied, but there was no punch to her words. Lobo had her boxed in and she knew it. "It's just hard to talk about." When she looked at me, her eyes held a deep sadness.

"Don't say anything that gives you a problem," I said to her. I felt bad about being the cause of her discomfort.

Carla sighed and said, "No, it's OK, really. Maybe Lobo's right. If what happened to me will smooth the way for your understanding of what might be going on here, then it's well worth the effort."

"First of all, from your description, it had to be Seloy, Lobo's cat. I believe that's possible because ... well ... I saw my mother at the moment she died with my dad in the Yucatan, even though I was here in St. Augustine. I actually spoke to her and felt her touch my hair. She also appeared to Lobo at the same moment. I'll tell you the full story sometime, but what you need to know now is that such a thing is definitely possible."

As her words faded away, a heavy silence filled the room.

"Wow!" I said softly. "That's ... amazing. Thanks for telling me." In my mind, Lobo's cat once again jumped down from the back of the couch and went to sleep next to Carla. Slowly, my mind began to accept that I had possibly seen something even more extraordinary than what Carla did to my Coke can. I wondered though, how Carla's mother's spirit could be in two places at exactly the same time.

"OK you two, join me at the dining room table and take a seat." Lobo could change gears quicker than anyone I had ever met. It made my aching head spin. Even before we settled into our chairs, the man started talking again, to me this time. "Before we look at what's in my little bag here, I need to explain a few more things to you."

"I'm listening."

Before speaking again, Lobo once more looked all around me, like he had been doing off and on since I met him. When he finished, he grimaced slightly and said, "My best guess is the knock on the head you got during your bike accident at the library made you sensitive to realities other than our own. It was an awakening of sorts. We'll talk about that dream some more after we get done here.

"Now, you've never had any experiences like the ones we've been discussing today before the accident, have you?"

"No," I replied, sure of my memory. I don't forget much, especially things that are strange and unusual.

"Uh huh, that fits." Lobo took a seat opposite me. "You and Carla both developed your abilities because of life events. You had your accident and Carla had her parents' deaths. They were triggers that set things off. Other people like me have their abilities starting at the beginning of their existences. In my case, I've had a lifetime to learn how to control those unusual gifts and Carla has had several years with me to learn to do the same. With you, however, things are very different, and that brings me back to the danger issue.

"You've recently been having a lot of headaches haven't you?"

The man's dark, deep-set eyes seemed even more penetrating than before.

"Yes," I replied, not sure where this line of questioning was going.

"You also sense someone is either following you, or you think you see someone out of the side of your eye. When you look in that direction though, there is never anyone there. Am I right?"

"Uh, yeah, once in a while." *How could he know that?* So?"

"Those two things," Lobo replied, "like the bayonet in your bed and the number twenty-eight you see everywhere, are attempts by someone long gone from this world to contact you."

"Wait, wait, you're talking about somebody who died, and it's this person's spirit doing all this?"

"Of course! That's one of the reasons I sometimes look in the air all around your body. Within your aura, I've been seeing a spiritual essence of a deceased person, a blur, actually, because he is moving so quickly. This rapid movement indicates he's extremely agitated. Why I don't know. I keep saying 'he' because I sense this person was an adult male during his lifetime."

Auras? Seeing a blurry image of an agitated man? My mind stumbled over itself trying to make sense of it all. In the middle of my mental confusion, Spock let out a low growl and started barking at me.

"What did I do to him?" I asked Carla, but she looked as surprised as I felt.

"Your dog can see this person," Lobo said to Carla before she could answer me, "and he doesn't like it. Put him on the porch so he won't disrupt things."

She did as Lobo asked, but Spock continued his barking on the porch, making me really nervous. I could see the poor dog's head from where I sat, moving on the other side of all that glass in the front door. When Carla came back, Lobo started talking again.

"I also get the sense that this spirit around you is desperate and blinded by fear. The bayonet heating up as it did was an indication of how intensely this man wants to reach you. However, such intensity also shows the potential for severe danger—danger to you, not us. From his viewpoint, it's as if Carla and I aren't even around. He is highly focused on you only. For whatever reason, he thinks you can solve his problem. Your headaches are the result of pressure from him trying to make contact."

"Contact? With me?" I squawked, looking all around the room but seeing nothing unusual. "Solve his problem? How can I do that? I don't know what the problem is."

"Lobo, are you sure?" Carla asked.

"To answer both your questions, we need to do some research. We have to sort this thing out and soon. Otherwise, this person, this spirit," Lobo said, staring directly at me, "may push you over the edge. The result for you could be destroyed health, insanity, death, or even worse. That's the danger, the blackness you saw at the bottom of my Ball of Realities."

"Come on, you've gotta be kidding." I tried saying those words calmly, but they came out all nervous like. The guy was really starting to freak me out. "You're telling me my life is in danger because of this, this ghost? Besides, what could be worse than death?"

"I hope you never discover that answer firsthand. Right now, however, you need to be aware that the paranormal sensitivities you have developed since your accident are very strong. To people and animals who have left this world, those abilities shine like a beacon. Seloy appeared to you for this reason, and it's at least partly why this man is hounding you so much. The problem is you haven't had time to develop defenses against unwanted contact. Once we gather more information, we can try to create a way to safely connect with this spiritual entity and convince him to leave you alone."

"Wait a minute Lobo," Carla said. What about Grandma's rule about no conjuring of spirits? She'll never let me come down here any more if she finds out."

"There won't be any conjuring. This spirit is already here. Nobody is calling him. Besides, do you have another idea about how to help your friend here?"

Carla took a deep breath, then blew it out quickly, shook her head and said, "No, I guess not." Outside, Spock still barked and whined.

I had no idea what they were talking about.

"Just so you understand," Lobo said, sliding his eyes over to me, "conjuring, or the calling of spirits, can cause tremendous problems sometimes. Carla's grandmother is correct. People can get in trouble doing it if they aren't extremely knowledgeable and careful."

"But what about your cat? What does this Seloy have to do with the person you say is trying to contact me?"

"Nothing directly. For a number of possible reasons, your natural sensitivities popped out this afternoon and Seloy just happened to respond. You meeting my cat simply shows how rapidly your connection with other worlds is increasing."

"Where did you ever get a name like Seloy for a cat?" Why that question came out of my mouth at that particular moment, I couldn't tell you.

Lobo got this disgusted look on his face, but to my surprise, he answered the question. "I named her after the original Indian village that existed here in St. Augustine when the Spanish first arrived. The important topic at this minute, however, is not my cat's background. What you must know is that St. Augustine directly links to all the various realities in existence. Here in this old city, we live right on the edge of many worlds exactly like you see in my multiple balls of carved ivory sitting there on the coffee table. The barriers here between our existence and all the other unseen existences are very thin.

"The thinning between realities in our town heightens the abilities of some people, especially people like the three of us, to touch those other worlds. This is especially so in the dream state. At the same time, beings from other realities, like Seloy, find it easier to make themselves known to us. The ghost tours of St. Augustine you laugh at may be money making machines that stretch the truth of spirit presences in this city, but they also indicate how much paranormal activity really occurs here."

Without saying another word, Lobo picked up the cloth bag lying on the table and turned it upside down. Out tumbled the most beautiful bunch of copper, silver, nickel and gold coins I had ever laid eyes on—a huge pile of them. From what I could see, the silver and copper coins that should have been tarnished sitting together in a bag like that weren't at all. And I'm not talking about any twenty-first century coins here. Those things were old, but looked new, almost freshly minted. Amazing.

I used to have a good collection myself, but that was in the days when my parents and I had a nice home and no money problems. During the seventh grade, my dad pawned my coins to pay for gambling debts like he did with lots of other things in our house.

Lobo spread his collection out across the tabletop until they were maybe three or four deep. Out on the porch, Spock gave a huge whine, but finally stopped barking. "We are going to use these coins," Lobo said, "to more precisely determine when the person who is trying to contact you lived. The bayonet you selected from all the other sharp edged weapons in my display case, came from a particular time in American history. The person trying to communicate with you created a copy of that weapon in your dream to get your attention, because he lived sometime during the era of its use. Now we need to determine the date a little more exactly.

"With your newly opened connections to other worlds, you should be able to sense enough from this person lurking nearby so you can pick a coin out of that pile that will give us a more specific date of his existence. This collection is from the United States, and none of it was minted later than 1950.

"What you are going to do in a minute is to put one hand out over the coins about six inches high, palm down. Then without looking at them directly, or touching them, slowly move your fingers in the air over the collection until you sense something, anything unusual. That's when you reach down and grab the first coin you touch. Is that clear?"

"Very clear." I tried concentrating through my headache.

"When you pick up that one coin, look at it and tell us the date. Are you ready?"

"I guess so."

"Good. Do it."

Keeping my eyes locked with Lobo's, I reached out my right hand and waved it over the coins. I did that for at least thirty seconds without feeling anything. I guess Lobo could see my frustration because he said, "It may take a little time so keep going." About ten seconds later, I got this tingly feeling in my index finger. Man that was so weird it made me not want to handle any of the coins, but Lobo nodded as if he knew I had found something.

Taking a big breath, I pointed my finger down until I touched one particular coin that felt different somehow and picked it up. "It's a U.S. dime, dated 1828," I said looking at the thing, shaking my head in disbelief. "Another number twenty-eight. See what I mean about that number?"

Carla raised her eyebrows in surprise but said nothing.

"Now we're getting close," Lobo said. "Maybe not exact but close."

"That's great, but this coin is starting to get hot, real hot." As soon as I said those words, Lobo reached over and grabbed the hand holding his dime. That sudden movement and the man's strong grip scared me even more than I was already. I tried to pull loose, but he held tight, making me panic. The coin kept getting hotter, and at the same time, my head felt like it would explode any second.

I just couldn't take it any more. I yelled as loud as I could and wrenched my hand away from Lobo's iron grip. Coins scattered everywhere as I did that. I tell you what, it wasn't easy to break free from the old guy, but I did and quickly stood up. Carla screamed my name as my chair crashed to the floor, and Lobo shouted for me to sit back down.

The stupid dime was so hot, I threw it at the other coins on the table. It skipped off the surface of the coin collection, hit the picture window with a crack, and fell to the floor. "You go to hell you son-of-a-bitch," I shouted at Lobo. "I've had enough of your crap. Nobody grabs me like that, nobody."

OK, I realize I was out of control, but I couldn't continue doing things Lobo's way anymore. I was so bent out of shape, I didn't even think about what how Carla might react to the words I used. I just wasn't able to continue dealing with Lobo, his rules and all that ghost talk, you know? I mean you try handling all that when the top of your head feels like it is going to blow off.

Well, I tell you what. I backed away from the table as both Lobo and Carla tried to get me to calm down. "No way!" I shouted at both of them. I ran back to the recliner I had been sitting in and grabbed my jacket. All I knew was that I had to get out of there.

On the porch, Spock barked even more wildly than before. Lobo looked like he wanted to shoot me and Carla's face had this pained expression on it I can't even begin to describe. "Sorry, Carla," I said heading out of the room. "I can't take this any more."

In seconds, I got to the front door where I could see Spock looking at me through the clear part of all those glass ovals, still barking. Light from the outside made the stained glass wolf on his cliff, the moon and the stars stood out against the dark background. I could see my angry face in the mirror-like sections of the door as I turned the handle.

When I opened the door, Spock pushed his way into the house as I escaped to the front porch.

9

Fog

I shut Lobo's door behind me without putting on my jacket and took a big breath of cold air. Standing there for a second, I felt like I had been running hard. God, my heart pounded so hard I thought it might split wide open, and that stupid headache throbbed even more. I hated leaving Carla like I did, but the time to get out of there had come. Being away from Lobo was such a relief.

With my eyes closed, I took another deep breath and let it out slowly. All that had gone on that afternoon rushed through my mind like a flooding river. Instantly, those panicky urges to turn around and run away while walking towards Lobo's place with Carla popped up in my head. I opened my eyes again only to see that everything had gotten a lot darker than it was seconds before. A massive fog bank had somehow moved in over Matanzas Bay and already covered most of Lobo's dock. As I watched, the rest of the dock disappeared into all that gray stuff as if it had never been there. Rapidly, a smaller wave of fog rolled over the tip of the peninsula and headed right for me at a speed fog should never move. It all happened so fast, I had no time to think or act. Long fingers of mist reached for the porch, and before I knew it, a cold wetness surrounded me.

"What the hell?" I whispered to myself. Talk about freaky. Yeah, it scared me—so much that I even turned around to go back into

the house. Believe it or not, right then, facing old Lobo seemed better than dealing with that awful, weird fog. When I turned around
though, I couldn't find the house. All I could see was fog in every
direction. Even so, I knew the front door had to be there directly
in front of me, right? I mean I hadn't moved more than a couple of
feet away from it. So I stretched my arms out and slowly stepped
forward.

After walking maybe five or six steps, I still hadn't found the
door or any part of the house. I know what you're thinking. You're
sure I must have been hallucinating all of that or something. I don't
blame you. To be perfectly honest, I thought the same thing at first,
but that cold, wet fog was very, very real.

"Carla!" I shouted, but my voice sounded muffled. "Lobo?" I
yelled. At any second, I expected one of them to open the door and
answer me. No such luck. I kept shouting anyway.

When I finally gave up yelling my lungs out, the absolute silence
startled me. Like a thick blanket of insulation, the fog no longer
allowed any sound in from the outside world—no birds chirping,
no noises from boats out on the bay or traffic in the neighborhood.
Nothing but total silence. I swear, it was so quiet I actually heard my
heart beating. As I listened though, I noticed a darkness creeping
into the fog. I'm telling you, it just got darker and darker as I stood
there frozen in fear, with my head still aching. In less than a minute,
I was in total blackness with only the feel of cold, wet fog all over
me. Strangely enough, I also smelled something like pine needles.
Pine trees. Pine needles. Something like that.

I didn't know what to do. Lobo's words about spirits and danger
still swirled through my weary brain, reviving the memory of that
deep blackness I had seen at the bottom of his carved ivory ball.
For a moment, I wondered if I was dreaming somehow, but the
feel of that cold fog all over my body told a different story. I turned
around several times, hoping to see or hear something, anything.
When that got me nowhere, the panic really started to build. Even

in the cold, I could feel sweat trickling down my back and under my arms. I had never felt so alone.

"Wait. Wait a minute," I said out loud, closing my eyes even though there was nothing to see. "Take it easy and think." After sucking in a couple of deep breaths of cold air, I put on my jacket. Funny how that helped. Doing that one little thing for myself also calmed me down a little. Even my headache eased up a bit.

No matter what, I said to myself, you still have to be on Lobo's porch. All you have to do is get down on your hands and knees and feel your way across the wood floor until you find the door. *Why didn't you think of that before, idiot?*

Listening to my own advice, I squatted on my heels and stretched out put my right hand. Instead of wood, I touched wet sand, dirt and what felt like a thick matting of pine needles. I pulled my hand back like it had been burned. As I thought about it, I didn't remember seeing any pine trees on Lobo's property.

"No way," I said out loud in my muffled voice. "I'm on the porch. I have to be." But the feeling of pine needles did match what I had been smelling and that gave me a tiny bit of hope, in a way. At least a couple of things connected in all that darkness.

An owl hooted loudly somewhere in the fog making me jump. Strange as it may sound, when I thought about the owl and the things I had touched, they all helped me feel better. I don't know why exactly, except maybe those items were solid, real things in that total darkness my mind could hold onto.

The owl hooted again, but this time I didn't jump. Instead, I wondered if maybe I had stepped off the porch into the fog and just got lost somehow. *If that's so*, I thought, *keep feeling around until you find the porch*. Once more following my own logic, I goton my hands and knees. Wetness soaked through my jeans and grit stuck to my hands. Again, all I could feel was dirt, sand and pine needles until something brushed my face, scaring the crap out of me at first.

When I felt around some more and found the thing, it was

nothing more than a palmetto frond, dripping wet from the fog. Following the frond all the way down to a palmetto bush, I found a shoe. The thing is, I hadn't seen any trash like that at all anywhere around Lobo's house except inside his truck. *A shoe?*

Continuing to crawl around and feeling with my fingers, I found even more pine needles, then some pinecones, and what felt like rough slivers of wood. To my sensitive nose, the scent of pine there was really strong.

Seconds later, I found a tree about a foot and a half thick and grabbed it with both hands. Why? It almost felt like a friend there in the dark, at least something big I could hold onto, you know? It didn't matter how rough the outside was. As my fingers explored the thing, I felt places that had no bark—spots of bare wood with splintery holes gouged out of it. Those holes oozed pine sap, and I wondered what had caused them. Yeah, my fingers got really sticky, but I could have cared less.

That's when it happened. Slowly the fog all around me started to glow. At first there was enough brightness so I could at least see my hands, the tree, and a shadow of the tree in the fog in front of me. The source of that illumination had to be coming from behind.

I whipped around and there it was, Lobo's front door not ten feet away. Light, wonderful light from inside Lobo's house pushing its way through those glass ovals and making the fog glow. "Yesssss!" I shouted long and hard, and started walking towards the door. All that brightness from inside really made the wolf on his cliff, the moon and Orion stand out brilliantly as fog swirled in front of them.

When I got there, I looked through the mist and the clear glass portion of the door. The hallway and room with the fireplace and weapons were on the left, right where they should be. I didn't see Carla or Lobo yet, but all I needed to do was open the door to safety. When I reached for the doorknob though, I couldn't find it. I couldn't even find the door itself—the wooden part. Reaching out with a shaking hand, I grasped one of the clear glass sections in my fingers, which should have been impossible.

10

Pine Sap

Someone called my name as if from very far away. It sounded like Carla, but I couldn't tell for sure. I kept staring at the stained glass window with its surrounding mirrors and the clear glass oval as it hung there in the fog all by itself.

"Jeff?" It was *Carla's* voice. Carla and Lobo somehow appeared directly in front of me with the stained glass window behind them set in its door as it should be. How that all happened so quickly I had no idea. The fog was gone and Lobo's house looked like it did when I first saw it. Once again, I stood on the porch.

"Are you OK?" Carla asked in a worried voice. "What is it? What's going on?"

I didn't say anything at first. Guess I was just too stunned. The change out of that horrible, dark fog had been so quick I found it hard to believe I had come back to Carla and Lobo. Where I had gone, I didn't know, but Lobo's words leaped into my mind. "Worlds-within-worlds-within worlds."

Instead of saying anything to either of them, I turned around to look behind me. When I saw Lobo's dock and Matanzas Bay, I breathed a deep sigh of relief. No fog out there either, not even way out on Anastasia Island or Villano Beach.

"Come on," Carla said, gently taking me by the arm. "Come back inside and sit down." She told me later how I stared out at across the bay for so long without saying anything that Lobo finally motioned for her to take me into the house.

She walked me all the way, holding my arm like I was a hundred years old or something. I didn't mind, really, because it was so good to be back with her and actually inside Lobo's place. I think after what happened on the porch, she could have probably led me anywhere, and it wouldn't have mattered.

"Lobo," she said, holding up a moist hand, "his jacket is damp."

"I can see that."

After I sat back down in the same recliner as before, Carla got me a fresh can of Coke.

I chugged a couple of cold, sweet swallows and blinked a few times, still not quite believing I had escaped that nasty, wet darkness. While I drank, Carla stood there next to me looking very worried. "I'm OK, really." I said the words, but I wasn't too sure they were the truth. In my mind, the only certainty right then, was how glad I felt to be back with her and even old Lobo. What a contrast to the way I left the house, so tough sounding and angry, right?

"He'll be all right." Lobo spoke from the opposite recliner, looking at me intently. It felt like his weird old eyes were boring into me somehow, touching places I didn't know existed. Strange sensation, one I can't begin to describe fully.

Assured by Lobo that I wouldn't die at any moment, Carla sat down on the couch. Even so, I could see the worry still in her eyes. She had left a replacement caretaker in her place though. Sitting on the floor next to me, Spock licked my hand. Since he wasn't growling and barking any more, I hoped maybe that meant he no longer sensed the ghostly presence Lobo kept talking about. I scratched him behind his ears, something he really likes.

For whatever reason, it took me until that point to fully realize I still wore my jacket. When I touched the zipper, I felt the moisture Carla had mentioned. Confirmation of my terrifying little trip outside Lobo's house covered my fingertips and seeped into my brain.

"What happened to you out there on the porch?" Lobo asked, his voice a distant rumble of thunder. Between us on the coffee table sat the Ball of Realities and my crushed Coke can like silent witnesses waiting to testify. Behind Lobo, his coins still lay in a big pile on the dining room table, and to my embarrassment, I saw a few of them scattered on the floor.

I tried to answer the man about what I experienced, but the words came out all garbled at first. My mind still wasn't working very well. Questioning by both Carla and Lobo over the next few minutes helped my brain get back on track, allowing me to tell my story about the fog. "I see," Lobo said when I finished, and Carla looked even more worried than before.

"I've never been that scared in my life," I said, meaning every word of it.

"No doubt," Lobo replied. "You were in a very dangerous situation. You, or part of you at least, went somewhere other than here, that's for sure."

"I know his clothes are a little wet, but he actually went somewhere?" Carla asked. "How could that be? He wasn't out the door for more than thirty seconds before he called to us?"

"Thirty seconds?" I yelped. "No way. I was … I was out there for at least five or ten minutes trying to get back to the house."

"Forty seconds tops," Lobo said, shaking his head. "Right after you left and closed the front door, you called our names as if you were in trouble. We both jumped up and found you staring at the door, but you didn't seem to be able to see us at first.

"Look at his knees," Lobo said, switching the conversation back to Carla. "He has sand and dirt on them as well as stains he didn't have before he went out the door."

As I looked down at my pants, I saw he was right.

"Show us your hands." To clarify what he meant, Lobo flashed the palms of his hands in my direction.

I put my Coke on the coffee table and held out my hands like he said. Up until then, I hadn't noticed there was some sort of discoloration and stickiness on both palms and most of my fingers.

Like a bullet fired from a gun, Lobo jumped up, rushed over to me and smelled one of my palms. "Pine sap," he said and returned to his seat.

"That's impossible." Carla sounded very certain. "You don't have pine trees on your property. And even if you did, Jeff didn't have time to run off somewhere and get it all over his hands."

"Nevertheless, your friend has pine sap on his hands. I don't have any palmettos around here either and he says he encountered those as well."

That's all it took for both Carla and me to start bombarding Lobo with questions. Instead of trying to answer, he put a hand up in my direction and one facing Carla, like a traffic cop trying to stop two lanes of traffic. Finally, we shut up.

"That's better," he grumbled. "Now listen, there are times, when a person becomes two people in a way. You, Carla already know this. It's what happens when you reach out and crush Coke cans without physically touching them. You also have seen this phenomenon in other ways, if you recall."

"Oh," she replied, making me wonder exactly what she knew.

"I'm sure you've read, Mr. Golden, or seen on TV, accounts of people who nearly died and came back to tell stories similar to what you told us about your bike accident and floating above your body."

"Yeah, sure, but I wasn't close to dying," I argued. "You're talking about what some people believe is the soul leaving the body at the point of death, right?"

"That final spirit separation from the body is similar," Lobo replied. "In your case, however, what you were dealing with after your accident is very much like when people have a *near* death event. In such a situation, one person becomes two people in a way. You have a duplication process where there is an original and a copy. Some people call it an out-of-body experience, but those words don't tell the full story.

"A double?" That really confused me, but not Carla. I saw her nodding ever so slightly as if she understood.

"Yes, in a way," Lobo said. "This happens naturally at times to everyone during dreaming, especially here in St. Augustine. Your physical being is asleep, but the consciousness wanders in a spirit body somewhere in the physical universe, into other realities, or even into the past or future."

"That's just too much for me to absorb," I said. "I mean, I can't even get my mind around people splitting into two parts."

"Two parts or more," Lobo elaborated.

I didn't say anything to that. The idea of human division, duplication or whatever, traveling to such crazy destinations, boggled my mind. All I could think of was a copy machine cranking out paper duplicates of people that somehow magically disappeared.

"In our world, the copy is usually invisible," Lobo instructed. "However, under very unusual circumstances, a physical duplicate develops that you can definitely see and at times, even touch. If such a thing occurs and the individual doesn't understand what's going on, it can cause severe mental trauma.

"This splitting or duplication is what you went through out on my porch. Your consciousness did indeed go somewhere else. I don't know where you went exactly, but since there was such a great time difference between what you remember and the actual time that passed, the probability is you traveled into a different reality instead of another place on earth."

"Uh, OK," I said, holding my sticky hands out in front of me. "But if I was traveling in this spirit body, duplicate or whatever, how could my clothes and hands bring back physical things like pine sap?"

"Excellent question," Lobo replied. "I have never seen such a thing happen. I suspect, your emotional outburst while working with the coins somehow helped to connect you with the spirit who hovers near you. The reality you visited must have a very strong link to that individual for you to bring physical evidence back from your journey. Beyond such speculation, I have no other answers for you."

Hearing Lobo say he didn't know something really startled me. The guy always seemed so self-assured. Thinking about that made me remember why I ran out of the old guy's house in the first place, and a twinge of anger shot through me. "Why did you grab my arm," I asked. "I mean after I picked out a coin from that big stack on your table?"

Lobo's usual frown deepened and he said, "I grabbed you in an attempt to get the coin out of your hand as quickly as possible. The hot coin, even more than the heat in the bayonet, showed a direct spirit contact that could have overwhelmed you. You were in danger and there wasn't time to explain. Whenever you are in close contact with this being, you are at risk. His spiritual essence is extremely intense and you haven't had any training in dealing with such things. I apologize for scaring you. Instead of helping, I brought about what I intended to prevent."

An apology from Lobo? Man, what a surprise. "Oh, OK. Now I understand." The increasing pain in my left temple caused me to pause for a few seconds and massage it with the few fingertips that had no sap on them. "Thanks, for uh, well, for trying to … protect me."

"You're welcome. I see your headache is still there. If you don't mind me touching you after our problem with the coin, I think I can help."

"Help?"

"He can make it better, really," Carla assured me.

"Um, I guess," I said, looking at Lobo. I wasn't too sure about my decision, but the intensity of the pain spoke louder than my uncertainty.

"Just stay seated where you are." Lobo came over to where I sat, scooted Spock away from the side of my chair and got down on his knees. After having me close my eyes, he told me he was going to touch my head and my upper chest. That's when I felt one big hand cover almost the entire upper half of my skull and the other one pressed gently against the area under my throat. That's when it started, a little tingling in my head and chest. Slowly, the tingling built into soothing warmth. Gradually, those two areas of warmth moved towards each other until they met right in the middle of my throat. In no time, the warmth spread over my entire body making me feel very relaxed. Even when Lobo took his hands away and went back to his chair, the feeling continued for a minute or so.

"The headache's gone, it's really … gone," I said, grinning like a fool. "I feel great, like I had a good night's sleep. Thanks, Lobo. Thanks a lot but how did you do that?"

"Too complex to explain," he replied with his usual sour expression. I wondered if the guy ever smiled or laughed. "What I accomplished, in addition to relieving your pain, was to share with you enough of my energy that it should shield you against unwanted spirit contact for a short while. It won't last long. For that very reason, we have to uncover as much information as quickly as we can about the deceased person who is putting you in danger. Make no mistake about it, he caused what happened to you out on my porch and interrupted your sleep with bad dreams. Understand?"

"I do." I startled myself with that instant response. I guess for the first time, I fully recognized how badly I needed the man's help.

"Good, but there's a large missing piece to your puzzle. It's something that you haven't told us yet, maybe something you've forgotten." Again, he did his little eye dance all around me and I wondered what he might be seeing. Instead of asking I waited for him to continue. "Your bike accident. Think about this carefully. When you felt yourself rise into the air and you looked out over Matanzas Bay and the city, did you see anything special or unusual?"

"Special or unusual? Oh … yeah, I did see something else but that part really had to have been my imagination or a dream."

"Everything's important in the limited time we have available. Now tell us."

"Well, as I was floating over the city and facing the bay, I glanced down to see if I could find my house and noticed a flashing of some sort, way off to my right. As I looked in that direction, I saw tall, dark clouds going way up into the sky with lightning popping inside every once in a while. When I looked at those clouds closer, I realized they actually covered the city south of downtown and even part of the river. It looked like a small thunderstorm with its base at street level. As I stared at it, the thing began to change and soon three glowing pyramids rose up out of the clouds. Weird, huh? Pyramids in St. Augustine? What a laugh."

At the mention of pyramids, Lobo pointed a big finger at me and said, "Now we're really getting somewhere." To Carla he said, "You do know where your friend's three pyramids are located?"

"Pyramids?" Carla asked with her faced scrunched up. "Oh, oh, of course," she replied, seconds later.

That really surprised me. "Aw come on, y'all!" I laughed nervously. "You've gotta be kidding me. There really are pyramids around here?"

"Uh huh," Carla replied. "You've really never seen them?"

"Nope. I haven't even been in the part of town where I saw the storm."

"Those pyramids appeared to you for a reason," Lobo said, looking all around me again. "The spirit hovering around you is very agitated, and as we speak of the pyramids he becomes even more so. I get the impression he put that storm and pyramid image into your mind as he did the bayonet. It fits. The pyramids, the bayonet and the coin are all from the same general historical period. A definite pattern is emerging and you need to take immediate action as soon as you get yourself cleaned up.

"Carla," he barked, turning to her. "Take him to the pyramids.

See if either of you can get any useful impressions and then return quickly. We'll need to take some time to process whatever you come up with there. It'll be dark soon. I want you both back before that happens.

"Now?" she asked, looking at her watch.

"Now! I have a definite feeling tomorrow will be too late."

PART TWO

Overwhelmed

11

Flying

As Carla and I rushed up San Marco Avenue, peddling hard in and out of heavy traffic, Lobo's words about tomorrow being too late still bounced around in my mind. At the time, no amount of prodding on my part, or on Carla's, got him to explain his meaning in more detail. The man's previous warnings about the danger surrounding me though, made the urgency of our little trip to the pyramids seem even more important.

We didn't waste any time dropping Spock off at Carla's house and picking up our bikes. By the time we got there, Lobo had already called Carla's grandmother. He explained to her how he wanted us to run an errand for him and then go to his house for dinner. Worked like a charm. All technically true, what he told her, but the three of us agreed not to mention the pyramids to Grandma. Doing so, we figured, might make her wonder about the conjuring of spirits and all that kind of stuff. Not the most honest of situations, but we didn't have time for detours. I know it wasn't easy for Carla to do that, but she pulled it off beautifully. No such problems for me at home. Mom planned to go straight from work and spend the night at her boyfriend's apartment.

Actually, I hated not telling Carla's grandma the full truth almost as much as Carla did. I mean, that lady had, well, adopted me in a way, I guess you might say. When she found out I eat most of my meals by myself, and out of cans, or at cheap restaurants, she swore she wasn't going to let it continue. After that, Carla's house became like a second home. I mean, I even went over there on Christmas Eve, but not inside or anything. Nope, I sat there on my bike looking at the little red, green and blue twinkle lights strung across the top of her front porch and the Christmas tree in the living room window facing the street. She and her grandma were having people over and I saw little glimpses of movement. Once I even spied Carla, but she didn't see me.

Every window in that house, even on the third floor, was glowing with light and I just wished I could be in there with Carla. It … well, looked comfortable and inviting, is all I can say—even more so than usual. A helluva lot better than being at home with my mom and her drunk-ass lover boy. That's where I was supposed to be, but they never knew the difference.

"So, why didn't you tell me about Lobo and all this spooky stuff of his before I met the guy?" I looked over at Carla sitting on her bike next to me. We were waiting for the traffic light to change down the street a little way from the grounds of the old Spanish fort. Oh, the Castillo de San Marcos to be more precise. Carla keeps trying to get me to call the place by its official name, or at least *The* Castillo.

She tried to reply to my question, but I couldn't hear her. A big old Harley kept revving up behind us, and a police siren nearby drowned out her words. You would think we lived in New York City. Too many tourists will definitely clog up the roads in a small town.

I shook my head and pointed to an ear to show her I couldn't hear.

"I said," Carla gave it another try, louder this time, "that I thought Lobo would give you a few ideas how to deal with your dream and we would be out of there. Telling you any more about him ahead of time, and you probably would never have gone to see him. Am I right?" Carla had the collar of her coat pulled up around her neck, and she blew into her cupped hands. Bike riding in that increasingly cold air chilled me, but I knew she had to be half frozen. That's why I didn't protest as she stopped at the red light when I would have plowed on through it. I realized she might need to warm up her hands a bit. She still wore a very worried look on her face, one I'd seen ever since I came back out of that God-awful fog.

"Yeah probably," I had to admit. In fact, I knew for sure I wouldn't have gotten anywhere near old Lobo if she had told me even a fraction of what I found out about him after we met. Traffic started moving again at that point, heading into downtown St. Augustine and cutting off any more conversation. As we rode single file, I caught the scent of Mexican food, burritos, I think. It smelled good and reminded me dinner awaited us back at Lobo's place. In the oncoming lanes, more and more headlights popped on as evening approached. Ahead of me, Carla's long hair flew and whipped behind her.

Luckily, no more traffic stops slowed down our progress. All along our route, little white lights covered buildings and trees as people choked the sidewalks on both sides of the road—Nights of Lights they call it in St. Augustine. Tourists flock here like migrating birds from November through January every year to ogle those bright little bulbs, absorb all the history of America's Oldest City during our extended Christmas season, eat in quaint little restaurants, and shop in the stores that stay open late.

Once we got past the Bridge of Lions, and the downtown plaza, the street we were on, Avenida Menendez, went from four lanes down to two, and traffic thinned out. We had finally entered the part of town I knew nothing about. Up until that point, I was able to keep my thoughts mostly on not getting run over and peddling my bike. Even so, memories of cold fog, a hot bayonet, and Lobo's warnings rushed back into my head, making me wonder if I was truly ready to visit the pyramids. As a chill ran up my spine, something happened so quickly I almost blew it off until I thought about my nearly instantaneous journey into Lobo's Ball of Realities. I'll do my best to explain it.

You see, I found myself … well, floating maybe five feet in the air looking down at the, uh, the me who was riding the bike. Yeah, the same floating-type-thing I experienced after my accident. This time though, I lay flat, parallel to the street, with my arms outstretched. When I looked, I could see them. Also unlike the time with my accident, I was *the me* riding the bike so that I saw my surroundings at the same time from two different viewpoints. Sounds crazy, I know.

Actually, that floating was more like flying since I kept pace with the me on my bike. The flying me felt no cold at all and my forward movement didn't ruffle my hair one bit. From the flying position, I lifted my head so I could see Carla, and there she was a couple of bike lengths away. Of course, I also watched her from where I sat on my bike. For whatever reason, looking at that girl from those two very different perspectives felt normal. It really didn't seem out of the ordinary at all. Don't ask me why, because I don't have any answers.

That's when everything changed again, and I mean very fast. The flying me felt this tug, a hard pulling sensation in my stomach. I knew it came from the me below, and I tried to resist, but couldn't. Like a stretched out rubber band being released, the flying me snapped back into that other Jeff riding down the street. When I say "into," I mean just that. It was like the flying me got instantly, and naturally, absorbed into a thirsty sponge. Even so, my whole body jerked—the body of the single, unified me. Without meaning to, I also jerked the handlebars of my bike, nearly smashing into a parked car on my right. For a split second, it felt very strange once again being a whole person instead of two.

Did I tell Carla about my little double-bodied, flying adventure. Hell no! I kept peddling and tried to ignore it myself. She had enough to worry about already without having to help me sort out another of my crazy situations. Besides, we didn't have the time.

On our left, the Matanzas River ran past the city marina and a place called the Santa Maria restaurant sitting out in the water on pilings. After the Santa Maria? Nothing there but sea wall, river, anchored boats, mudflats, and oysters. Beyond the river over on Anastasia Island, the beam from the St. Augustine Lighthouse flashed briefly from time to time, reflecting off the darkening water. A slight breeze coming over the sea wall brought with it the crappy smell of low tide. To our right, just the usual mix of houses, motels and inns—and little white lights. Believe me, those lights are every-where at that time of year.

Up the street, directly in front of us, an American flag, and one other I couldn't identify, barely moved on top of a tall flagpole. The road appeared to end there, but didn't. Instead, it turned sharply to the right. When we turned with it, we rode by a couple of large pillars and a low wall on our left. As the road took another sharp turn, this time to the left, a large, cream-colored building loomed into view in front of us. Large black letters across the front of that place identified it as the "St. Francis Barracks." A sign on the parking lot wall directly across the street from the building said, "Headquarters, Florida National Guard." Right in front of that wall, two old-fashioned cannons aimed outward towards the road. The flagpole, I discovered, was inside the National Guard parking lot containing a few cars and two modern looking cannons pointing out towards the river.

When Carla and I got to the St. Francis Barracks, a young sol-dier ran out of it into the street all dressed in his multi shades of green outfit and hat. Because he was talking on his cell phone and not paying attention, he almost ran into us. Luckily, he stopped in time. As we swung around him, he grinned and waved but still stayed glued to his phone. I figured he had to be talking to a girl. U.S. Army it said in black letters printed on the upper left side of his jacket, coat, or whatever you call it. On the opposite side was the word, "Basinger." I knew that had to be the guy's name, but for some reason, reading it made me stop and look back at him when he sprinted towards his car.

"Jeff, come on," Carla called, looking back at me, but still peddling. In seconds, I caught up with her.

On our right, we passed four tidy looking, two-story houses painted white, each of them with a small American flag on its front porch, and more little white lights. A large historic marker identified the houses as Officers' Quarters. Beyond those houses a short distance sat a large two-story coquina building surrounded by a metal fence made of skinny bars painted black. Down the road a little way, the fence ended, but immediately, another one started—a thick one, about waist high. Looked like it might be made of plastered coquina, brick or maybe even concrete block. I really couldn't tell from that distance. That's where Carla pulled to a stop, got off her bike and pushed it up onto the sidewalk. I did the same.

"How are your headaches?" she asked, leaning her bike against her hip and blowing on her fingers some more.

"No problem so far. Looks like whatever Lobo did is still working." I wanted to ask her how the old guy seemed to be able to read my thoughts, but decided to wait until after I got to see the pyramids.

"Good," she said, but her face still had that tense and worried look. "Let's keep moving, have you see the pyramids, and get back to Lobo's as soon as we can. They're right up here." She was definitely in a no-nonsense mood.

As I followed her, I looked between the metal bars of the fence on the other side of the large coquina house and saw tombstones. "We're going to a cemetery?" I croaked. Now I'm not afraid of cemeteries or anything, but they aren't the most positive places in the world, right? Besides, with Lobo talking about death and all, it, uh, startled me, you know?

"Um, yes." Carla looked over at me uncertainly as we walked. "It's a cemetery all right. I didn't think you needed to know that ahead of time."

12

Pyramids

The place wasn't very large, as cemeteries go. Maybe a couple of hundred feet long and a hundred wide with some really large oak trees inside. In the increasing darkness, small white tombstones seemed to march off through the surrounding grass in perfect order.

"So, the pyramids are actually in there?" I asked as we got closer. Guess I still couldn't accept the idea our destination was a cemetery. Up until then, I thought ghost stories in movies about such places were just silly inventions by screen writers.

"Look carefully." Carla pointed at an angle across the cemetery.

"No way," I whispered when I finally spied them. Near some of the taller monuments at the far end of the enclosure sat three grey, triangular shapes side-by-side. To me, they looked like they had thrust themselves up out of the ground somehow. God, it was startling to see those things truly existed, but they were a little disappointing. "They're kind of tiny."

"Not when you get near them," Carla replied. "Besides, what were you expecting? Huge buildings the size of the Giza pyramids in Egypt?"

"I'm not sure what I expected, except the ones I saw right after my accident were a lot larger."

"What does it matter? Your vision or whatever you want to call it, led you right here. That's what's important."

I couldn't argue with her. She had it right.

"St. Augustine National Cemetery," a sign said to our right on a closed metal gate. Instead of stopping, Carla led me a little farther until we stood in front of a large historical marker pointing out towards the sidewalk alongside the street.

"Lobo told me to have you check this out before we go inside."

Now normally I don't read historical markers. This time was different though. I really wanted to see what the one in front of me had to say. Turned out, it had a short, but interesting story to tell. Here is the exact wording:

Major Dade and his
Command Monuments

On December 28, 1835, during the Second Seminole War,
a column of 108 U.S. Army soldiers dispatched from
Fort Brooke (Tampa) to relieve the detachment at
Fort King (Ocala) was surprised by a strong force
of Seminole Indians near Bushnell in Sumter County.
Except for three soldiers and an interpreter, the entire column
of 108 men, led by Major Francis Langhorne Dade,
perished in Battle that day.
On August 15, 1842, Dade and his command,
as well as other casualties of the war,
were re-interred here under three coquina stone pyramids
in a ceremony marking the end of the conflict.
Among those buried with Dade are
Captain George W. Gardiner, U.S. Military Academy
(U.S.M.A.) 1814, first Commandant of Cadets at
West Point, and Major David Moniac, U.S.M.A., 1822,
a Creek Indian and first Native-American graduate
of the Military Academy.

"Wow!"I said when I finished reading. "So the pyramids are

tombstones for a mass grave."

"Yup," Carla agreed. "And the date of the battle, as you read, was December *28*—one more twenty-eight for your list."

"I noticed." I noticed all right, but I had tried to ignore it without much success.

"That number does tend to follow you around. Lobo sure thinks it has some significance. Wonder what it is?"

"Yeah, you and me both."

"Uh, you do realize tomorrow is the 28th of December don't you?" she asked.

"It is?" I had to think for a few seconds, and as I did, the oddest feeling slithered through my gut. "Oh crap... you're right. You don't think—?"

"That something is going to happen tomorrow?"

I swear, just then the girl sounded like Lobo—as if she had read my exact thought. No matter what, she had to be at least thinking the same thing. Instead of replying to her, I shrugged. Unfortunately, Lobo's warning about the next day being too late fit what we were saying much too nicely.

"Maybe," she said, answering her own question, "but don't get too wrapped up in possibilities yet. We simply don't know enough."

"OK," I replied, "but it could be, right? I mean you brought up tomorrow yourself and so did Lobo." Again, that odd sensation shot through my gut.

"True, but don't drive yourself crazy thinking that's the only possibility. Besides, I have another little wrinkle in all this to tell you."

"Wrinkle?" I asked, not sure I could stand any more wrinkles in my day than I had already experienced.

"Take it easy. It's nothing upsetting. Remember that line on the marker about an interpreter escaping the battle?"

"Yeah. What about it?" My words came out with a little more intensity than I had intended. "Sorry, guess I'm a little stressed."

"Don't worry about it. Understandable. I'll quick finish my story and we'll go see the pyramids.

"That interpreter, the one mentioned on the marker? His name was Luis Pacheco, a slave rented out to Major Dade for $25 a month by a Spanish lady who owned him. Luis was very intelligent and spoke three languages other than English—Spanish, French, and Seminole. Dade used the man as an interpreter and even a scout against the Seminoles. Luis didn't necessarily want to do those things for Dade, but he had no choice."

"OK, but why do I need to know this right now?" I really didn't see the point of listening to another one of her history lectures when we needed to get back to Lobo's before dark.

"I'm telling you this because I'm related to him, Luis Pacheco, not Major Dade." She said those words about her long gone relative so casually. OK, the girl is brainy and loves history. That's one thing. But for her to have someone from her family who had lived through an important historical event was really startling—especially one involved with the same pyramids we were visiting.

"You, uh, never told me that before."

"Um, with your lack of interest in history, I thought what happened to a member of my family in the past would be boring for you."

"No, I am interested, really. Go ahead and finish what you were going to tell me about this Pacheco guy."

"OK, short and simple. Luis was captured by the Seminoles during the battle you read about, one of the few people to actually survive it. They didn't kill him because he spoke their language, and they understood that as a slave, he had to carry out whatever orders the white soldiers gave him."

By the time Carla finished talking, it fully registered on my brain that somebody had owned this Luis Pacheco guy. And rented him out like you would a piece of equipment! To the United States army! An actual relative of Carla's? *Good God!* Of course, I had read about slavery and heard about it in history classes, but that was the first time it had any real meaning for me. "I can't get over your ancestor being owned and rented out." That's all I could think of to say. I knew there had to be a better way of saying that, but that's all I came up with.

"Tell me about it." The look on her face showed an intense mixture of sadness, disgust, and even anger.

Listening to Carla brought to mind a talk I once had with her grandmother. We were munching cookies in Carla's kitchen while I waited for her to come home from school. When the conversation shifted to race relations in St. Augustine's past, Grandma pointed out the window across Matanzas Bay. "Right out there on Vilano Beach one night back in 1964," she said, "the Ku Klux Klan burned a huge cross as a warning to the African American community. I remember that night so clearly. You could see those flames over much of St. Augustine and nearby areas. Scared black folks around here silly. It scared a lot of whites as well, if you want to know the truth. That was back in the days of Jim Crow and the civil rights movement—dangerous times when you never knew who the Klan might come after."

When Grandma said what she did, I looked where she had pointed and imagined I could see a giant fiery cross lighting up the city and Matanzas Bay across from the Castillo with its hatred.

"Earth to Jeff," Carla said, snapping me away from my memory about her grandmother.

Picking up the conversation again, I said, "That's quite a coincidence, isn't it? I mean how I saw pyramids during my accident, and the fact that your ancestor is related to their history."

"No kidding, but don't ever say that to Lobo. He constantly lectures me about there being no such thing as a coincidence." Not giving me a chance to ask her what Lobo meant by that, Carla put her bike down in front of the closed cemetery gate. In no time, she had reached down through the bars, unlatched one side of the gate somehow, and shoved it partway open. Once we both pushed our bikes inside, she said, "We'll leave it this way since we won't be here long."

"You do have a talent for getting things done," I replied, admiring her knowledge of St. Augustine and her ability to make things happen.

"Watch and learn, Golden Boy." She said this not with a smile, but a tight little grimace instead. Carla sometimes tends to try and cover up worry with efficiency, and a not very convincing expression of cool detachment. This was one of those times.

"Yes ma'am. You're the boss. Well, on this trip anyway."

In reply, she just snorted.

Without talking for a little while, we walked our bikes up the wide driveway and turned left down a central sidewalk leading to the pyramids. A row of low bushes to the left and right of the walkway separated us from the rows of tombstones. On the ground between two of those bushes, a huge floodlight pointed up at large American flag barely fluttering on its pole behind us, high up in the gloom of decreasing daylight. The light breeze making the flag move brought the strong scent of freshly cut grass to us. Houses surrounded the cemetery on three sides, and I wondered what it must be like to come out of your door everyday and see gravestones.

Ahead of us about 100 feet, the sidewalk ended at a very tall monument, and behind it stood the pyramids—my pyramids, the ones I saw come out of a storm as I floated above St. Augustine. All three faced us, close together and mainly showing one flat side.

For whatever reason, seeing those things right in front of me caused my thoughts to flash back to that dark, cold fog at Lobo's place once more. For an instant, I again held onto a ripped up tree like it was a life raft or something. I mean I could feel the moisture of my face and those weird, sticky, pine sap covered holes rubbing across my fingertips. What I could feel most of all though, was the terror of being stuck there in such a weird, unknown place without anybody else around. Not what I needed to have happen right about then.

"Sorry, what was that?" Carla had said something I didn't catch because of my wandering mind. "My brain keeps shifting out of gear."

"Are you OK?" she asked with an intense stare through crinkled eyes as if she might be able to see how I felt no matter how I responded. Behind Carla, on the other side of the cemetery wall, a silver colored pickup truck roared past us heading towards downtown, country music blaring from an open window.

"A lot of stuff keeps running through my head, that's all," I replied as honestly as I could. "It's hard to not let it drive me crazy."

That seemed to satisfy her, to some degree anyway, but the worried look on her face didn't go away. "Hang in there," she said, reaching over and squeezing my arm. Seconds later, we arrived at the tall monument in front of the pyramids where Carla proceeded to tell me how it honored all the soldiers who died in the Second Seminole War.

Interesting as that was, to her, I only had eyes for what sat behind the monument. Maybe eight feet across and five feet high, the pyramids definitely looked a lot larger than when I first saw them. In the diminishing light, it took me a few seconds to realize that the construction of each of those objects consisted of shaped pieces of coquina, held together with mortar, or cement maybe.

Part of me couldn't wait to get closer, but another, smaller part wanted to hold back. After my recent experiences with Lobo's hot bayonet and coin, all from the same general period of history as the pyramids, I didn't know if something else weird might happen. On top of that, the memory of flying above myself on the way to the cemetery still had me spooked. In the end though, curiosity won over. Carla and I left our bikes at the war monument and walked across the grass to the central pyramid. Nothing out of the ordinary occurred when we got there, so I relaxed a little and read the first few lines of the small historical maker in front of us:

**These three pyramids cover vaults
containing individually unidentified remains
of 1468 soldiers of the Florida Indian Wars,
1835-1842.**

1,468 soldiers, I said to myself with a shiver. So much death.

"As the marker says," Carla explained, "these pyramids weren't made only for Dade's men. After the Second Seminole War ended, the military collected the bones of soldiers who died during that entire seven-year conflict from all over the state and brought them here. Back in 1842 they had a huge ceremony with muskets firing and bugles blowing. I think it lasted an entire day."

"Wait a minute." With her eyes wide, she pointed at the pyramid. "The spirit Lobo says is hanging around you. I'm wondering if it could be from one of these soldiers."

Again, I felt that odd slithering sensation in my gut, but this time it even crept up into my chest. I didn't comment on what Carla had said one way or the other. I didn't need to reply because she kept on talking. Besides, I didn't want to think about what she said.

"It all fits together somehow—the pyramids, tomorrow's date as the Dade battle's anniversary, the bayonet, the coin, and even the connection to Luis Pacheco."

"Now look who's getting locked into possibilities," I replied. Instead of trying to figure it all out, I reached down and touched the rough surface of a coquina block with my fingertips. A slight tingling prickled up through that hand and I quickly pulled it away.

"What?" Carla asked, as I straightened, rubbing my fingers and staring at the pyramid.

It's cold out here, I told myself, ignoring Carla's question at first. *The coquina was just cold, dummy. That's all you felt. God, you are really letting your fears take over. Wimp!* "It's nothing," I said to her, finally deciding to overcome what had to be my imagination. To prove to myself there was nothing to be afraid of, I bent over again, and put my whole hand flat against a different piece of coquina.

As soon as I did that, a painful rippling, like a strong electric current, surged up through my arm and throughout my body. At the same time, my vision erupted in a blinding flash of white.

13

A Cloud of Vultures

Oh man, at first when I took my hand away from the coquina, I thought I had somehow touched a live electric wire. After that brilliant white light and the pain going up my arm, I knew there had to be high voltage connected to the pyramid somehow. Thoughts of underground power lines leaking electricity and fallen electric wires resting on the pyramid wet from the rain earlier in the day flickered through my mind. *Not likely*, I said to myself, since I was standing and conscious. No matter what though, I still couldn't see. That's what really scared me. My eyes moved, but my field of vision showed nothing but pure, eerie white.

"Carla?" No answer. Why wouldn't she answer? "Uh, something just happened." My voice sounded as shaky as I felt. "Carla? I ... can't see." Even as I spoke, I noticed the white in front of my eyes slowly starting to fade—a hopeful sign. Again, no answer.

As I listened desperately for a response, I thought I smelled pine needles and something else—not very pleasant. Pine needles? "No way! Don't start this again," I whispered to myself.

Pine needles were not what I needed to be sniffing at that moment. "Carla, talk to me," I yelled. "This isn't funny. I really need your help." I tell you what. When she didn't answer that time, I really freaked. I knew if she could answer, she would. Either something had happened to her, or she just wasn't there. Both choices scared the hell out me, and I stood there not knowing what to do.

Slowly, vague images started appearing in the white I was seeing. When I lifted my hands in front of my face, I wiggled my fingers until I finally saw them—blurry, but there. "All right!" I shouted, and when I did, my vision suddenly snapped back to normal. My hands stood out perfectly in focus. What I didn't see though, is what made my insides do a flip-flop. Carla, the pyramids, the cemetery, and the rest of St. Augustine were … well, gone. Spread out in front of me was nothing but pine trees and palmetto bushes extending out as far as I could see. Across the cloudless sky above, a big bunch of vultures drifted around in soundless, lazy circles. Yeah, vultures. "Damn!" I whispered. "Damn, damn, damn."

All those pine trees and palmettos cast long, deep shadows running away from me in the yellowish, orange color of either a sunrise or sunset. I swallowed hard as sweat trickled down my left side, and that stupid headache returned. "Lobo, where's your protection?" I wailed loudly. My voice sounded strange, as if it didn't belong to me.

Realizing I was barely breathing, I inhaled deeply and got an intense whiff of that bad smell again, in addition to the scent of pine needles—a really weird combination. Deciding to turn around, I found more pine trees, palmettos and shadows. On the horizon, half a sun glared in my direction. I still couldn't tell if it was rising or setting. In the sky right above the sun floated a few high, wispy clouds the color of gold. I felt like I had been tossed into a vast sea of vegetation ruled by a one-eyed god.

"This can't be happening," I kept saying to myself. With each passing second, the reality of what my senses continued relaying to my brain told a different story.

As a light breeze rippled through the treetops, a red winged blackbird stared at me from his perch on a dead branch lying on the ground about ten feet away. With a squawk, it flew off, heading off over that endless wilderness. Into the clutter of trees and bushes on either side of me, someone had long ago hacked out what appeared to be a wide path or a small road. Weathered tree stumps, rotting logs and dried-out palm fronds littered the opened up landscape in both directions as far as I could see.

Frantic to bring some sort of sanity into everything around me, I closed my eyes for a couple of minutes, hoping that when I opened them again I would somehow magically be back in the cemetery with Carla. Yeah, right. No such luck. When I opened my eyes again, something had changed all right. The yellowish, orange light from the sun had disappeared and so had the shadows. "No," I whispered hoarsely, but the sun had sunk out of sight. "No, no, no. Don't do that," I pleaded, but of course, the sun didn't listen. The idea of me being there, wherever there was when it got dark, shook me up even more than before.

I got so desperate I even pulled out my cell phone, but the thing wouldn't turn on even though I had charged it that morning. Did I really think it would work so far from everything? No, not really. But for it not to even turn on startled me.

The shrill hoot of an owl echoing through the pines didn't help my jittery nerves one bit.

The sound reminded me of the dark fog on Lobo's porch and I shivered with the memory. "Well, at least there isn't any fog here," I said, trying very hard to make the best of a really bad situation. Night was coming and I had to do something. Even so, nothing came to mind except Carla. What if somehow she actually came with me to this place, I wondered, but was somewhere else on the road. "Carla!" I shouted at the top of my lungs knowing that it probably wouldn't be worth the effort. No matter what, it felt good to yell. I think it was just the idea of taking action, any kind of action.

When I shouted Carla's name, a strange, tremendous whooshing noise like soft, distant thunder came from up the road to my right.

As I stared in that direction through the treetops, I saw a huge cloud of vultures rising up into the air. There had to be hundreds of them. The whooshing noise was all those wings pounding the air.

Vultures usually mean only one thing. "Dead critters," I said to myself, using Carla's word. That's when I started getting scared for her. Could she have come to that place with me but ended up somewhere else? Could she be in trouble? Did those vultures attack her?

My mind raced with all the possibilities.

"Carla!" I ran up the road towards where the vultures had risen from the ground. The closer I got, the more that strange, nasty smell filled my nostrils. It was so disgusting I finally realized it must be whatever the vultures had been eating. Reminded me of opening a package of rotting chicken once. Really gross. The air around me on that road though, had that old chicken smell beat by a thousand times. I covered my mouth and nose with both hands.

"Carla!" I yelled again, taking my hands away from my face just long enough to get the word out. No response, but even more vultures rose up into the air not very far away up the road. Frantic, I ran even faster. Problem was, I found it difficult to breathe through my hands.

As I stopped for a second to catch my breath, I spotted a shoe lying in the sand and pine needles ahead of me. A short distance away stood a large pine tree. On the ground scattered near its base, I saw little slivers of wood. Bypassing the shoe, I walked quickly up to the tree and stared at it. From the bottom of the trunk up to seven feet high or so, much of the bark had been ripped away. In the bare wood, exactly as I had felt on the tree in the dark at Lobo's place, jagged holes oozed sap. "No way," I whispered.

The woods by that time were darkening quickly. Vultures filled the dimming sky above me as they silently circled and circled. At first, I couldn't help but stare at them until I forced myself to look away. When I did, I saw a man lying on his back up a little farther up the road. I hadn't noticed him at first, I guess, because of my focus on the shoe and tree. On his chest, sat a huge vulture with flies buzzing all around. It didn't register in my mind right away what the bird was doing until I saw the thing pecking and pulling at the guy's face. I mean, I was so surprised to find anybody else around there except maybe for Carla, you know? And then to see that! God it was awful.

"Get off !" I shouted once I got over the shock of that scene. The stupid bird turned its ugly head and looked directly at me, but with something in its beak. I won't tell you what it looked like. Believe me, you don't want to know. Even though I yelled at that damned bird, the thing didn't move. Well, that made me mad and without even thinking, I ran right at him, yelling and waving my arms. When I got about half way there, the vulture made this weird squawk, and dropped what was in its beak. With wings flapping, it slowly hoisted itself into the air and flew off.

Once more I clamped both hands back over my nose and mouth. In my anger at the vulture, I had taken them away from my face. Looking at the poor guy's mangled head, I knew he had to be the source of that really putrid smell.

When I heard noises coming from up ahead, I decided to bypass the dead guy and get away from the stink. As I walked by him, I avoided looking at his face, but noticed he wore what looked like a light blue or gray uniform. Gold buttons ran up the front of his jacket. White belts crisscrossed his chest and one went around his waist.

Uniform? Carla's words about me possibly being haunted by one of Dade's soldiers flashed into my mind. *Oh man, what am I seeing here?* Instantly, my stomach started to rebel. I had to get far away from that body, so I walked away quickly only to run into what I thought might be the back end of a large, partially burned, wooden wagon. Resting on their sides, just in front of the wagon, I saw three very large cows, rust colored, with big horns.

Beyond the wagon as far as I could see, lay more men dressed like the first. On top of the cows and men, vultures ripped flesh, buried their heads into bodies and flapped their ugly wings. In the distance, there was a barricade of some sort, made out of logs.

"Oh God." I tried hard not think about all those dead people being the source of that horrible stink. It didn't work. What little I had left in my stomach fired out through my mouth.

14

Brightness and People

I puked and puked until nothing came up but air. It seemed like my stomach was going to come right out of my mouth. Through closed eyes, I could feel hot tears drop away. All I could think of was those bodies on the road, vultures feasting, the stink, and being alone in a place I didn't understand.

A voice just behind me said something I couldn't quite hear. At the same time, I felt a hand touch my back and come to rest there. Part of me wanted to whirl around and see who it was, thankful somebody, anybody, had found me. The thing is, I wasn't even able to turn my head because of the heaving. The hand on my back moved over to my shoulder and gently squeezed. "Are you OK?" the person said, the voice louder and sharper this time. It sounded vaguely like Carla.

"Carla?" Her name came out all raspy sounding, but the possibility it might really be her calmed my stomach a bit. After retching one more time, and bringing nothing up, I found I could turn my head. When I opened my eyes, there she was, beautiful, wonderful Carla. Couldn't believe it. I had never been so glad to see someone in my life, but part of me feared she might fade away in a flash of brilliant white. All the while, my stomach kept twisting, but I didn't puke any more.

"You had me so scared." In her voice, I could hear a mixture of deep worry, almost panic. For Carla, that's saying something. She doesn't do panic.

I dropped my head between my shoulders a bit and took in a deep breath. That's when I smelled it. Sure enough, there was my puke all over the grass. I had been throwing up in front of the middle pyramid back in the cemetery.

"Oh man." I wiped my mouth with the back of my hand and stood up. Talk about embarrassing. "Sorry Carla," was all I could manage to say. The thought of me throwing up in front of her made me feel worse. In order for me to get both of us away from all that mess I'd made on the ground, I walked into the grass around the tall war monument and squatted with my back to the pyramids. I barely made it, my legs were so wobbly.

Carla came over and sat next to me, again putting her hand on my shoulder. That felt so good, but my mind kept going back to all I had seen on the lonely wilderness road.

"We've got to get you to a doctor," she said gently, but with urgency in her voice.

"No... I'll, ah, be OK, really." I took another deep breath, realizing for the first time, there was no horrible stink in the air, and I don't mean the puke behind me. I've never been so glad to inhale clean air in my whole life.

"Come on now," Carla argued, "one minute we're talking and the next minute you're throwing up. There has to be something really wrong with you, food poisoning maybe."

"It isn't anything like that." My mouth tasted terrible. I knew my breath must smell awful so I tried not talking to Carla directly. As my mind began functioning better, it dawned on me I had started throwing up on the road with the bodies and finished back in the cemetery with Carla. I was beginning to think I really was losing my mind. "Tell me what happened."

"What do mean?" she asked.

"Please," I begged her, "just ... just tell me what you saw from the moment I touched the pyramid until I started puking."

"OK, but there really isn't much to tell. You, ah, touched the pyramid with your fingers at first, and then you put your whole hand on it. You backed up a little bit right after that, and quivered, like you were cold. The next thing I know, you bent over and started throwing up. That's it."

That's it? My mind raced through the memory of all I experienced after I touched the pyramid the second time. All of that was not my imagination, a dream, or a hallucination, I kept telling myself. Lobo's words about spirit bodies traveling to other places also thundered inside my head, as if he was standing next to me. Talk about confusion.

"Something else is going on with you you're not telling me isn't it?" Carla asked.

"Well … yeah, but this is going to sound even crazier than what I told you about all that fog on Lobo's porch." It only took a few minutes for me to spill my story about the road, and what I found there, but it felt like an hour. As I talked to Carla, the fear I felt during my time on that stinking road once again forced its way into my mind, and my hands shook. Seeing how agitated I was getting, she took both my hands in both of hers, immediately calming me down.

"Fascinating," she said wide-eyed when I finished "Unbelievably fascinating."

"That's not exactly the word I would use, but at least you're not ready to have me committed to a mental hospital, right?"

"Hardly. I think your experience here has really pointed you in the right direction."

"To hell with direction, I want it to stop. If I get any more direction like that I may really go freakin' crazy."

Surprisingly, Carla didn't even blink when I forgot and used the word "hell." "I hear you, really I do," she replied, "but Lobo sent us here to see if we could pick up any information that might put an end to all this for you."

"Maybe so, but you haven't gone where I have and neither has Lobo. Look at me," I said holding up my hands that had started shaking again. "My head is killing me, and it's really hard for me to sit here and talk about all this in a calm, logical way."

"OK, OK, take it easy. You don't have to do any more talking, but let me quick tell you something, and then we'll go. Whether you know it or not, you just described to me the battlefield where Major Dade and his soldiers lost their lives in 1835. You nailed it right down to the road they used, their uniforms, the burned out wagon, the cows that were actually oxen, and even all those vultures. Jeff, it was as if you truly were there somehow."

"Really?" As interesting as what she had to say was, it scared me even more.

"Really. You were right on the money. Like I said before, I wouldn't be surprised if it's one of those soldiers from the battle who's trying to grab your attention. I'm sure Lobo can now help you to find—"

I don't know what happened while Carla talked. For whatever reason, I felt completely overwhelmed. Maybe I suffered a panic attack or something, I'm not sure. What I do know is that after she mentioned the possibility of one of Dade's soldier's being the source of all my trouble, I had this uncontrollable urge to get away from those pyramids as fast as I could. Carla or no Carla, I had to get out of there, and I did. When I say overwhelming, I am not kidding.

Without a word, I jumped up, hopped on my bike, and roared off down the sidewalk. Behind me, I could hear Carla calling my name, but I was blinded by so much pain, confusion, doubt, and fear that I flat didn't care. After coasting through the small opening Carla left in the cemetery gate, I hit the street pumping the old pedals for all I was worth. My butt didn't get anywhere near the bike seat until I pushed well past the National Guard building. Only when the lights from the marina, the Santa Maria restaurant, and the Bridge of Lions reflected in the Matanzas River did I slow down a little. Those lights gave me a target, a place to head for, as far away from that cemetery as possible. It felt so good to move, to use all my strength and energy and feel the cold, clean wind on my face.

In front of me, a horse drawn carriage with a couple of tourists in it plodded along, its red taillights and little side lanterns glowing. The driver looked up from talking to his passengers just in time to see me approaching at a high speed. I ignored him, whipped into the left lane and found myself facing the headlights from an oncoming car. I was going too fast to slow down in time, but luckily, the driver swerved to his right and partially into a vacant parking spot with breaks squealing. Barely threading my bike between the car's rear bumper on my left and the horse on my right, I heard a horn blare behind me.

Not for a second did I consider slowing down, but that didn't last long. When I swung back into the right-hand lane, a line of cars came to a gradual stop on my side of the road up at the King Street traffic light near the Bridge of Lions. Red taillights burned with fiery warnings of danger meant for me and nobody else—warnings about the past somehow coming alive and threatening to swallow me whole. Paranoid thinking? Sure, but can you really blame me?

OK, I did slow down quite a bit when I approached all that traffic in my way, because I had no other choice. Instead of being completely reckless, I glided by the driver's side of the cars in front of me as oncoming traffic, with their headlights glaring, rushed past on my left. It took until then for me to recognize I had no idea where I was going. Panic had shoved me this far, but I no longer felt that mindless need to move and distance myself from the cemetery. Safely behind me, the pyramids were no longer the problem.

So now what? Returning to Lobo's place, waiting for Carla and talking to both of them about my experience over dinner was definitely not an option just then. No way I was going to talk about all those bodies any more. I thought about going home, but I sure didn't want to sit there all alone. To tell the truth, part of me wanted to turn right across the Bridge of Lions out to Anastasia Island, head south on highway A1A along the Atlantic and get away from St. Augustine as fast as I could.

Ahead of me on my left, the plaza and all its little lights glowed brightly. All those thousands of tiny shining white bulbs everywhere, the huge Christmas tree, and all the people walking around looked kind of inviting. Yeah, even the tourists. Brightness and people, that's what I needed—well, people I didn't know anyway. Nobody there would know or care about any of my dumbass experiences. To me, the plaza looked like this brilliant oasis of warmth and sanity.

As I got to the first car in line ahead of me at the King Street intersection, the traffic light turned green. Immediatley, I turned left and shot in front of the oncoming cars and up King Street. I went against the one-way traffic flow there, but at least those cars had a red light. For me it was the quickest way to get to my oasis where I could feel anonymous and safe.

At the plaza, I got off my bike and walked it past the old public market place across the grass. There were way too many people on the sidewalks for bike riding, and besides, the cops frown on it. The last thing I needed was a problem with St. Augustine's finest. Exhausted and with my nerves shot to pieces, all I wanted to do was find a bench and sit down. People already occupied most of them, but finally I spied an empty one near the bandstand and the Christmas tree. Trotting next to my bike as fast as I could without bumping into people, I rushed to claim the seat before anyone else did. When I got there, I threw my bike up against the bushes behind the bench and then collapsed on it, sweating and panting like crazy. Slowly, my headache began to ease a little.

Across the sidewalk from me, two old people, a man and a woman, sat on another bench. Nice enough looking folks, but they just stared at me as if they were sure I had robbed a bank or something. So much for the plaza being as perfectly warm and cuddly as I had hoped, right? Even so, it still felt good to be sitting there, and for the first time in a long while I began to really relax. My breathing slowed, and soon I realized my thoughts weren't as wild and threatening as they had been minutes before.

That's when I saw her. Carla I mean. Walking her bike on the sidewalk towards me from the other side of the plaza. I have no idea how she found me. "Oh crap," I whispered, realizing I had left her without a word in the cemetery while she attempted to help me in every way she could. In my blind need to escape, I had let her slip into the far background of my overloaded mind. *Idiot!*

When she got to my bench, she stood in front of me for a moment without expression or saying a word. Instead, she closed her eyes for a few seconds, took a deep, shuddering breath, and swallowed hard. I thought she was going to cry, but she didn't. Only at that point did I begin to understand how truly worried she was about me. God I felt awful.

What she did do was to prop her bike on its kickstand, fold her arms across her chest, and arch a slender eyebrow. She wanted an explanation and she wanted it fast. Funny how much she can communicate with those eyebrows of hers. The two old people across from us stared in our direction, probably wondering what was going to happen. I could see the man thinking, son, whatever you did, you're gonna get it now. I figured he had it about right. As compassionate and caring as Carla is, you don't mess with her.

"I am so sorry," I said. "I really I am."

In response, her other eyebrow went up. That meant, "Umm, OK, go on, convince me."

After stumbling around to find appropriate words for a minute or two, I did get her to sit down. Slowly and painfully, I worked hard to explain what had happened to me back in the cemetery. It was so difficult because I wasn't really sure I understood it myself.

When I finished what I had to say, Carla's eyebrows came down, always a good sign if she's angry or upset at all. Instead of saying anything right away though, she breathed deeply again and turned her head to gaze out over the plaza. The two oldsters were still staring at us. It looked like they were listening to our conversation, and that I did not like.

"So are you doing better now?" Carla asked once she turned her attention back to me.

"Better than I was back there in the cemetery."

"OK, that's good, but we really have to get to Lobo's. He needs to know what happened at the pyramids. Remember, Jeff, what he said about being out after dark and the danger you face. You've had two serious … events, where you, or at least part of you, has gone somewhere else. Who knows what might—"

"Tell me something I don't know!" My reply came out a little stronger than intended. Her talk about Lobo, pyramids and danger instantly made my entire body tighten. Just thinking about going back to Lobo's place twisted my stomach into knots, and again my hands started to shake—not a lot, but enough to tell me what I could and could not do. "There's no way I'm going back and see Lobo right now. I'm OK sitting here for a while."

"How can you say that? You're putting your life in even more jeopardy. Remember what Lobo told you about the danger you're in and getting back by dark?"

"Damn him," I exploded. "Who is this Lobo guy anyway? It's Lobo this and Lobo that. I'm sick to death of Lobo. What do you really know about him, huh? Well, I'll tell you who he is. He's a weird old guy who likes to scare kids, that's who. I've had enough of him." Even before the words were completely out of my mouth, I knew I had gone too far in so many different ways. I really didn't want to offend Carla, but I knew I had.

Before I could try repairing the damage, a hard look spread over her face, and she stood up like a giant spring had shot her into position. With hands on her hips, she started in on me.

"Now you listen here, Jeffrey Golden. Don't you ever go damning one of my friends, especially Lobo. That man is probably the only thing standing between you and destruction. But if you want to ignore his expert advice and try dealing with all this on your own … " Her eyes welled with tears, but her voice rose as she shook a finger in my direction. "If you want to do this your way, be my guest. I'm finished. I've done all I can." She grabbed her bike, smacked the kickstand with her foot, and walked away through the crowds of tourists.

That was not what I wanted to happen. "Oh crap," I moaned.

Across from me, I noticed the two oldsters whispering to each other and glancing over at me. After a few seconds, the man shrugged, pulled out his wallet and handed the lady some money. They hadn't just been listening in, I figured, they had bet on the outcome of our conversation.

"You two have fun did you?" I shouted at them, standing up. "Huh?"

Well, tell you what. Those two looked like they had been terribly insulted. I don't think anybody had ever nailed them while they played their little game. In a snooty huff, they both got up and walked down Cathedral Place.

15

Lyle

I sat there on that cold concrete bench feeling sorry for myself trying not to think for quite a while. Tons of people walked by, most of them looking happy, some with Santa Claus hats on even though Christmas had come and gone. Laughter and conversation floated all around me in the early evening air. Across the plaza on King Street, a tram full of tourists came to a stop in front of Potter's Wax Museum. In a loud, electronic voice, the driver explained how in its long history, St. Augustine had been burned to the ground more than once by pirates and other invaders.

No matter how hard I tried not to think about my argument with Carla, as well as what drove me to the plaza in the first place, it all came gushing back into my mind. Regret at treating Carla so horribly mixed itself with the fear and panic that still bubbled deep inside me. Just as thoughts of bodies, vultures and fog threatened to take control of my brain again, church bells started ringing—first, the ones from the Catholic Cathedral nearby and then from the Episcopal Church across the plaza. Dueling church bells I call them, keeping time for the city. 6:00 p.m.

Seeing how focusing my attention on the bells helped divert my thoughts for at least a short time, I decided to watch the kids in the plaza. Yeah, the little guys with their families. They made me smile with their big eyes staring up at the huge lighted Christmas tree. Some wanted to open the fake presents there while others wanted to sit on the nearby cannons and have their picture taken.

Cannons. They're everywhere in St. Augustine. As I thought about it though, Christmas and cannons didn't go together—at all. I mean Christmas is supposed to be about peace and brotherly love, right? I wondered if any of those cannons had killed anybody. No doubt about it, finding those bodies out on that lonely, stinking road had really gotten to me.

As I alternated between watching the kids and staring at the cannons, a homeless guy I know named Lyle walked up to the bench opposite me where the old couple had been sitting. How come I know a homeless person? Why not? Yeah, sure homeless folks have all kinds of problems, but they're people too. Lyle and I just happened to share a bench together in the plaza soon after I moved to St. Augustine. We started talking and I later met some of his friends.

When he took off his backpack, Lyle flipped it, along with a big old plastic yard bag full of what he calls, "stuff," onto the bench. "Yo, Jeff. How's it going, brother?" He was wearing a heavy orange colored jacket I had never seen on him before.

"I'm cool," I lied. I really didn't feel like talking to anybody, but I decided to force myself. "We match tonight." I pointed at my at my mostly orange University of Florida jacket.

"Yeah man. Go Gators!" Lyle grinned and did the Gator Chomp, his arms outstretched in front of him, going up and down.

"You bet. Go Gators! How's life treating you, Lyle?" I knew better than to ask, but the words were automatic. At times, Lyle can become a little too chatty.

"If it was any better, I couldn't stand it." He smiled, showing a big gap where his top two front teeth should have been. Dropping the smile, he scanned the plaza for police officers as he usually does. "You a cop, Jeff?"

"Naw, I'm no cop. Not quite old enough." It's the same answer

I give every time he asks, but he likes to hear the answer just the same.

Lyle nodded, reached into his backpack and pulled out a paper sack with a can of beer inside. Keeping his drink in its sack, he popped it open. "Smart you are, not being a cop." Once more, he scanned the area for his enemy, the police. Satisfied there were none nearby, he took a long swig and hid the can behind the bench where he sat.

Lyle's a white guy, fifty-six years old, but he looks a lot older. He's got this long, grey beard that he keeps squeezed together in the middle with a rubber band. I can always tell it's Lyle from way off because he wears this bright red baseball cap. His good luck hat, he calls it. I always wondered exactly what type of good luck it had brought him, but never asked.

The first time I met Lyle, I got him talking and found out all kinds of things. Years ago, the guy used to be a business executive, but he had an accident of some kind that gave him brain damage. When he couldn't work anymore, his wife left him. After the accident is when he became an alcoholic—bad combination, alcoholism and brain damage.

"Got a dollar I can have until tomorrow, Jeff?" Lyle asked as usual.

If I have some extra change, sometimes I'll give it to him or one of the other homeless folks I talk to, but not that night. Of course, Lyle doesn't pay it back, but I don't expect him to. We're not talking about much money here. I just don't have it. I always hoped he used what I could give him for food and not for beer or drugs.

"Sorry, Lyle, not tonight." For some reason, I thought I had better hold onto what little money I had on me.

"I can handle that." Instead of pestering me, he reached around the bench for another swig of beer. After taking a long gulp, he held the can in his lap still camouflaged by the sack. The guy never sips. For him, it only takes about three long pulls to finish one of his secret beverages.

Now, how can I explain what happened next? You see, after Lyle took his gulp of beer, he, well, wasn't Lyle anymore. I say that calmly at this minute, but believe me, I about jumped out of my skin. Instead of him sitting there, I was facing a man, probably in his mid to late twenties, dressed in a long, high-collared, dark coat with gold buttons running down the front. Around his waist I could see a white belt with a sword attached. He wore black boots and light colored pants. A full head of dark, messed up hair merged with long sideburns that stretched almost to his lips. His face was square looking, and he had wide set eyes that seemed to glitter just like Lobo's. They were dark, but I couldn't tell the color.

After what I had seen back on that nasty smelling road with all the vultures, I knew without a doubt that the guy in front of me was one of the soldiers I had found there. I wanted to run away, but for some wild reason I kept looking at the guy, my head throbbing and heart pounding like crazy. I could feel the sweat start pouring out of me. My hands shook, and I felt glued to my seat. I mean, I flat could not move. The closest I had ever felt like that before was in dreams when I can't move, or I move much too slow, just as the worst thing in the world is about to attack.

As this soldier and I stared at each other, something began happening to the guy's coat. A red stain slowly blossomed in the middle of his chest and then erupted in a spurt of blood that shot outward and drenched his pants. More blood then gushed from the man's mouth right as a crack appeared in the top of his head threatening to split it in half.

The plaza, my safe oasis, had turned into a house of horrors. I couldn't take it anymore. Shaking off the paralysis, I bolted from my seat on the bench and ran across Cathedral Place ignoring honking horns and the sound of brakes locking.

16

Spitting Coffee

Once on the other side of Cathedral Place, I pushed through tourists strolling along the sidewalk until I reached the bank building opposite the plaza. I whirled around to see if the bloody soldier still sat on the bench. No soldier. Instead, it was Lyle who stared back at me as if I had totally lost my mind.

Leaning against the wall behind me, I breathed a big sigh of relief. People going by on the sidewalk though, looked at me with questioning glances. I ignored them. What they thought didn't matter. Still gulping air from my dash across the street, I closed my eyes to erase from my mind that bloody scene in the plaza. Didn't work. The recollection of what I had witnessed combined with the memories of being lost in fog and in a wilderness filled with vultures. Behind my closed eyes, I fought a losing battle with memories and fear.

Right in the middle of all that mental pain though, I got a whiff of something good. I smelled food. French fries to be exact. I had forgotten about my hunger and the fact that a lot of restaurants surround the plaza. Despite all that had happened to me, my mouth started watering and my negative thoughts gave way a bit to the possibililty of eating. My mom says I like food so much I could probably wolf down a full meal on a sinking ship. Guess she was right.

Dinner with Carla and Lobo was definitely not going to happen, but now I had options.

One more look to make sure Lyle was still Lyle, which he was, and I walked the short distance on the sidewalk towards the Bridge of Lions to the Athena restaurant. It's a nice little Greek place. My granddad and I ate there a couple of times before he died. I'm not really that much into Greek food, but they have all kinds of other things to eat. When I walked in the front door, nice warm air and even more good smells came my way. Packed with people, the low rumble of conversation buzzed in my ears.

A server, not much older than me, came up and asked if I was by myself. When I told her I was alone, she grabbed a menu and seated me in what looked like the last booth in the place—right in front. On each of the side walls, the murals I liked when I was little still showed those historic street scenes of St. Augustine. Taking the seat facing the windows made me feel more secure. I figured in that way I could see if whoever Lyle had turned into was coming back after me. What I would do then, I didn't know, but I did feel a lot safer.

After looking at the menu and checking my wallet, I revised my hopes. "Crap," I muttered and ordered a cup of soup, bread and coffee. Something hot to drink sounded really good after being out in that chilly air so long.

When the steaming coffee came, I put in three sugars, but no cream, like I always do. Oh, man, that tasted so good. Felt good on my throat too. Too much puking will definitely rub your throat raw. My enjoyment of the coffee didn't last long though, when I remembered I had left my bike out in the plaza. Worried that someone might steal it, I almost ran out to get it. Almost. The thought of Lyle changing back into that gory soldier stopped me cold. Retrieving the bike would have to wait.

In front of me, a short distance on the other side of the Athena's front window, all kinds of people walked back and forth on the sidewalk—male and female of every age, size, shape, race, face type, and color of hair. We get 'em all in St, Augustine, we really do.

Created out of small rectangular panes of glass with white painted wood between them, the Athena's windows made me think of multiple TV screens. I imagined them providing me with an infinite televised version of what lay outside of the restaurant. OK, silly, but what can I say? It kept my mind busy, right?

By the time my soup and bread arrived, I did feel a little more relaxed. Lyle hadn't transformed again into that bloody soldier and charged through the door. Feeling more comfortable than I had in quite a while, I dug into my lemon chicken soup. It was wonderful.

About halfway through my little meal, I decided I better figure out what I was going to do. I mean, I couldn't stay in the restaurant all night. Going home to an empty house still wasn't an option. As much as I wanted to see Carla, I knew that wouldn't work. She and Lobo were a package deal. As lonely as I felt, I didn't want to talk to Lobo again. Not that night, anyway. I even started toying with the idea that maybe Lobo somehow staged everything I experienced that day. I even went so far as thinking maybe he slipped a hallucinogenic drug into my Coke or hypnotized me with those eyes of his. Pretty wild thinking, I suppose, but it shows you how whacked out I had really become.

No matter what, I still worried that maybe the December 28 date really did have some meaning for me. That's when I started hatching a plan to get out of St. Augustine, away from everything and everybody, at least until after the next day. I had enough food money and cash left over from what mom gave me on my birthday at home so that I could get a bus ticket to Orlando. One of my friends there, I hoped, would give me a place to sleep for a day or two.

Happy I had a plan, I took another sip of coffee. As I did, I happened to look out the window again. What I saw, caused me to choke and spit coffee all over my soup, part of the table and the opposite booth seat. Some of it even squirted out through my nose. God, that hurt. Still staring at me with his blue eyes through Athena's window was ... well ... me. That's what I said ... me. Outside on the sidewalk sitting on a little bench in front of the window, sat a kid who ... looked exactly like yours truly—shaggy blond hair, crooked grin and all. I am not lying. Where he came from or when he sat down without me noticing, I had no idea.

Maybe you think because I saw myself riding my bike on the way to the cemetery I shouldn't have been so startled, but I was. I mean, that experience with the bike happened so fast I really didn't have time to react. At the Athena though, the whole scene played out slow enough for me to absorb it more completely. I'm telling you, that duplicate of me even had on the same type of orange and blue Florida Gator jacket I had taken off when I sat down in the restaurant. Mine was still sitting in a heap next to me. Talk about being freaked out! Another me? As Lobo's words about how human beings produce other versions of themselves shot through my mind, I stared at my double in disbelief, choking and dripping coffee from my nose.

Before I had time to stop gagging and do anything, this kid, this other me, got up and stood there for a few seconds as people walked around him. Next thing I know, he winked at me, of all things, slowly turned and then joined the sidewalk crowd heading in the direction of Flagler College.

PART THREE

*Forced
to
Understand*

17

The Chase

Inhaling hot coffee when you've just been startled out your mind is definitely not a good idea. Guess I made so much noise, even people on the other side of the restaurant kept looking in my direction, probably wondering if they needed to do something to keep me from choking to death. Embarrassing? Yeah, but all that time I was so frustrated because I couldn't do anything about the other Jeff, until I stopped coughing.

Seeing my double was a helluva shock, but it didn't scare me down deep like some of the other things I experienced after meeting Lobo. No, totally weird as it was, that situation showed a hard reality connected to everyday life even though I didn't understand it. What I mean is, people out there on the sidewalk actually walked around that kid who looked like me, so they wouldn't bump into him. Without a doubt, he physically existed, yet I didn't feel threatened. Maybe it was also because of my flying experience on the way to the cemetery.

Yeah, now that I think about it, looking down on myself riding my bike definitely set the stage for at least a partial acceptance of seeing that other Jeff in the Athena's window. In fact, I felt energized and ready for action. Up until encountering that other me while eating, my fried brain had left me with a sense of hopelessness. Not anymore.

When I finally caught my breath, I slapped money on the table, grabbed my jacket and rushed out of the Athena's front door. By then, I had this wild idea maybe somebody was impersonating me, and I needed to catch the kid to find the truth. As I thought about it, I figured Lobo had something to do with that other Jeff. Don't ask me why, I just did, even though I had the distinct memory of flying over myself as I rode my bike to the cemetery. Confused thinking? Absolutely. But hopeless? No way. I now had a goal to find that other kid and maybe start making sense out of all the craziness.

In front of the Athena, I looked to the right, the direction my double had gone. At first, I couldn't see him because there were so many people. When I looked again, there he was, facing me, standing in the middle of the sidewalk—down near the end of the block in front of the Catholic Cathedral. People there walked around him even more than before, because this time he blocked their way quite a bit. *Damn, he's waiting for me.* God what a weird sensation to stare at myself again.

The instant I saw the guy, I ran towards him. It wasn't easy because of all the people, so I trotted and danced around those who were in my way. I had no intention of losing that guy, but when I got about half way there, he turned and slowly walked up the cathedral steps and went inside.

"Gotcha!" I whispered to myself. I figured finding the guy in the cathedral would be a lot easier than chasing him all over town at night. He had to be boxed in. When I got to the cathedral, I hesitated for a few seconds before opening the large, brick red door in front of me. This was Carla's church, the oldest in St. Augustine. So many times she and her grandma tried to get me to join them there for Sunday services, but I refused. Now I was going to roar into the place of worship on my own, searching for someone who looked like me.

To be honest, my reluctance didn't last very long. I had to find out what connection that kid had to all of my experiences that day, so I grabbed the door's cold metal handle and pulled. Tell you what, that thing didn't open easily—very heavy wood, probably oak. Seconds later, I was inside in the warmth, listening to the door click shut behind me.

I expected a big, open church, but instead, found myself in a much smaller, semi-dark, rectangular room. What little light there was in there came from the main part of the cathedral through glass panels set into curling wrought iron in front of me. Peeking through those panes of glass, I saw how freakin' huge the place actually was. On either side of a wide central isle, long rows of pews stopped just in front of a brilliantly spotlighted white altar decorated with gold angels and other religious figures.

Surprisingly, there didn't seem to be any people around, including my double. I thought sure there would be at least a few tourists in there, or maybe people praying. Music echoed softly all around me—men chanting, to be specific. With no one around, it had to be a recording, I figured, set up in case people wandered inside—very eerie sounding, no matter what. The only movement in the place came from lighted candles, lots of them, sitting on tables in a large niche set into the thick walls on either side of the pews halfway to the altar. They explained the slight burning smell I detected as soon as I came in from outside.

Anxious to find that other Jeff, I chose the door on my right, one of four leading from that little room out into the main part of the cathedral. As I opened it, a figure standing there in the shadows made me freeze in mid step. At first, I thought it might really be that other kid, and then I definitely knew it was the bloody solider from the plaza. Man, fear can really play tricks with your mind. It turned out I was looking at a statue of a monk. That's when I discovered another aisle going down to the altar next to the right hand wall.

Once I walked by the fake monk and entered the cathedral itself, the place looked even bigger than before. Have you ever been in a cathedral? I mean, those ceilings had to be at least fifty feet up there or more. Big ceiling lights hung from high rafters, set into each wall all the way to the front of the place. For whatever reason, only a few of them were turned on, making most of the cathedral, except for the altar, pretty gloomy. Large stained glass windows set high into both walls let a little of St. Augustine's Nights of Lights brightness shine through, but not much. Nighttime had settled in across the city.

Heading down the right hand aisle as quickly as I could, I looked in all the pews for my double, thinking he might be lying down, trying to hide. As I searched, the gentle chanting continued, making the place seem more and more spooky. I kept wondering if a priest or somebody might come running up and ask what I was doing. "Where are you?" I whispered to that other Jeff ever so slightly, knowing the music would drown out my voice.

When I got about three quarters of the way down the aisle, I noticed two huge dark areas on either side of the altar were actually other big rooms with their own pews and dimly lighted stained glass in those walls as well. In the back of the darkened room to the left, candlelight flickered beyond what looked like a large arch showing there was even another room beyond. The place appeared to go on forever.

"Oh man," I whispered with a little more volume than I intended, "that guy could be anywhere."

"Are you lost, Mr. Golden?" Lobo's voice boomed and echoed through the cathedral so loudly I thought I had been shot or something. My heart raced as it had done so many times that day and my headache increased its throbbing. I swear, I thought I was going to have a heart attack.

18

Fighting the Problem

Without saying anything else, Lobo emerged into the dim light from the darkness to the left of the altar, walked briskly in front of the left-hand row of pews, and stood there with his bare arms crossed. He was dressed just as he was when I last saw him. Evidently he didn't wear a jacket or coat no matter what the outside temperature might be.

I stared at him in amazement while taking deep breaths, trying to calm my pounding heart. Even though I suspected him of somehow being behind the appearance of that other Jeff, I never expected to see him there in the cathedral.

"You going to stand there all night?" he asked, breaking the silence of the place. "Or, are you going to come over here and talk to me?" The man's deep voice again echoed throughout the cathedral as if he was using a microphone. For whatever reason, the chanting had stopped. Somehow, even in that low light level, the man's eyes still glittered, but it seemed, not quite as much as they had at his house.

The palms of my hands were so damp by that time I wiped them on my jeans. I looked all around, expecting someone from the church to come see who was making so much noise.

"Nobody here but us right now." After speaking, Lobo sat down in the first pew closest to him and waved me over.

"Wait one freakin' minute!" I yelled back at him, surprising myself. The shock of seeing the man there had worn off enough for me to challenge him. Sick and tired of whatever games he was playing, I yelled once more. "What about the kid who came in here a couple of minutes ago?"

"Oh him. Your twin's not here anymore."

"Oh, I'm sure," I fired back at the guy. "How convenient." I walked quickly to where he sat and stared down at him waiting for an answer.

"Don't get mad at me because you can't accept the fact you encountered your double."

"And of course you had nothing to do with it, right? You magically appear where I last saw him? Give me a break. How would you know about his appearance if you didn't set this whole thing up somehow?"

"Do you really think," he replied shaking his head slowly, "that in the short time I've known you I somehow found a young man who looks exactly like you, dressed him the way you're dressed, and had him intercept you at precisely the right minute? Besides, tell me how I somehow created your experience of flying over yourself riding your bike this evening?"

"How did you know about that? I didn't even tell Carla?"

"You answer my questions and I'll answer yours," he replied.

Of course, I didn't have any good answers to what he had asked me—especially ones that fit my little conspiracy theory. What really made me wonder was how he could be at that very spot right after I entered the cathedral looking for my double. Did I ask him? No. In complete frustration, I took off my jacket, balled it up, threw the thing on the pew a few feet from Lobo, and slumped down next to it. As good as it felt to sit down again, that wood seat had a real hardness to it.

"I don't know what to think any more," I said. Instead of looking at him, I rested my neck and aching head against the back of the pew, and stared up at the gloom far above. "So much has happened ever since I met you, you can't blame me for being suspicious."

"You've had a rough day," he replied, "no question about that. Carla told me what happened at the cemetery. That's partly why I'm here. I owe you another apology. I should have foreseen the possibility of my energy protection wearing off so soon, but I didn't.

"Now, as to the escalation of events in your life since you came to my home, that is simply because of your connection to Carla and me."

"I don't understand."

"What you've experienced today occurred sooner than it would have otherwise. The collective energy the three of us emit into other worlds is very strong and it attracted this spirit somewhat more quickly and forcibly than would have happened if you were alone. Make no mistake, however, and think you might have escaped all this if you had never met me. Rest assured that you would have experienced similar events but later in the evening, *and* you would have been unprotected.

"Unfortunately, the link between you and this soldier's spirit is much stronger than I suspected. That connection eroded the barrier I put around you at an exceedingly high rate. Very unusual."

"Soldier's spirit?"

"Surely you understand by now how correct Carla was in suggesting that possibility to you."

After what, or who, I had seen Lyle become, I didn't argue with the man. Lobo's words made me think he somehow knew about my experience in the plaza. He couldn't have learned about it from Carla though, because she left before it happened. My head throbbed as I tried to sort everything out.

Eying me carefully, Lobo said, "If you wish, I'll transfer some more of my energy to you. Besides helping with your headache and clearing out some of the cobwebs in your mind, it will protect you for another short span of time."

I didn't understand that energy thing of his, but I did know it could make me feel better. Besides, any protection from bloody soldiers sounded pretty good right about then. "Yeah ... sure," I told him, "but where does this energy of yours come from anyway?"

"Long ago, I was the shaman for my people. In those days, I picked up a lot of tricks by working with various sources of power."

"Shaman? Like in medicine man?"

"Something along those lines." He shifted close to me on the pew, and, as he did before, placed one hand on my chest and the other on my head. Instantly the same soothing warmth I had experienced at his house swam throughout my body. In no time, I felt like I had been washed clean of all pain and tiredness. Even my anger, doubt and fear lost some of their grip on my mind.

"Better?"

"A lot, thanks." *Amazing how he does that*, I thought, but the question of the other Jeff hadn't gone away. "As much as I appreciate your help, I gotta know about that other kid? Who was he? Where did he go?"

"Simple, although you might not think so. That other young man was an exact, but temporary, physical copy of you and produced by you."

"You're out of your freakin' mind. I didn't produce any such thing."

"Not consciously, no, but a wiser and more powerful portion of who you are did. What occurred is an extremely rare event. Very few people in the world possess that talent."

"Oh, so, you're telling me I ... created this ... this other me, clothes and all, but I just wasn't aware of doing it, right?"

"Yes," he replied, his eyes flashing, "clothes and all. Can I explain the exact process to you so you would understand it? No, but I will tell you this. You most likely produced a second Jeff more than once because of all the shocks you had today. That and you were also badly in need of help. You forget our conversation about the natural human capacity to produce duplicates after Carla crushed your Coke can."

"No, I didn't forget but—"

"But you don't believe it. *That's* your problem. Now listen to me. I came here only after talking to Carla and also sensing the presence of another Jeff Golden. I not only perceived his presence, I also communicated with him in ways you could never comprehend. To put it simply, he asked me to meet you here so we could talk in peace. He is a part of you, which means you set this whole thing up yourself even though you have no memory of doing such a thing."

"Wait a minute, how could you—"

"Forget how I do things. It's a shaman thing. Leave it at that. All you need to do is to stop fighting the problem."

"Fighting the problem? What the hell are you talking about?" Only after that one little word left my mouth did I think about my surroundings. Lobo didn't bat an eye, but I was glad Carla didn't hear what I said inside her church.

Lobo stood up, walked a few steps towards the altar as if he was thinking and then turned back around."Take a deep breath," he said, "and listen very carefully. When you hear or see something you don't believe, don't like or don't understand, you tend to jump on it like you are trying to wrestle an alligator. Or you run away from it, or you do both—wrestle first, then run away. What that does is to erect within you a wall against your ability to deal with the issue effectively. Instead, you get yourself all tied up into emotional knots. It's like quicksand. The more you resist, the deeper you go."

"But that's who I am, Lobo. I can't change that."

"Not true. Nobody is stuck in such emotional cement. You can restructure your mind if you really want to, but you have to work hard to make it happen—especially with that hair trigger anger of yours. You must start making that change now, and as fast as you can. If you can't, with what you are now facing, you could end up dead. Did you hear that? *Dead.* You've heard me warn you about the danger you're in before, but now is the time to start really believing what I'm telling you and taking corrective action." As if to see the impact of his words, Lobo abruptly stopped talking, and gave me one of his hard stares.

The sudden silence around me made the air feel thick, as if I could reach out and touch it. Memories of the day's events flooded my mind and my hands began to shake again.

"Trust yourself," Lobo said, breaking into that dense quiet. "Your inner self that produced another Jeff Golden is showing you the power you have to do whatever it takes."

He made it sound so easy, but I knew it couldn't be true. Oh, believe me, I wanted him to be right, but I had no idea where to begin. "So what do I do exactly?"

"Excellent question. First of all don't resist whatever problem or negativity life presents to you. Accept it for what it is and work through it. Simple as it sounds, tell yourself repeatedly to, *not fight the problem*, so that you get the concept through your head. I know you've heard people say, 'Count to ten when you're angry or upset before you react.' It's good advice. In your case, you might want to try breathing slowly and deeply while concentrating on each breath you take as you count just to five. If you can start doing those few things now, you'll discover within yourself a wealth of strength. You truly have the choice of making your life a heaven or a hell.

"Now," he said, changing the subject, "Carla told me about your experience with the pyramids. Even so, I want to hear it from you directly. Tell me everything that happened from the time you touched the pyramid until you came here to the cathedral."

I really didn't want to go through all that, but his words, "Don't fight the problem," echoed in my mind. So instead of making his request into a *problem*, I did as he asked.

We talked for about fifteen minutes as I explained everything the best I could with Lobo asking questions. When I was done, his wild eyes flickered all around me as they had done many times before. I wondered how those eyes could still flash so much when there wasn't much light in the cathedral for them to reflect.

"What?" I asked.

After a long pause, he stood up and finally gave me an answer. "First of all, the nearness of the Dade battle anniversary tomorrow, December 28, at least points to why all this is occurring now. Second, you and Carla guessed correctly when you concluded the man pursuing you might be from Major Dade's command. In life, he was one of Dade's officers."

"How do you know?"

"He's no longer rushing all around you at a blinding speed like before. This change allows me to perceive him more clearly now. He has slowed down because he senses he has your attention and he even wants you to see him."

"So that was him I saw Lyle turn into." As I said those words, I felt that same slithery sensation in my stomach I noticed at the cemetery with Carla.

"Your friend Lyle didn't actually change. What probably happened is this officer projected an image into your mind. From what you said, I think he was trying to show you how he died, bullet wounds in the chest, and finally having his head split open."

I shuddered with the memory of what I had seen in the plaza. "Well, he did a good job of it. Wait a minute. You said officer. How do you know that's what he was?"

"Officer's wore dark blue coats, over sky blue pants," Lobo replied in a lowered voice as he pointed to the pew behind me, "just like what he has on right now."

19

The Officer

Hearing Lobo's words and seeing his big old finger showing me where to look gave me a very tight feeling in my chest, like a giant hand squeezing my heart. When I breathed, the air came and went in little bumpy chunks. I knew without a doubt somewhere behind me sat the officer from the Dade battle, and I flat did not want to turn around.

"Looking at him won't be easy for you," Lobo said quietly, but it is necessary. Your soldier has materialized back there in order to solidify his contact with you. If you don't acknowledge him, he could get even more agitated than he has been up to this point. That, you do not want, so—and hear me on this one more time—*do not fight the problem!*"

"Right." My voice came out as a shaky whisper. "Easy for you to say."

"It's all in the mind." Pointing to his temple, Lobo nodded ever so slightly. "Besides, if you recall, the energy boost I gave you a short time ago, just like the previous one you received, also protects you to a great degree."

"Yeah, that's what you said when I went to the cemetery and look what happened."

"See how you fight the problem? Blaming me isn't going to help. It's time for you to breathe deeply and slowly. Focus on five of those breaths. For right now, ignore the past and the future. If you stay with the present moment, you can deal with anything."

"OK, OK. I'll try." And I did. Closing my eyes for about ten seconds, I followed his instructions. After finishing the fifth breath, I felt a little more relaxed and not quite as afraid to look behind me. That small success gave me just enough courage to open my eyes and turn around. When I did, I found myself staring into the face of the man I had seen Lyle become sitting two rows directly behind me, looking as real as Lobo. No blood, no gore. *Thank God!* Even so, I could not get my mind around the idea he no longer actually lived. I wondered if other people could see him if they happened to walk into the cathedral—like how people saw my double out on the sidewalk.

It was so strange, because for whatever reason, I felt more recognition than fear—probably, I figured, because Lobo stood fairly close to me. I mean, it went beyond seeing him in the plaza dressed as he was then with his dark blue coat and gold buttons. Why? I had no idea, but he looked … like an ordinary guy with long sideburns. I tried, but in that dimly lighted place, I couldn't see the color of his eyes.

As we stared at each other, those shadowed eyes widened, and he tilted his head to the side as if studying me. He stayed that way for probably half a minute, opening and closing his mouth. It looked like he might be trying to say something, but no words came out. In response, I shook my head to help him understand I couldn't hear his words. When I did that, he got this very frustrated look on his face. The next thing I know, he lifted a hand and extended it in my direction as far as his arm will go. Scared me a little, but he sat two rows back. I knew he couldn't reach me. Or so I thought. Two seconds later, his arm shot out twice its normal length or more, putting the tips of his fingers only inches from my chest.

Tell you what, I shoved myself out of that seat backwards so hard I fell on the floor beyond where Lobo stood, close to the railing in front of the altar. Hurt my butt something terrible, but I got away from that hand.

Almost at the same time, he … the officer … well, he, uh … popped. That's the only word I can use to describe what happened. His body sort of … well, divided into a bunch of big circular pieces bunched all together. Within each of those clear circles, I could still see the guy, the ghost or whatever you want to call him—his entire body from head to toe. Those individual circular images looked like bubbles floating there for a few seconds before they popped again into even smaller bubbles—with the officer inside. All the popping happened simultaneously, and when it did, it sounded like a giant ripping noise, so loud it hurt not only my ears, but I somehow felt it deep inside my head.

The popping happened again and again, each time the bubbles got smaller and smaller until there was absolutely nothing left. It reminded me of watching foam disappear after you've poured a Coke into a glass. The officer went from looking perfectly solid to nothing in a matter of seconds as if he had never been there.

That's when I looked at Lobo. He was about to say something, but I interrupted from my seat on the floor. "I know, I know. Don't fight the problem." He nodded his agreement and helped me up.

"Was he as real as he looked?"

"If you had reached out and tried to touch him," Lobo replied, "you would have felt solidity, but that would not have been a safe thing for you to do in this circumstance. You were wise to react as you did and get away from his extended reach. I still don't sense he intends you any harm, but his aroused need for your help is where the danger lies.

"I always thought ghosts were supposed to be filmy things you could see through."

"They are at times. The solidity you witnessed, and its disintegration, are most unusual. This all speaks to the intensity of what's developing here. His appearance moments ago, your being lost in the fog, and your experience at the pyramids all show how strong the connection between you both is getting the closer we move towards December 28. If you aren't exceptionally careful, you could find yourself permanently sucked into this officer's world."

"Twice now, once on my porch and once at the cemetery, a part of you stepped into his living memories of the Dade battlefield once the fighting was finished. Evidently, after he died, the man's spirit also stayed for some time with the bodies and the vultures you saw. I sense he has been clinging to those terrible memories ever since, and for him, they're like a bad dream from which he can't fully awaken. For all practical purposes, where his spirit exists is a physical parallel world to the one in which he died, battle and all."

"What I experienced both those times was definitely real, Lobo, not just some kind of memory." I surprised myself when I said those words, but I believed them to be absolutely true.

"Worlds-within-worlds-within-worlds. You have heard it from me before, and you will hear it from me again, and again until the concept truly penetrates your mind. Thoughts and memories have realities all their own. To that officer, his dream of the battle and after would no doubt seem as real as me standing here in this cathedral now seems to you. Your own experience in his reality proves my point. It is indeed so real that if you go there a third time, you might not return. That's what I mean by 'permanently sucked into his world.' "

"Oh man, this all gets worse and worse," I moaned.

"The good news is what I already told you. I still don't sense this man actually intends you any harm."

Thoughts of catching a bus to Orlando tiptoed back into my mind. Lobo's words about severe danger lurking everywhere impressed me a lot more than his good news.

"You can't outrun this," he said, once again picking up on my thoughts in his irritating way. "Taking a bus to Orlando will do you no good. Wherever you go on this earth, that officer will still be with you, and the danger will still stay the same. The thinness of the barriers in St. Augustine between worlds has already allowed him to attach himself to you, at least through tomorrow."

"What can I do?" I asked slumped in my seat feeling doomed.

"Do you pray?" He replied, looking up at the lighted altar.

"Who me?" I snorted. "No."

"Too bad. You're going to need all the help you can get."

20

Solidity

Prayer? I'm going to need all the help I can get? Lobo sure had a way of making a bad situation worse. Not what I needed to hear. Was my situation really that hopeless, I wondered, or was Lobo just being Lobo and trying to keep my attention highly focused? Or, maybe, I thought, the guy might simply be very religious and believe in the power of prayer. No wonder he and Carla got along so well together. Carla! I wasn't sure if she would ever speak to me again after our argument in the plaza. "Uh, Lobo, how's Carla?"

"She hasn't edited you out of her life yet, if that's what you mean." Lobo sat down on the pew and looked up at me. "Miss Carla came back to my place mighty unhappy. However, I explained to her the depth of your emotional distress. As a result, her own anger, shall we say, no longer consumes her as it did."

The breath I held as Lobo talked came out in a big whoosh. "Oh man, Lobo, thanks. You saved my life."

"Not yet I haven't."

"Yeah, well, I didn't mean that literally." Still those chilling words jerked me back to the long dead military officer who had just tried to touch me. I still couldn't get over how real he looked. "You said the officer we saw was ... solid, right?"

Lobo nodded.

"And my double, he was solid too, wasn't he? Because I saw

people walking around him."

"And you want to know how a separate part of you and the spirit of a dead person can become as solid as this?" When he said the word "this," he reached over, grabbed my shoulder hard, and held his hand there with the same amount of pressure. The muscles in his bare arm stood out in clear definition.

That hurt. Believe me, the guy is strong.

"You would do well to simply accept the solidity you speak of as one of those little mysteries of life. Like right now. At this juncture in time, you feel my hand on your shoulder and we have been talking for a long time. You see me, you hear me, and you even hear my voice echo around this cathedral. You would never suspect I am a double of the original Lobo, would you?" He removed his hand from my shoulder, held it up, and wiggled his fingers.

"Oh come on." I laughed, but it came out like a ragged burst of nervousness. "You telling me you're not ... what? the, uh, the real Lobo?"

Instead of a response, I got one of his penetrating stares as he folded his arms.

"No way. No ... freakin' ... way!"

"You have a cell phone and Carla has a cell phone. Call her and ask her where I am."

His challenge to prove him wrong gave me an intense sinking feeling in my stomach. On top of that, my brain seemed to twist in on itself trying to absorb what the man was telling me.

"Go ahead," Lobo prompted. "You're wasting time."

Don't' fight the problem, I said to myself. After taking a few deep breaths, I dug into my pocket and pulled out my phone. It hadn't worked on that stinking road, with all the bodies, but it worked right there in the cathedral. I punched Carla's speed dial number. In seconds, she answered.

"Hi Jeff. You calling to apologize?" She didn't sound too angry.

"Hey, Carla. Ah, yeah. I really am sorry about how I acted in the Plaza."

"Um hm. Well, Lobo helped me understand the pressure you're under, but why are you calling. Just come on back here to his place and we'll all have dinner, O.K?"

"Ah, right. OK. I'll be there … soon, but—"

"Are you still in the plaza?"

"Wellll, right now, I'm, ah, in your cathedral."

"What?" Carla yelled into my ear. Then in a calmer voice, she said, "What are you doing there and how did you get in? The cathedral should be closed."

"I'll explain later. But listen, do you know where Lobo is right now?"

"Lobo? Sure. He's sitting with me in front of the fireplace. You need to talk to him?"

That's when my stomach really started turning in knots. "Uh, yeah, thanks."

"Do you believe me now?" Lobo's voiced boomed out of the phone, making me jump.

Sitting next to me, Lobo said nothing. He didn't need to. Two Lobo's. *Not possible*, I kept saying to myself. Or was it? After all, I had seen my own double.

"By the way," Lobo said on the phone, "a person's double is called a doppelganger in German." I slapped my phone shut like it was a rattlesnake trying to bite me.

"Convinced?" the Lobo next to me asked. He unfolded his arms, made a fist with his right hand and pounded the back of the pew. "Solid, but temporary I am."

What do you say to something like that? I didn't know. That's why I kept quiet. Stunned. Yeah that's the word. It about sums up what I felt, even after all the totally crazy things I had experienced that day.

"Oh please," Lobo said. "You saw your own double. How is communicating with a Lobo double any different?"

When I still didn't say anything, he got up, walked back into the darkness of the room to our left and yelled, "Come with me." His voiced bounced and echoed throughout the cathedral one final time. At first, all I could see back there was the red glowing letters of an exit sign, and then a door opened to the outside with a bang. Light from downtown St. Augustine showed Lobo waiting for me.

Taking a deep breath, I grabbed my jacket and walked back to the exit.

21

Doppelgangers

Lobo, his double I mean, stood next to me near a low wall, part of a grassy courtyard along both Cathedral Place and St. George Street. Above us, the cathedral's huge bell tower stood out against the night sky bathed in floodlights. I breathed in the cold night air and caught a brief scent of pizza. On the other side of the courtyard, nightlife in the city went along as usual. People on the sidewalk to our left strolled past slow moving cars, and shoppers wandered back and forth across traffic-free St. George Street in front of us. For a split second, everything all around me seemed almost like a dream world—unreal compared to the startlingly weird experiences I'd had that day.

"From here," Lobo's double said, "you can see between the trees and parked cars to the crosswalk and Flagler College." He pointed up Cathedral Place on our left to where it dead-ended a short block away at Cordova Street with Flagler College on the other side.

I heard him, and I looked where he directed me to, but my mind was a jumble, still trying to understand the idea of human beings producing temporary duplicates of themselves—doppelgangers, Lobo's double had called them—called himself. I wondered if the Lobo next to me would just disintegrate in a burst of little bubbles like the officer in the cathedral had? I thought my head would explode trying to figure all that out. I even had this wild urge to yell at all the people walking around outside of the courtyard, "Do you have any idea what's happening in my life?" but I didn't. Instead, I kept listening to the man's explanation.

"I'm showing you this because I have a very simple task I want you to perform. All you need to do is to exit through the gate here in the wall, go down the sidewalk to the right all the way to Cordova and cross it. Once you're there, turn around so you can look back in this direction. I'll be standing here so that you can see me at any time during your journey."

"What's this all about?"

"Just do it," he growled, "and I assure you it will become clear very soon."

One thing about doubles I discovered. They have the same personalities as the originals.

Breathing a sigh of exasperation and confusion, I did as he asked and walked the short distance down the street past a bank building on the right and Government House on the other side of the road to my left. On the way, I turned around a couple of times and there was Lobo, I mean his double, still standing in the cathedral courtyard.

I ran across Cordova Street avoiding traffic and onto the sidewalk in front of Flagler College. For whatever reason, that old, familiar building seemed alive, like it wanted to tell me something. With its big chains containing spiky iron balls, the place always seemed more like a castle to me than a college. The thing had been built sometime in the 1800's as a hotel or something.

As instructed, I turned around and looked back down Cathedral Place. In the glare of oncoming one-way traffic, I saw that Lobo's double still hadn't moved. What I was doing standing there looking at him, I had no idea.

"What do you know, you can follow orders." The all too familiar voice came from behind me. As I whirled around, Lobo stepped off a walkway leading to the college. I stared at him in disbelief, and without speaking, turned my head so I could look back up Cathedral Place. There was Lobo's double right where I had left him.

"Having fun are you?" the Lobo coming from the college asked. Before I could say anything, he walked up to me, looked up Cathedral Place himself and waved. The Lobo in the courtyard did the same.

"Good God." I kept looking back and forth between the two identical men.

"Oh, I'm another duplicate all right," the Lobo next to me said, answering the question that had just started to form in my mind. "Want to call Carla and talk to the original to confirm it?"

Three Lobos? I couldn't fully get my head around the idea, but I didn't doubt its reality. "Ah … no," I replied. "That won't be necessary."

"Mm. Good. Progress. This little demonstration was a wake-up call for you—a way to get you to accept the infinite possibilities possessed by the human mind, body and spirit. It looks as though we're getting somewhere."

"Oh, believe me, you made your point."

A group of Spanish speaking tourists swept past us on the sidewalk all bundled up in coats and jackets. As they went by, a couple of them stared at Lobo and shook their heads, looking I'm sure, at his bare arms.

"All of the people here tonight," the Flagler College Lobo said, pointing at the group once they were out of hearing range, "and all of the people on earth have within them wonderful abilities, paranormal and otherwise. The problem is, most of them never recognize that until they die, and even then, many of them don't figure it out. In life, or after death, many stay stuck in their own little mental prisons, exactly like the officer who won't let you alone did to himself after he died so long ago. They each have a key to their cell door, but they don't realize it.

"Like all those people, you have lived in your own mental prison your whole life. Now, however, you have experienced so many unusual events you find yourself continually overwhelmed. As understandable as that is, you don't have the time to nurse your confusion and fear. You can no longer afford to let strange occurrences like more than one Lobo throw you off track. It's time for you to expect the unexpected, and it's time for you to stop *fighting the problems* that arrive on your doorstep. I assure you, more are on the way and time is short. December 28 is almost here, and you, sir, will be facing the crisis of your life."

When he finished speaking, those dark eyes of his flashed in my direction. I felt little pinpricks inside my head as if he had somehow penetrated deep into my brain—not painful but like when your arm falls asleep and you try to wake it up again. My mouth went dry and the palms of my hands started sweating, even in the cold.

"Up here," the Lobo next to me said," tapping me between the eyes with a big forefinger, "is where your answer lies. You have the ability to create your own reality and help that poor soldier change his. Otherwise … " Instead of finishing what he had to say, he shrugged.

I nodded instead of saying anything. His words made sense, but I didn't quite know how to respond. As I struggled to think of a reply, I again glanced at the other Lobo still standing by the cathedral. He waved, walked across the courtyard and entered St. George Street where I lost sight of him as he merged with all the people. When I brought my gaze back up to look at the Lobo next me, he was gone, just flat gone. He couldn't possibly have walked off and there was no place for him to hide.

Even with noisy traffic rumbling past and tourists walking by, I stood there feeling very much alone.

22

Little Switches

Not knowing what to do, I just watched the cars and trucks heading directly towards me on Cathedral Place. The glare from all those headlights didn't help any because they reminded me how so many absolutely crazy things had come charging my way since I first arrived at Lobo's house. It was like all of that happened had somehow filled me up and pushed my old world right out the window. OK, my old world wasn't so perfect, but at that point I would have taken it back in a second.

"Up here is where your answer lies," the Flagler College Lobo had said, tapping me between the eyes a short time before.

"Yeah, right!" I said standing there. With my brain so overloaded, I didn't see how any answers or direction could come from it. Anyway, according to Lobo's duplicate at Flagler College, I only had until the next day to figure it all out while he, well, both Lobos really, then upped and disappeared on me. "If I'm in so damn much danger here," I grumbled to myself, "why didn't at least one of you guys stick around?"

When I said those words though, I shook my head at how completely I seemed to have accepted the fact that Lobo could be in two or even in three places at one time. Then I thought about how I had seen myself outside of the Athena and gave up trying to figure it all out. While lost in my thoughts, some teenagers in an old green

Chevy Lumina turned way too fast onto Cordova Street in front of me. The car's tires screeched and its horn blared. Some guy in the back seat on my side of the road leaned out of his window and yelled, "Get a life zombie."

"Screw you!" I shouted back and gave him the finger.

"Zombie," I snorted.

Breathe deeply. At first, I thought someone had spoken those two words, but I wasn't really sure. Little pinpricks of sensation inside my head made me wonder if one of Lobo's doubles had come back. A quick look around showed me that hadn't happened. Even so, I found myself taking five full breaths and concentrating on them as much as I could. When I got done, I had to chuckle. While focusing on my breathing, I realized how truly stupid I must have looked standing there staring vacantly into the headlights of oncoming traffic. At that point, the zombie tag didn't look far off the mark.

"Now hold on a minute," I said to myself. I had also noticed how quickly my emotions changed during that encounter with the kids in the Lumina. From being lost and full of fear at the time, I had quickly became angry, very angry. It filled my mind. No room for anything else—an instant and complete shift in attitude. It was almost as if someone had flipped a little switch inside my head. Who was this someone? I asked myself. I wanted to pin it on the kid in the Lumina. Even so, down deep, I knew if I did blame that guy, I had actually *let* him do it.

For the first time in my life, I recognized how *choice* played a huge part in my reactions. As clear as could be, I sensed a whole bunch of those little switches in my head I had never noticed before. I could let people or situations into my brain to run wild with those switches, or I could … learn to decide … how best to flip them myself.

"So that's what Lobo's been trying to tell me," I whispered. Why I whispered, I have no idea. With all that traffic noise, I could have shouted and no one would have heard me. "OK zombie," I told myself, "it's time for you to get your act together." Taking it a couple of steps at a time, I decided to retrieve my bike and get to Lobo's place as quickly as possible. Carla and the original Lobo were there and I needed to be with them. Beyond that, I wasn't sure what to do, but Lobo would no doubt have some suggestions.

At the plaza, I found both Lyle and my bike gone. "Crap!" I startled two middle-aged women sitting on the bench where Lyle had been. Too bad. "Crap! Crap! Crap!" I didn't want to believe Lyle had taken my bike, but it didn't matter who the thief was, right then. I could sort that out later—if a later existed for me beyond December 28.

Not feeling like walking all the way back to Lobo's place, a little fire of anger welled up in my stomach at whoever swiped my bike. *The bastard!* Yes, I remembered the switches in my head, and I even tried focusing on my breath, but it sure wasn't easy. My switches felt then more like rusty, hard to turn dials. "This is going to take a hell of a lot of practice," I muttered. After inhaling deeply a bunch of times and focusing on each breath, I calmed down a little, and found I really could think a little more clearly.

The walk through the rest of downtown on my way back to Lobo's place was kind of a blur. My mind kept firing off in so many directions that I couldn't concentrate. Of course, still being a some-what pissed off didn't help either, no matter how hard I worked on turning it around. For some idiotic reason I decided to take St. George Street. Dumb! You might think with traffic not allowed on St. George there would be plenty of room. Ha! It seemed like all the tourists in the world were in my way. During that whole time, I kept looking all around, afraid the Dade officer might put in another appearance. Never happened, luckily.

It took me about ten minutes until I neared the city gate at the end of St. George Street. The number of people in my way there thinned out, and I was able to move much faster. Once through the two old coquina columns that make up the gate, a break in traffic on both sides of South Castillo Drive allowed me to cross. On the other side of the road to my right, the Castillo itself, with its high coquina walls, stood out in the glare of floodlights. As I looked at it, my mind flashed back to the pyramid and touching its rough coquina surface. Not what I wanted to think about at all!

When I got to the sidewalk on the other side of the street, I started running. It's what I do sometimes when my brain gets filled to overflowing—like what I did on my bike with Carla after being at the cemetery. It felt so good to concentrate on nothing but moving at full speed even though I had to slow up when a few tourists got in my way from time to time. Ahead in the near distance on my side of the street, the lights from Ripley's Believe It or Not Museum were getting closer. You can't miss those big old white globes. They're about the size of bowling balls set on top of a white picket fence. They made perfect targets for me to keep my eyes on as I ran. When I got almost to the Ripley's entrance, I stopped dead in my tracks. Behind the white fence stood Carla and Lobo.

I guess by then I should have known to expect anything from Lobo, but seeing both him and Carla there still startled me. After all, I had experienced that day, I didn't think I could be surprised by anything else, but I was definitely wrong. Sucking in a few deep breaths, I walked over to the fence. When I got there, Carla wore an expression of worry mixed with irritation.

"Hi," she said. "Lobo told me you had an even rougher time after I left. Sorry about your bike."

I realized then that Lobo must have told her about everything that had gone on with me since Lyle transformed into a soldier including the doppelgangers. In the calm way she said what she did, I felt sure things like three Lobos weren't unusual experiences for her. How she knew about me losing my bike though, I couldn't figure out. OK, of course Lobo told her, but how did he know? Neither of the Lobo doubles was around when I found my bike gone.

"Uh ... hi," I replied, breathing hard from my run. "Yeah ... it's been ... well ... interesting since you left, that's for sure. What are you all doing here?" I noticed this time Lobo wore a jacket, a grey one that looked pretty heavy. This time? Ha! For whatever reason, it had been his doubles who hadn't worn jackets. Didn't they feel the cold? I wondered. When I first met Lobo in his chilly workshop and at his house, he didn't have a jacket. Did that mean I had been talking to one or more of his doubles from the beginning?

"You're going to blow a mental fuse if you keep trying to figure out every little thing." Lobo's unblinking eyes flashed as usual when he spoke. "We thought you might need a ride."

For some reason, his reference to my unspoken thoughts didn't rattle me. It just didn't seem to matter. "Sure," I replied to his offer, giving up on trying to understand him and his doppelgangers. "Why not? Thanks." It wasn't a long way back to his place, but I figured riding, especially with Carla, wasn't such a bad deal, you know?

"Come on," he replied, waving me to the other side of the fence where he had parked his rusty old truck. "Let's head back to my place like we planned and cook up some dinner." When we got to the truck, I saw he had cleaned all of the crap out of the cab making room enough for the three of us. It was still a tight fit with big old Lobo taking up a huge amount of space. OK, I took up a good-sized piece of that seat as well. Poor Carla got scrunched in the middle. When Lobo started the engine, it ran very smoothly, pretty quiet, really. I had expected it to rumble as much as he did.

"Uh, could we make a stop at my place?" I asked right as Lobo started backing his truck out of the parking space. "I could really use a quick shower and a change of clothes." I felt bad enough sitting next to Carla so sweaty and all, but I sure didn't want to go through dinner that way as well. Lobo grunted in reply and off we went.

When we got to *The Dump*, as I call where I live, Lobo parked in front of the house and shut off the engine. The place was dark since mom wasn't coming back until the next night. I was about to get out of the truck when I thought about Carla and Lobo having to sit there and wait for me. That didn't seem too cool, but I had never invited anybody inside my house before.

I call it *The Dump* for a reason. The place is really small, old and everything we have is sort of ratty. I live in the same neighborhood as Carla and Lobo, but where I live, well, isn't anywhere near as nice as Carla's place on Water Street. That's where the more expensive houses are located.

"You want to come in?" I asked them both, knowing I would regret it, but figuring I had no other choice. I suddenly remembered I hadn't done the dishes, or picked stuff up in the living room and kitchen. Too late.

"Sure," Carla said, and my heart sank. I really didn't want her to see how I lived, but I couldn't take the invitation back.

"Cool," I lied, and popped open the passenger side door. If this has to happen, I thought as Lobo also opened his door, let's get it over with. Lobo, if you're reading my mind, have fun. He didn't say anything back.

My front yard is tiny, only about six feet deep, so in no time we were on the little porch as I fumbled in the dark for my keys. Once I unlocked the door, it stuck as it does sometimes. With a good shove from my shoulder, the stupid thing opened all the way. When I flipped the wall switch to the left of the door, the living room came to life in all its cruddy glory. A pile of laundry I hadn't yet sorted lay in a heap on the couch, and a TV tray with my half-eaten breakfast stared me in the face. A slight odor of cooked bacon still hung in the air from that morning along with the smell of stale cigarette smoke. An ashtray overloaded with my mom's partially used cancer sticks sat on the coffee table along with a couple of her empty beer cans.

All that mess and smell didn't usually bother me much, but walking in there with Carla and Lobo made my house seem really nasty. I'm telling you, I wanted to bail out of there so bad. Of course, I couldn't. I just had to suck it up, and try not to appear too embarrassed. On our left, The Ancestor, as I call him, stared at me as always. The eyes from my long lost relative in the old dark oil painting on that far wall seem to follow me everywhere.

I threw my keys into the brass bowl on the little table near the front door, quickly got rid of the laundry, and took my dishes into the kitchen. With room to sit down made available, I told Carla and Lobo to make themselves comfortable—while trying to hide my embarrassment. As Lobo sank into the old recliner and Carla sat on the overstuffed couch, I said, "I won't be a minute," and ran for the bathroom.

Once I got into the shower, I stood there for a little while, with my eyes closed letting the water splash me in the face and flow down my body. As memories from that day I wanted to forget edged their way back into my mind, I focused on my breath and tried imagining the rushing water washing them away. It helped, a little. Still, I hated thinking about Carla and Lobo sitting in the living room without me there, so I quickly finished showering, toweled off and put on some fresh clothes. I could hear conversation when I arrived back in the living room, but it stopped as I entered the room.

"I'm doing better now," I announced, "thanks for waiting." As usual, the Ancestor's eyes seemed to look at me as I spoke. That time though, something seemed oddly familiar about him. As Carla started saying something to me, I really didn't hear her because I was staring so intently at the old portrait, something I never do. That's when I recognized the person in the old painting. "Lobo!" I shouted, pointing at The Ancestor. "He's the, the ..." I was so startled, I couldn't get the words out.

"It's about time you noticed," Lobo said, shaking his head.

23

A Blood Connection

W hat's going on?" Carla called from behind me.
I stood in front of my ancestor's portrait, looking up at it wide-eyed. The square face, and long sideburns matched perfectly. "This painting is of one of my relatives going way back. His name was Walton ... and ah ... he's the man I saw in the plaza and in the cathedral with Lobo."

"You're being haunted by your own ancestor?" Carla quickly joined me so she could study the picture.

"Looks that way. He seemed familiar, but why I didn't see the resemblance before this ..."

"It's a very old painting," Carla said, "badly cracked and very dark. From where I was standing, I could barely see his features. Just his eyes seem to stand out. Besides, here he isn't wearing a uniform."

"Yeah, but I've seen that portrait ever since I was a little kid." Only then did I notice for the first time The Ancestor's eyes were dark brown.

"No one in your family ever told you about Walton's background?" she asked.

"Not really. My parents never cared about things like family history. Years ago my grandfather told me Walton served in the military and died in some war, but I didn't really pay attention. I was pretty young."

"Now," Lobo said, "we see the primary reason why so much happened to you today. Your blood connection with this man means you and he have a direct channel to each other. After your bike accident and your abilities to link with other worlds instantly blossomed, your ancestor increasingly attached himself to you using this channel. As December 28 approaches, and all that it means to him, his agitation threatens to engulf you. As I have told you before, I don't believe that this is his intention. He simply clings to you like a leech in hopes you will help him."

I didn't like how Lobo used the words, "blood" and "leech," together in his statements. At first, I thought about how The Ancestor gushed blood in the plaza. That made me think about vampires, and I hoped to God there wasn't actually anything like that in Lobo's worlds-within-worlds. Crazy thought, I know. By then, I guess, I might have believed about anything.

Lobo paused and studied me intently before going on with his explanation. "Most of today's strange events have simply been your ancestor's way of making you sit up and take notice. He even led you back here to this house tonight so you could rediscover his picture."

"Jeff just wanted a shower," Carla protested, echoing my own thought.

"Wrong!" Lobo shot back, his voice filing the room. "The very fact that we are here looking at this picture proves the point. Walton's influence manifests itself in your friend here through sub-conscious mechanisms."

"You mean he's influencing my mind without me knowing? Come on, Lobo, that was a coincidence," I said.

Tell you what, the guy bounced out of his chair and got right into my face. "Hammer this into your head once and for all. Everything in this world connects with everything else in all the infinity of worlds that exist. You discount what you call coincidental events at this point in your life to your peril."

"Oh man, Lobo," I said, looking away and rubbing my temples, "you make my head ache with all that stuff."

"Your blood connection to Walton is the cause of your head-aches, not my words. Make no mistake about it. Your entire body feels the pressure from your ancestor as he attempts to contact you in order to stop *his* pain. Along with that pressure, you are definitely sensing whatever agony *he* endures."

"Oh," I replied. Such a thing never occurred to me. "But what kind of agony could cause him to be so, well, blindly dangerous?"

"We don't know exactly. There is one thing I can tell you. A Lieutenant Walton died during Major Dade's battle with the Seminoles in 1835. His agony no doubt relates to that event which occurred on December 28."

"Of course, that Walton," Carla said, her eyes bright with recognition and surprise. "I recall reading his name somewhere."

With her love of history and the involvement of her own ancestor in the battle, I had no doubt she knew every detail about what happened back in those days. My thoughts though, flowed in a slightly different direction than hers and it dawned on me that Walton was buried under one of those pyramids in the National Cemetery. The memory of what seemed like an electrical charge running up my arm when I put my hand on the central pyramid fired through my mind.

"Another thing," Lobo said, this time to Carla. "There is a high probability that through you, your ancestor, Luis Pacheco, adds to the intensity of this situation. Pacheco's spirit might somehow be supporting the contact between your friend here and Lieutenant Walton."

"Pacheco? Through me?" Startled, Carla looked at me like she had done something wrong.

"Relax," Lobo scolded her. "We haven't established that as a fact yet. Even if it is true, you couldn't have controlled it."

"But I can make certain it doesn't impact Jeff anymore by staying away from him until after tomorrow."

"Forget about that!" I blurted. "No way!" Unlike how I felt in the plaza, I couldn't stand the thought of not having both Lobo and Carla around to help me figure out what to do.

"Not necessary and even detrimental at this point," Lobo said to her. "If that linkage exists, it has already been solidified. Your absence would not change it in the least. Besides, your young man here can greatly benefit from your presence and your insights."

"There you go!" I told her. "You gotta stick around. Please?" I gave her one of my sad-eyed puppy looks.

"Oh stop it with the eyes and the long face," she replied. "If you're sure, Lobo."

"I'm sure."

"OK, all right, but I do have an idea if you want to hear it."

"Go for it," I told her.

"I was thinking that sometimes people write or attach information on the backs of old pictures and portraits. Maybe your grandfather or somebody along the way in your family recorded some information that could tell us a little more."

"Smart lady!" I rushed to take the picture down. In no time, I had the portrait sitting on the floor. Kneeling in front of it, I looked on the back as Carla suggested. There, covered with dust I found a large, ratty old envelope taped to the canvas.

"Carla, you are so right!" I yelled. The envelope came loose easily when I pulled on it—old tape holding the thing in place just fell apart. While still balancing the portrait upright with one hand, I held up the dusty envelope triumphantly in the other. That's when *it* happened. Everything in the room started … flickering … as if someone was quickly turning the lights off and on. No, that's not completely right. All sound also stopped for a split second at the same time everything would go dark. Carla said something, but her words got chopped up so much they didn't make any sense.

Into those spaces between seeing and hearing what went on in my living room, came other vague, unfamiliar images and sounds. That flip-flopping back and forth between the known and unknown sped up until nothing remained but those unfamiliar sights and sounds. They also flickered on and off but at a slower rate than before. It was like watching and listening to a whole bunch of extremely short film clips strung together. Think of turning your TV from channel to channel every second or two and you'll get an even better idea of what I experienced.

I'm telling you, what I saw was a wild mixture of places I had never been, things I had never seen before, and people I didn't know. Images maybe? No, even that word doesn't explain it properly. No, what I saw seemed more like ... memories ... random memories... someone's memories ... thin slices of a life I had never known.

Weird? No kidding. I mean, within each of those life slices, there were also emotions, touch, smells and sounds coming at me so rapid-fire, I couldn't make sense out of them. Through it all though, one thing became crystal clear. Those flashing, living images were not from the twenty-first century. No way. In that world, horses transported people and many streets went unpaved. The clothes people wore, the hairstyles, absolutely everything screamed, *distant past*.

On and on it went until the whole mess blended into a massive painful blur.

24

Pipelines

I kept wondering why I had nothing better to do than look at a big chunk of wood. It took the smell of food cooking to shake me into a hazy understanding that I was lying on my back, staring at one of those big, hand-cut rafters in Lobo's ceiling. *Hamburgers?*

"Hi," Carla said from somewhere very close. "Just about to wake you up."

Slowly, I turned my head towards her voice. I wanted very much to look at her instead of that stupid rafter. Turned out she was sitting in a little folding chair next to me where I lay on Lobo's couch. "What the hell?" I mumbled. The last thing I remembered was holding the oil painting of my ancestor at my house.

"Take it easy," she said gently, putting a hand on my shoulder. "You've been asleep for well over an hour." Behind her, I noticed a fire cracking away in Lobo's fireplace. I could even feel the heat on my face. Carla had shed her coat and now wore a long sleeved green sweater. God, she looked good.

"Asleep?" I mumbled, my mind still not very clear. On the coffee table next to us, Lobo's Ball of Realities and my crushed Coke can acted like an alarm clock. As soon as I saw them, I woke up all the way.

Carla tilted her head to the side a little and squeezed her lips together for a few seconds before saying anything. "You, ah, got zapped after you took that envelope off the back of the portrait. It was full of information about Walton, even old letters he wrote. Lobo said your ancestor more or less tried to pour his thoughts and memories into you through the picture and some of the items in the envelope that actually belonged to him. All of that overloaded you, like an electric current. It knocked you flat on the floor, but you didn't fully lose consciousness. I'm so sorry I suggested you look there."

Electric current? Oh man, that made me think about what happened as I touched the pyramid, and images from another century trickled back into my awareness from when I handled the envelope. "Oh, oh yeah. I remember some of that. You couldn't have known there would be a problem, but ... but what about my house and the painting?"

"When he realized what was happening," Carla replied, "Lobo jumped up and pulled both the portrait and the envelope away from you. He says you're OK, but you had a major overload with that connection to your ancestor. If it had gone on for much longer, it could have been a real problem. You were so woozy from that experience, we walked you to the truck and then into the house here. When we laid you on the couch, you went right to sleep. Oh, we locked up your house and left the portrait there."

I had no recollection of walking out of my house at all. "Thanks for, ah, taking care of everything," I replied, sitting up and rubbing my eyes. Feeling hot, I flipped the blanket covering me onto the back of the couch. As I did that, I saw I had no shoes on, and my jacket was missing. I hoped Carla hadn't been the one to take off those smelly old sneakers of mine.

"Oh," Carla said, "I looked up Lieutenant Walton in a book and confirmed what Lobo said about him dying on December 28 along with Dade and most of his men. By the way, his first name was Robert. Lieutenant Robert Walton."

"I don't know if that is good news or bad," I replied. "I mean everything keeps speeding up and I can't seem to absorb it enough to make sense of it all. Talk about overload. I mean look at me lying here after collapsing at my house. This is the third freakin' time you have had to take care of me when I've been either sick or just plain out of it in some way."

"And wouldn't you have done the same for me?"

"Well, of course but—"

"This has got to be hard on you, but Lobo told me after all you've been through, you've shown how strong your mind really is. He said if most people in the world had experienced what you have been through in such a short amount of time, they could have gone crazy. You might want to think about that."

"Really?" I asked, feeling a little encouraged.

"Uh huh, and you know by now Lobo doesn't say something unless he really means it."

"I hear that," I replied, accompanied by a rumbling in my stomach. The delicious scent of hamburgers had gotten to me, and I remembered how I hadn't finished my little meal at the Athena restaurant. Of course, when I thought about the Athena, an image of looking at myself through panes of glass popped into my mind.

With a worried look on her face, Carla said, "But also according to Lobo, your ancestor is trying even harder to make a connection because you've finally recognized him. When you touched the portrait and that envelope, he was ready and waiting to make a serious link. It's easier for him to contact you through things that belonged to him, see?"

"Oh," I said, still overwhelmed with the day's incredible chain of events.

"Dinner!" Lobo called from the dining room table after putting some things on it.

I couldn't see any coins on the table or scattered on the floor. Either Carla or Lobo, or even the both of them, had picked up the mess I made. That fact made me feel a little guilty. By the time Carla and I stood up, Lobo had gone back into the kitchen. Under the red and blue, hanging Tiffany lamp, somebody had set the dining room table for three people. A plate of hamburgers in buns, a big bowl of potato salad, and smaller plates of lettuce, tomatoes and pickles all sat there making me really hungry. Bottled water stood next to each plate.

"Come on," Carla said, tugging on my arm gently until she made me sit in the chair facing Lobo's picture window, even pulling it out for me. I guess she wanted to make sure I didn't collapse or something. Who could blame her? How many times had she helped me as I bumped into Lobo's worlds-within-worlds knocking myself silly?

As she sat in the chair to my right, I looked out into the darkness through Lobo's window. There in the distance, the lights from the bridge to Vilano Beach, the Bridge of Lions, and Anastasia Island glittered brightly. Several seconds after that, the beam from the St. Augustine Lighthouse out on the island swept across Matanzas Bay and out to sea.

"Here's your salad," Lobo said to Carla, coming back into the dining room with a bowl full of lettuce and vegetables in one hand and in the other, ketchup and mustard. Since Carla is a vegetarian, I figured he had created a special meal just for her. She definitely doesn't do hamburgers.

Seeing Lobo with those things in his hands looked really odd. To me, after running into more than one of the guy at the same time, and hearing all of his scary explanations, it looked weird seeing him doing such ordinary things. You understand? What I mean is, the man was so completely out of the ordinary in so many wild ways I had trouble seeing him involved in the everyday task of cooking and serving food.

Anyway, after he finally sat down, it didn't take long for the thought of eating to grab my full attention. I dove into my meal like I hadn't eaten in a week. Gotta admit, I stuffed myself with everything I could find while Carla and Lobo had this long discussion about Tiffany stained glass. Borrrring.

When I had gotten half way through my second burger, Lobo started talking directly to me. He and Carla had already finished their dinner.

"As Carla already told you, contact with that portrait of your ancestor and his papers knocked you partly unconscious."

"That's not all of it," I said and went on to explain to both him and Carla what I experienced at the time.

Lobo nodded and said, "That was a very dangerous situation indeed, one you don't want to repeat. We almost lost you."

As he said that, the bite of food going down my throat sort of stuck there. I had to gulp some water to help the stuff go down. When it did, I said, "So, ah, I could have, what? died or something?"

"Yes, or as I told you before, your consciousness could have been pulled into your ancestor's reality without any escape. One possibility is that your physical body in our world would then appear as if you had fallen into a deep coma. For right now, you can't afford to touch anything from your ancestor's time, especially personal items of his, like letters and so forth. Such things are quickly becoming direct pipelines that allow him dangerous access to your mind in addition to the blood connection that already exists."

Direct pipelines? Great! Just freakin' great!

25

Muskets and Rifles

Lobo dropped the big old envelope I took from the back of my ancestor's portrait right in the middle of the dining room table, startling me. Carla and I had been sitting there chatting and waiting for him after clearing off the dinner dishes when he came up behind me like he did. For whatever reason, I thought he and Carla had left the envelope at my house with the portrait. My enthusiasm for looking at the envelope's contents evaporated the moment I touched that thing when I first found it. "What's that doing here?" I asked.

"As long as you don't touch it, or anything in it, you'll be all right," he replied after sitting back down with us.

"OK, fine, but you didn't answer my question." With all I had been through, I found it hard to fully trust the guy's judgment.

"A bit edgy are we now?"

"Not edgy, just wary. Can you blame me?"

"Nobody's blaming you," Carla said, sliding into the conversation, and glaring at Lobo. "We brought the envelope back because the idea of you finding out more about your ancestor is still a good one."

"Like it or not," Lobo said, "*you* are in a battle of survival! Not me, not Cara, just *you*. Without a doubt, you will be encountering your ancestor again, and the more you know about his personal life, the better prepared you will be to deal with the situation in a positive manner. Your very existence could well depend on what you might learn here."

Lobo's never-ending words about my survival were like a constant drumbeat bouncing around inside my head. "I got it, OK? So go ahead and show me what's in the freakin' envelope." At that point, I didn't care how irritated I sounded.

"Hold on a minute." Carla jumped up, scooted over to one of Lobo's bookcases and quickly came back with a book. "Here," she said, handing it to me. "Take a look at the cover."

When I took the book from her hand, my eyes locked onto a full color, artistic recreation of a raging battle scene. It began on the front cover, continued across the book's spine and ended on the back cover. Desperate looking men in sky-blue uniforms with white belts crisscrossing their chests fought for their lives. Sprinkled among them were other men in dark blue coats with gold buttons. *Dade's Last Command,* it said on the front with a guy named Frank Laumer as the author.

Yeah, those uniforms looked very familiar to me. What really hit me even more than that though, were the expressions on those soldiers' faces. *My God!* I mean, those men looked exactly how I felt—scared and trapped with no way out. Don't know how long I stared at that picture in a daze of recognition. Finally, I pointed at the tall, leather looking hat on one man's head and said to Carla, "I saw some of those. I remember them now. They, those hats, were scattered on the ground with all kinds of other stuff."

"See how valid your experience at the cemetery was?" Carla smiled, obviously trying to encourage me to be more positive without actually saying so. "That's why I wanted to show you the book cover. Somehow, you were able to gather incredible, firsthand insights into the Dade battlefield soon after the fighting ended. Now you can merge that information with whatever you might find useful in some of your ancestor's documents in the envelope. It's a great combination. That's all Lobo is trying to tell you."

"Mmm, yeah. Makes sense, I guess." And it did, really. What also made sense was how Carla had a key or two to some of the little switches in my head I hadn't yet learned to flip on my own. Good and bad keys in other people's possession, I said to myself, and I wondered when, or if, I would ever be the one turning the switches on my own. When I handed the book back to Carla, she put it on the coffee table. Glancing at the book once more as she came back to her seat, I thought about the large historical marker at the cemetery and its simplified version of the Dade battle. "I still can't get over both our ancestors being part of all … that." I jerked a thumb back in the book's direction.

"I hear you," she replied, shaking her head.

"What started the battle anyway? And how did such a large group from the U.S. Army get wiped out so easily?" For some reason, my curiosity had gotten all fired up. Yeah, me asking a couple of questions about history. I even surprised myself. Guess it was seeing that book cover combined with my ancestor and Carla's both having been part of what happened so long ago.

"Uh, well," Carla said, clearly surprised by my interest, "there's no doubt about it. The defeat of Dade and his men was the worst loss by the U.S. Army to Native Americans until Custer and his people died at the Little Big Horn about forty years later.

"You see, back in the early 1830's, the U.S. was in the process of moving Native People out of the eastern part of the country and sending them west of the Mississippi whether they wanted to go or not. Horrible stuff. A lot of those folks died on the way. By 1835, the only land the Seminoles had left in Florida was a reservation 60 miles wide by 120 long. It only stretched from just north of Tampa to Ocala, but even that the government wanted to take that away from them. At the time, the U.S. had a fort where Tampa is located today called Fort Brooke. There was another one named Fort King where present-day Ocala is located."

I remembered seeing those names on the cemetery's historical marker.

"Eventually, the Seminoles, and their black allies had had enough and decided to resist."

"Black allies?"

"Free blacks, escaped slaves, and their families."

"Oh." I'm telling you, sometimes all that Carla knows about history just astounds me.

"When December of 1835 rolled around, the Seminoles were getting restless and causing the whites problems. When a message arrived at Fort Brooke from Fort King asking for reinforcements, Major Dade and his soldiers were quickly sent up the military road on the 23rd of December."

"Military road? That's the one where the battle took place, the same location where I saw all those bodies?"

"Yes, Mr. Golden," Lobo rumbled, "the locations are identical, but we don't have time for the pampering of your newly awakened fascination with history."

"OK, but wait a minute," I protested. "You said the more I know about my ancestor's private life the better prepared I'll be. What's more private than the circumstances of the man's death?"

"He's got you there." Carla snickered and looked at Lobo with both eyebrows raised. "*Your move*," she said to him without using words.

Letting out a sigh of exasperation, and frowning deeply, Lobo said, "Here's the quick version of what happened, so pay attention."

"Absolutely." I had to flash Carla a tiny victory smile when I said that one word. She winked at me as Lobo took over the storytelling.

"The Seminole chiefs, Micanopy, Alligator and Jumper laid an ambush for Dade and his men about half way between Fort Brooke and Fort King. The great war leader, Osceola, wasn't able to participate. Armed with rifles they got from the Spanish in Cuba, 180 Indians formed a semicircle going across the military road with a pond and high grass on one side. No escape for the soldiers once they entered the jaws of that trap.

"Major Dade allowed his troops to keep their muskets under their heavy overcoats on that morning of December 28 to keep them dry. In the chilly air, the pine trees and palmettos still dripped water from an early morning rain. Dade also thought the Seminoles wouldn't attack in such a wide-open area. He couldn't have been more wrong, obviously, putting his men at a great disadvantage in case of an attack."

"Muskets?" I asked. "That was the soldiers' main weapon, but the Seminoles had rifles, which were more modern, right?"

"Rifles didn't become the weapon of choice in the U.S military," Carla answered, "until much later in that century. In 1835, rifles and muskets both had their advantages and disadvantages."

Just as Carla finished her sentence, the fire in the fireplace popped loudly and showered sparks into the living room about half way to the coffee table. I wondered why Lobo didn't use one of those screens to protect the room and furniture from damage. Both Carla and I jumped, but old Lobo never flinched or even blinked, as usual. He did gripe at us though.

"Enough digression and talk of weapons," he grumbled. "We need to finish this discussion quickly, and get to the envelope."

I apologized for getting us off track and Lobo launched back into his explanation—at a much faster pace.

"Commanded by Captain Gardiner, a short barrel of a man, most of Dade's men walked up the road in two columns. Lieutenant Walton's post was there as well, but he had no horse, unlike Gardiner and Dade. An advance party pushed ahead of the column consisting of Lieutenant Mudge, Carla's ancestor, Luis Pacheco and several soldiers, all led by Captain Fraser. A rear guard followed the main force with a cannon and supply wagon, Lieutenant Basinger commanding."

"Wait! Lieutenant ... *Basinger*?" I knew I couldn't have heard the man correctly.

"Yes, why," Lobo asked, but he had this look on his face that made me think he already knew the answer.

"The soldier at the National Guard Headquarters, the one we almost ran into," I said to Carla, "his name was *Basinger.*"

"Really?"

"I'm not kidding! I saw the name on his uniform when we rode by."

"How ..." She seemed at a real loss for words. Unusual, but true.

"Carla," Lobo said, "in that instance, you directly shared with your friend here, one of his many odd experiences of the day. That particular coincidental event, as some people would describe it, was part of a unique unfolding of patterns set in motion that have great importance—even if none of us ever discovers its ultimate meaning."

To me, he said, "Perhaps the soldier was a descendant of the Dade battle Basinger, unconsciously channeling a warning from his ancestor to beware of your contact with the pyramids by almost running into you. Or, your own inner self might have put you at that exact place, and at that precise time, as a subconscious warning of what was yet to come. The possibilities are infinite."

"Uh, Jeff, Lobo ..." Carla didn't finish her sentence. She had her head turned to the side, staring intently at Lobo's picture window.

"What?" I asked, looking straight ahead of me across the dining room table. I couldn't see anything out of the ordinary—nothing but darkness outside of Lobo's house and the usual lights on the other side of Matanzas Bay.

"Don't either of you say another word, and above all, don't move," Lobo ordered, his eyes locked onto the window just as Carla's were.

26

Begging for Help

Lobo's warning sent shivers up my spine. I still couldn't see anything unusual, but that strange sensation in my stomach I first noticed at the pyramids returned. This time, it felt like a snake sliding through my insides and wrapping itself tightly around my stomach. When the squeezing moved upward towards my heart, I saw them in the window—two wide-open eyes and nothing more—dark brown eyes, looking all around the room. They appeared to be very real and seemed to be imbedded somehow in the glass itself—no eyelids, no eyebrows, only those brown irises set dead center in a background of white. *What the hell?* I wanted to say something out loud, but after Lobo's warning, I didn't dare.

Very slowly, a shape formed around those eyes, extended itself downward to the bottom of the window, and snapped into focus. My ancestor, Lieutenant Robert Walton, in his dark military coat with gold buttons, looked out from all that glass directly at me—not at Lobo or Carla, just me. His legs in sky-blue pants only went down to about mid-thigh level where the window ended.

Carla said nothing, but a sharp intake of her breath made me forget Lobo's order to stay perfectly still. I didn't move much, nothing more than a little shift of the my head and eyes in her direction. That's all it took though, for me to find myself in deep trouble. It happened very quickly when I think about it now, but at the time, it felt like it took forever.

As soon as I made those two little moves, a sound came from the window, a sound like something ... being stretched—rubber or plastic maybe. When I moved my gaze back to the image of Lieutenant Walton, I saw he had partially emerged from the glass in three-dimensional form. He stared at me even more intently than before, and tilted his head slightly like he did at the cathedral. Slowly, he lifted his hands outward in my direction with an expression on his face that looked like ... I don't know ... he might be begging for help or something. It reminded me of when he extended his hand unbelievably far in the cathedral, and I got ready to shove away from the table as fast as I could if he did it again.

I tried to focus on my breath to reduce the instant fear bubbling up inside me. It didn't work. Not enough time. That tight, slithery feeling in my stomach and heart quickly switched to the same kind of tugging sensation I experienced when I flew back into myself on the bike ride to the cemetery—only much stronger.

Before I knew what had happened, I uh, well ... felt my body ... slide forward a couple of feet. Of course, that was impossible since the dining room table sat directly in front of me. When I looked down though, I saw ... ah, well ... just half of me, the top half, and I seemed to be sitting on the dining room table like some sort of partial statue. I mean, I couldn't see any part of my body below stomach or elbow level—no forearms, hands, hips, crotch, legs or feet. The only thing I saw nearby was that envelope from the portrait on the table inches from my stomach. Man, I sucked my gut in so quick you would believe.

Talk about freaked out? I wanted to scream, but couldn't for some reason. The thing is, I also watched all that happen while still seated in my chair in front of the table. Besides the horror of seeing another me emerge from myself like that, I also knew beyond a doubt that my ancestor was trying to reel that other Jeff in like a fish.

In the next instant, though, instead of staring into the eyes of Lieutenant Walton, I saw … Lobo. Somehow, he had gotten to the other side of the table, putting himself between my body, uh, both my bodies, I guess you would say, and my ancestor. When he did that, whatever connection Walton had established with me disintegrated, and I went back to being one incredibly scared kid, sitting in a dining room chair. At the same time, it sounded like something hit the window, hard, followed by a tremendous splitting sound. Only when Lobo stepped aside did I see Walton had vanished. In his place, were maybe a dozen large cracks that zigzagged outward in the picture window from a central point—looked like somebody had smacked it with a baseball bat.

"Dear God!" Carla stared at the damaged glass wide-eyed, as if my ancestor might suddenly reappear.

Believe me, I felt the same way. On top of that, I realized my body was as rigid as a board, and I was barely breathing. I'm telling you my heart thumped in my chest so loud, I thought for sure Carla and Lobo could hear it.

"Relax, both of you," Lobo said. "He's gone, for now, but what just occurred is an indication of how very intense and threatening this situation has become."

Breathing deeply and then exhaling long and loud, I slumped in my chair feeling like a balloon somebody had let loose until it ran out of air. "I thought I was toast," I said to Lobo. "If you hadn't—"

"Toast?" Carla asked, tearing her eyes away from the window. "What … what are you—"

"She didn't see the separation," Lobo said to me instead of speaking to Carla.

"Really?" I replied, startled that only Lobo and I knew exactly what had happened to me.

"Will you two stop that?" Carla protested, getting even more upset. "Separation? Somebody talk to me!"

"Uh, sorry," I replied, and went on to tell her, in a shaky voice, about my experience of once again splitting in two. While I spoke, I found it difficult to keep my eyes off the spot on the dining room table where another terrified me had looked down to see only half a body. Carla, on the other hand, kept glancing at Lobo's battered window with fear and worry clearly written across her face.

"Well, now at least, you've actually seen him," I said to her, trying to lessen the tension in the room. Didn't work.

"Oh, no doubt about it, I, ah, saw your Lieutenant Walton all right." Carla kept nodding mechanically for a few seconds. I think she was in shock.

Pointing at his cracked window, Lobo said to both of us, "This attempted intrusion into the physical world is one of the most forceful I have ever seen. It tells us we don't have a lot of time to dillydally."

"You mean because Walton could return?" Carla asked.

"Precisely."

"But I thought Jeff would be safe here."

"He is to a degree, but I'll need to take some further precautions relatively soon."

"Like what?" I asked. That didn't sound good. I thought I was safe too.

"You'll see, later," he replied. "To save time, however, we need to put a stop to the Dade battle history lesson and get to the contents of the envelope."

"No," I said, softly, but firmly. Don't know where that came from, but it just popped out of my mouth. "It's … important that I hear the basic facts. Not sure why. I can't explain."

"But Jeff—"

"Hmm," Lobo said, ignoring Carla and looking all around me the way he does. "In that case, we'll make the time."

Surprised how easy it was to turn old Lobo around, I nodded and he picked up where he had left off. Carla didn't look too pleased, but she kept quiet as Lobo told his story.

"As the advance party with Captain Fraser in command moved deep into the ambush site at approximately 8:00 a.m. on December 28, Major Dade trotted his horse up and down the two columns of his men strung out on the road, occasionally talking to them. Finally, he arrived at the head of both lines for the last time, his big, black beard blowing in the breeze, and shouted encouragement to his troops. He told the men that all the danger was behind them, and their long march would soon be over. To encourage them even more, he said that upon arrival at Fort King, he would give them three days off duty to relax and celebrate Christmas. As the soldiers cheered his remarks, he saluted them and rode off towards the advance party.

"Just as Dade got to Captain Fraser and Luis Pacheco, who were also approaching the rest of the advance party, Chief Micanopy stood up and shot Dade through the heart. As he fell from his horse, 180 Seminoles in their semicircle around Dade's soldiers opened fire with their rifles. It was a turkey shoot. Especially with their muskets under their overcoats, Dade's people never had a chance. Many soldiers fell in that first volley of fire, and as gun smoke filled the air, the remaining men either froze or tore wildly at their overcoats to uncover their muskets.

"In the middle of all that chaos, Captain Gardiner yelled and cursed to shock the men back to their senses. Eventually, he got them to take cover and start shooting back at the Seminoles. Soon after that, he called for Lt. Basinger to bring the cannon from the rear of the column and start firing into the pines and palmettos where the Seminole hid on the other side of the road.

"After close to an hour of battle, the Seminoles retreated for a small period of time.

"When Captain Gardiner counted his men, only forty out of Dade's 100 plus soldiers survived that first attack in good enough condition to continue fighting. Major Dade, and all of the advance party, except for Luis Pacheco, died in that initial exchange of gunfire."

"Forty soldiers?" I asked, finding what Lobo had said hard to believe. "That's over sixty men killed or wounded—in an hour?"

"It was a very good ambush," Lobo replied in a cold tone of voice. "When the Seminoles withdrew, Captain Gardiner ordered his men to chop down pine trees and create a little triangular fort. It wasn't much of a defensive position, but it provided the only protection they could muster at the time. You saw such a structure during your encounter with your ancestor's living memories of the battle."

"Oh, yeah," I agreed, remembering.

"Soon after the completion of the fort, the Seminoles attacked again. One of the first shots when the battle resumed caught your ancestor in the chest, and he went down, mortally wounded. The fighting raged on again, until one by one, the remaining soldiers died, were badly wounded, or simply ran out of ammunition. When the cannon finally stopped firing, and there were no more musket shots from Dade's men, the Seminoles and their black allies moved in and finished off those who still lived. Over one hundred soldiers died that day with the loss of only three Seminoles."

While Lobo spoke, all I could think of was how Lyle turned into Lieutenant Walton in the plaza with blood soaking his chest, and his head splitting open. I didn't want to know what caused Walton's head to fracture like that, and even though I tried not to think about it, I imagined all kinds of possibilities.

"Out of all the soldiers participating in the battle, only two lived to tell about it. One was Ransom Clark. Shot five times, Clark played dead and painfully dragged himself the sixty miles or so back to Fort Brooke. The reason we have accurate accounts of what happened on that day, came from interviews later given by Clark and his fellow soldier, as well as the Seminole leader, Halpatter Tustenugge, known to the whites as Alligator, and, of course, Carla's ancestor, Luis Pacheco."

"After taking only the soldiers' weapons, but no money or jewelry, the Seminoles went into the Wahoo Swamp, and had a big celebration. That battle began the Second Seminole War, which lasted for another seven years and took many lives. During those years, the army captured the great war leader Osceola, when he came to peace talks under a flag of truce—a disgraceful act of treachery by the Americans. He and other Seminoles were for a time held prisoner in our St. Augustine Castillo—Fort Marion, they called it in those days. At war's end, most of the surviving Seminoles gave up and agreed to go out west. The few who still resisted fled to the Everglades."

"What about their black allies?" I asked.

"Eventually," Carla answered for Lobo with a more than a touch of anger in her voice, "most of them ended up back in slavery."

"Oh ... I see. And your relative ... Luis Pacheco?"

"Luis? Well, that's quite a story," she replied, looking once more at Lobo's badly cracked window with a shiver. "We don't have time for it now. The main thing is that he lived a full life and died a free man in the Jacksonville area right around 1895."

"Which brings us back to *your* ancestor," Lobo said, putting a hand on the envelope in front of him and sliding those fiery eyes of his in my direction.

PART FOUR

*Plunging
into
the Unknown*

27

Spiritual Insanity

Lobo pulled my ancestor's documents out of its raggedy old envelope and put them on the dining room table in front of him. "A number of men under Major Dade's command," he said to me, "including your ancestor and Captain Fraser, sympathized with the Seminoles, had Seminole friends, and also hated slavery."

"At least he had the right idea," I said, but not feeling very comfortable being so close to all those dangerous "pipelines" to another world lying on the table.

Carla nodded in agreement to what I said about Walton.

"He did indeed," Lobo replied. "Being a good soldier, however, like the others, he did his job as ordered and on December 28, paid the ultimate price for doing so."

After searching through all those old looking papers, Lobo picked out one item and held it up for me to see. "Lieutenant Walton sent this letter to his mother in New York City before he left Fort Brooke with Major Dade. In it, he told her he intended to resign his commission in the army because he couldn't stand being a part of what might happen to the Seminoles and free blacks."

Now that surprised me. I really wanted to read the letter for myself, but just looking at it and knowing what could happen if I touched it made me wince.

"It must have been very hard for your ancestor to even consider quitting," Carla said. "According to the documents we found, Lieutenant Walton was a graduate of the U.S. Military Academy at West Point. The army was probably his whole life."

"In addition to the army, however," Lobo said, "he did have a wife and also a daughter. The daughter's name was Elizabeth. At first they were at Fort Brooke with Walton, but when things started going sour with the Seminoles, he sent them by ship to safety in Key West."

"A daughter?" I asked. "So this Elizabeth—"

"Elizabeth," Lobo said, "was your great, great, great, great grandmother. She and her mother eventually moved to St. Augustine after the Second Seminole war ended in 1842. When Elizabeth came of age, she married a businessman here by the name of Golden."

It was very strange listening to someone I had only met hours before educate me about my own family history. I mean, especially when he got to the name Golden. Up until then, what he had said could have been about anybody's family, you see? At that point, it all became very real to me.

Lobo again sorted through the papers until he found an old picture. "This," he said holding it up, "is a photograph taken of Elizabeth with her two children during the Civil War. Look at it closely but *do not* touch it."

I got as close as I dared until I could make out the black and white images. The picture was warped and very faded, but I clearly saw a woman and two little boys. The woman wore one of those big old floor length dresses they used to have in those days. She had a long face with her hair parted down the middle and pulled back behind her ears. The picture had faded so much I couldn't really tell if she was pretty or not. The two little boys looked to be about maybe five and six years old, dressed in dark suits with white shirts and floppy bow ties.

"The boy on the right," Lobo said, "is William Golden, your

great, great, great grandfather."

It felt so strange to see those three faces out of the past, specially the little boys who would grow up, have families of their own and … die. Pain and death swirled all around me no matter where I turned.

Lobo put the picture back on top of the document pile with the envelope on the bottom and shoved it all to the far side of the table towards the cracked window. "Those two pieces of information I gave you," he said, "are all you need to know about your ancestor from his papers at this moment. Now, you have a couple of decisions to make."

Oh oh, here it comes. "Decisions? What type of decisions," I asked, wondering why we so quickly went from talking about Lieutenant Walton and his family to making choices.

"When I took the portrait of your ancestor away from you at your home," Lobo replied, "I sensed some things about the man that might be of value to you. First, when Lieutenant Walton died, his spirit left the body, but stayed near it. After the battle was over he observed his physical head being split open by an ax as the Seminoles and their black allies made sure all of Dade's men were dead."

"Oh man," I complained, my memory of Lyle turning into Walton popping back into my head. "I didn't need to hear that." As I looked over at Carla, I could see Lobo's words had affected her as well. On her face was this pinched, painful expression.

"On the contrary," Lobo growled, "you definitely did need to hear that. It will help you understand at least part of why your ancestor has latched onto you with such fierceness."

"Wait, I don't understand."

"The horror of watching what was done to his body," Lobo replied, "combined with Lieutenant Walton's deep concerns regarding his participation in America's policies toward Native Americans and slavery, was too much for him. His death began what you might call a spiritual insanity of sorts. His fear and guilt created a special after-the-battle dream world back in 1835 causing him to relive his memories of that battle every December 28 afterward. In his mind, he is still alive struggling to survive on that lonely road all by himself, but a part of him knows what is about to occur tomorrow. In ignoring the fact that he no longer lives, he is actually punishing himself."

"So," I said, "he kind of sent himself into his own hell without realizing it, right?"

"Exactly," Lobo replied.

"OK, that's really sad, and I feel bad for him, but what does he think I can do about it?"

"He has no idea." Lobo replied as he got up and started pacing back in forth in front of his cracked window. Again, all he knows is his pain and the possibility you could be his savior. To him, you are like a dream of hope that could possibly save him from going through all that again tomorrow. You must understand that Lieutenant Walton is like a drowning person. He has grabbed onto the only thing he thinks might keep him afloat and that thing is you. The danger with helping drowning people of course is, if you aren't careful, you may end up going under as well.

"Now, as I told you before, the Dade battle started around 8:00 a.m. That means you can expect your ancestor to summon all his energy tomorrow at exactly 8:00 a.m., or even earlier, in a last desperate effort to get you to help him. When dawn breaks is the point at which the danger to you will begin to escalate dramatically. The only way for me to fully protect you before then, however, is if you stay here with me."

"Stay … with you?" I croaked, very surprised. A sleepover at Lobo's place didn't sound like a whole lot of fun, but waiting for my ancestor back at *The Dump* all by myself didn't sound like a good alternative either. So, I agreed to stay with the old guy. Yeah, I know. It was an amazing shift from when I stormed out of Lobo's house into that creepy fog, but a lot had happened since then.

"Good, that's settled," he replied. "Now, as to the next decision you need to make. Tomorrow, you can stay here with Carla and me until well after 8:00 a.m. and perhaps together, we can give you the protection you need. Or, we can all go to the cemetery and you can be in direct contact with one of the pyramids."

"No way I'm going back there!" I squawked. "I'm not touching one of those things again."

"Why would you want him to do that again, Lobo?" Carla asked. "You know what Jeff went through the first time."

"It has its risks," he agreed. To me he said, "But it would give you the best opportunity to make contact with Lieutenant Walton on your terms, convince him he's dead, and that he is living in a memory. If you can do that, you have a much better chance of getting the man to permanently leave you alone than if we simply try to defend you here."

"Come on Lobo," I pleaded, "can't you contact him for me?"

In a softer voice than usual, Lobo said, "I have tried on a number of occasions to contact your ancestor and convince him he is no longer living. Unfortunately, he looked right through me each time as if I didn't exist. He is focused just on you, which means you are the key to your own survival."

"*I'm the key to my own survival?* You've got to be freakin' kidding. If that's true, I'm outta luck."

"I don't kid people," Lobo replied. "If you decide to return to the pyramids, Carla and I will go with you as added help and protection, but we must do it shortly after dawn, well before 8:00 a.m. We'll have no time to waste. If, however, you want to take the safer route and stay here with us, we will do what we can. Either way, whatever you decide, you face the possibility of becoming lost in Walton's dream world like I've told you before. As a result, both of you could be doomed to endure the annual recreation of that battle and live with its results over and over, year after year, perhaps forever."

Lobo's words made me feel like somebody had kicked me in the stomach. The word "forever," I guess is what really did it. OK, he had used the word "permanently" before but somehow it didn't make quite the impression the word "forever" did. Don't ask me why. I couldn't possibly tell you. I also thought about my poor old ancestor maybe having to roam that stinking road and reliving the massacre, possibly *forever*, unless I helped him. My decision, I fully realized for the first time, could affect him as well as me.

"When I say dream world," Lobo said, "make no mistake about it. If you somehow become involved in the battle, it will seem as real as anything you have experienced in your life. Remember how real your two short trips to that battlefield seemed at the time?" Here he paused, stared at me hard and said, "Rifle balls and axes will be able to do to you what they do to everyone else there. You will feel all of it exactly as you would have if you had been part of the original battle in 1835. There's a whole world of continuous hurt and mental agony waiting for you if you make the wrong choice here. That's why I'm suggesting you take the extra risk of going to the pyramids. It is truly your best bet for avoiding all of that, but only you can decide."

It's hard to explain what went through my head with both Lobo and Carla quietly staring at me. My thinking seemed to short-circuit and endlessly spin around and around, getting me nowhere. Talk about decision-making. I knew I couldn't just sit there in Lobo's house the next day, waiting for things to happen. Not only that, I kept thinking about Lieutenant Walton. By that time, he had become very real to me. After all, I figured, the guy was my five times great grandfather, right? How could I not give him the best chance possible to get out of the hell he had built for himself? "OK OK, I'll do it. I'll go to the pyramids tomorrow," I said, startling myself as well as Carla. She looked at me like I had lost my mind. Even as I said the words, "I'll do it," I wondered how they came out so easily.

"Jeff, are you sure?" Carla asked, shaking her head like she wanted me to change my mind.

"No," I replied honestly, "but I really don't see I have a better choice."

"Good," Lobo said and stood up. "That settles it. Carla, it's time for you to go. We'll take you home and then pick you up in front of your house at dawn."

Carla stared at him without moving, and with both eyebrows raised, she said, "*Mr.* Lobo, sometimes you are a bit too abrupt."

As serious as things were, I had to stifle a laugh. Carla's words of "*Mr.* Lobo" had the same sarcastic tone the man used when he first called me, "*Mr.* Golden." And, to hear her describe him as "a bit too abrupt," was too much. I mean the guy was all about abrupt, you know?

"Since when do you need to *take* me next door to my house?" Carla asked, looking indignant, yet a little alarmed.

"Since that happened," Lobo said, pointing at his cracked window.

"Walton's a danger to Carla now as well as me?" I couldn't stand the idea of my situation affecting her.

"We're in uncharted territory here," Lobo replied. "We simply don't need to take any chances."

I didn't like hearing Lobo had limited experience with something like my ancestor's increasing aggressive behavior. "Will she be OK at her house?"

"Yes. Besides attaching himself to you, your ancestor has also temporarily attached himself to my home and a large area all around it. In his crazed condition, it's remotely possible he would try to connect with Carla in a similar manner if she walked out of here alone. With me going along for protection, and you to keep his focus elsewhere, we can safely deposit her outside the circumference of danger. When you return here with me, Lieutenant Walton will lose interest in her and follow you."

As you might imagine, Carla didn't offer any resistance to being escorted after Lobo's explanation. With all of his outside floodlights turned on, including some on his dock, we quickly walked her to Lobo's gate and came back to his house. As soon as we got inside, the old guy didn't waste any time getting down to business.

"Go over to the coffee table," he said. "Sit down on the floor right in front of it with your back to the fire."

"Why?"

"The same reason I gave Carla," he said, pointing towards his cracked window like he did with her.

"Oh," I replied and did exactly as he told me to do. After I sat down, he brought more firewood into the house, stirred the coals in the fireplace, and threw on the fresh wood. Next, he turned off two of his stained glass lamps, leaving only the blue one with the dragonflies lighted. That one he turned down to a very low level using a dimmer switch. Instead of turning off the outside floodlights, he left them on and then squeezed his big, old body between the couch and the coffee table, reminding me how Spock had done almost the same thing. There, he sat on the floor directly opposite me. With the fire starting to crackle again, he said, "We need to get begin."

What the hell is all this? "Get started with what?"

"You'll see," he replied. Sitting with his back to the arched doorway and the couch, he moved the Ball of Realities, the smashed coke can, and *Dade's Last Command* towards one end of the coffee table. After that, he put his big old muscular right arm on the coffee table as if he wanted to arm-wrestle me, his eyes glittering even in that minimal light.

No way. I knew he could break my arm in a second. What was the guy trying to do?

"No, we are not going to arm wrestle," he replied to my unspoken thoughts, "but you need to put your right hand in mine and your elbow on the table as if we were."

After what happened with the coin when Lobo grabbed me, the idea of holding his hand wasn't very appealing, but I put my arm on the table and did it anyway. Man, that guy had a grip. My hand looked like a doll hand compared to his. He then put his other elbow on the table and covered my right hand with his left. After that, he told me to do what he had done with my left arm and put my left hand over his right hand. It sounds complicated, I know, but when we were done, we each had both elbows on the table, all four hands clasped, and our faces were very close together, not a very comfortable situation.

"When Carla was here," Lobo said as we stared at each other across our hands in the dim light, "I said I could protect you until morning. The only way for me to do so effectively, however, is for us to remain in this connected position all night."

All night? Oh damn!

28

Fear

Staring into Lobo's weird eyes for such an incredible amount of time, even in that small amount of light, was not something I looked forward to. But what real choice did I have? His iron grip on both of my hands made it very clear he had no intention of letting loose for a long time. *What if I have to go to the bathroom?* I wondered, just as Lobo pulled his hands away from mine. I figured he must have read my mind again, thinking I needed to go immediately, but I was wrong.

"That's it," he said, sitting back against the couch with his big old arms folded. The room seemed a lot darker than it had the second before, but I couldn't figure out why. "You made it through the night, and I've been able to saturate you with as much protective energy as possible."

"What do you mean, 'I made it through the night'?" I asked. "We sat down just a few seconds ago."

Very slowly, Lobo shook his head. "No, it's morning," he replied and pointed towards his picture window.

"No freakin' way!" I said, looking at his window with all the cracks in it. Instead of finding the dock under the glare of floodlights, I saw darkness, a slight glow of what had to be dawn, and an arcing string of light orange blobs in place of the bridge to Vilano Beach.

"Timer switch," Lobo said to my unspoken question about his outside lights on the dock. "Too bad you also have to deal with fog this morning on top of everything else."

"Oh, God ... you're right." I said with disbelief after staring intently at the orange blobs in the distance that had to be fog covered streetlights.

Fog and dawn. The two concepts really split my brain in two different and confusing directions. The fog, of course, brought back bad memories of stepping off Lobo's porch into a dark, wet wilderness of pines and palmettos. It was the undeniable sight of early morning struggling to light up St. Augustine that shook me up even more. I had just been thinking what a long night it was going to be grasping hands with old Lobo so close. *Not possible.* When I glanced at the fireplace behind me, there was nothing left but ashes. The room smelled of wood smoke, and I felt a definite chill. There hadn't been a fire burning for quite a while, no matter what my memory told me.

"How can that be?" I asked Lobo as I stared out the window once more in disbelief.

"You have very limited ideas about time," he replied. "Speaking of which, we leave in ten minutes to pick Carla up and head to the cemetery. Do what you need to do in the bathroom and grab anything you want to eat or drink out of the fridge." Without waiting for me to reply, he stood up and walked out of the room. I sat there on the floor for at least a minute, looking at the fireplace and trying to collect my thoughts. Somehow, December 28 had arrived and I wasn't ready for it—at all.

My gaze drifted back to the misty darkness outside the picture window with its orange blobs and slight glow and then back to Lobo's coffee table. Again, I looked at his Ball of Realities, the book Carla showed me on the Dade battle the night before, and the crushed Coke can. I tell you what, those three things were unwanted reminders of what the rest of the morning might bring, and I closed my eyes, wishing it would all go away.

Of course, that didn't happen, and as I opened my eyes again, my restless mind drifted to the bayonet hanging in the display cabinet. I couldn't really see it in the gloom, but I knew it was there. Part of me wanted to look at the thing up close once more, but another part wouldn't let me do it. I didn't want to think about why Lieutenant Walton had been trying to make contact.

Even so, the memory of scaring away a vulture and walking close to the dead soldier dressed in a sky blue colored uniform bubbled up into my mind. Somehow, I could even smell the horrible stink that went along with all those bodies in the woods. Even though I knew the smell couldn't be real, my stomach lurched. Right on the edge of nausea, I struggled to watch my breathing until the possibility of another puke fest went away. Still, my restless mind flashed back to seeing my ancestor in the plaza. Once again, he stared at me as blood flowed down the front of his coat and once more, his head starting to split wide open.

A shiver passed through me and I wrapped my arms around myself trying to get warm. As I looked again at the darkened fireplace wishing it still had a nice fire, I realized how scared I really was. The ashes are what did it, got me even more fearful I mean. You see, I kept thinking about that big stack of wood burning brightly the night before and then in no time it was nothing but ashes. Maybe this makes no sense to you but that's kind of how I felt when my dad died. One minute he was full of life and the next minute ... gone. Ashes.

I suppose everything had been moving so fast, I never let the possibility of me actually dying truly sink into my brain. December 28 had arrived and I couldn't avoid it. There it was, death or whatever, ready to gobble me up. Lobo's warning about what could happen on that day made me feel like a rat caught in a trap.

"Are you really so afraid of dying?" Lobo asked. He stood there behind the couch staring at me with those wild, fiery eyes of his waiting for an answer.

"Yeah … I'm scared," I replied to his question, glancing down, not wanting to look into his eyes any more. The idea that I might no longer exist, or continue to exist insane, or even caught forever living in a dream battle, terrified me. I mean, wouldn't you feel the same way? As screwed up as my life was though, thinking about not being alive, or worse, made me feel like I had dropped into a deep, dark and bottomless pit.

"A little fear is a good thing. It keeps you alert," Lobo said, but still I didn't look at him, "Too much of it, however, slices the mind painfully over and over again. If you live in constant fear, you die in spirit time after time before anything negative actually catches up with you, if indeed it ever does. You weaken yourself so that you stand little or no chance of winning whatever battle you're fighting."

I nodded instead of saying anything, but I still didn't look at the man. What he was saying made sense. Still, my nerves were so jittery I felt like I wanted to jump up and run somewhere, anywhere. I tried focusing on my breathing and not fighting the problem, but it wasn't easy. Lobo had shown me there were "worlds-within-worlds-within-worlds," as he put it, but somehow that wasn't helping me figure out how not to be so completely afraid.

"By now," Lobo said, sitting down in his recliner, "you know that death doesn't mean you cease to exist, don't you?"

I thought about his question for a second and said, "I guess so." Before meeting Lobo, I would have told people when you die, that's it. End of story. But, after seeing Lobo's long lost cat and Lieutenant Walton both looking real as anything, I knew there was definitely something more to death than nothingness. Exactly what though, I had no real idea.

"Look at me," Lobo barked, and I did. "This life you are living is only a tiny, tiny fraction of who you really are and the same is true for every being on earth. One of the differences between you and most other people, however, is that you have the ability to connect with other existences, as I've said before. When you saw your double at the Athena restaurant, you were showing yourself possibilities beyond the self you think you know so well. When you saw your body lying in the street after your accident at the library, you were doing the same thing. Those two events were lessons you were taught by a deeper, wiser part of yourself."

The more the guy talked, the better I felt. Not good, you understand, but better. The panicky, jittery feelings eased up a bit, but I had to ask Lobo the thing that really disturbed me the most.

"OK, but you told me before … something worse than death could happen to me … like getting stuck in my ancestor's dream forever. Man, that's what really—"

"Lieutenant Walton exists in his self-created hell, but you certainly don't want to share it with him."

"You got that right."

"The only way such a thing could happen now is if you don't concentrate, and you let your fear build up ahead of time. Doing so would damage your mind's ability to deal effectively with the situations you may face. If you allow that to happen, when the time comes to handle Lieutenant Walton, you will definitely make mistakes that could very well doom you both.

"Remember, what I said to you, 'It's all in the mind.' You know this, because you finally discovered what you call the little switches or dials inside your head that allow you to chose how you feel and act."

His words made me think back to seeing an old green Lumina full of teenagers sliding around the corner near Flagler College and hear the guy on the passenger side yell at me. Looking at how I reacted then, I sensed even more clearly than before how my white-hot anger had burst out of me directly from a core of my own fear, confusion and embarrassment. I let it happen, let it control me. "Yeah," I finally replied to Lobo in a low, hoarse voice, no longer amazed at his ability to pick up on my thoughts. "Yeah, you're right," I said again, my voice stronger and clearer, "I do remember." *Don't fight the problem*, I said to myself as I tried to focus on my breath. Up until then, I hadn't been doing such a great job of repeating that important selection of words.

"Good, because the deeper you live in fear this morning, the more bad decisions you will make while in contact with Lieutenant Walton and the more chances you have of not coming back to this life. Am I getting through to you?"

"Yes."

Nodding, Lobo said, "Obviously, when you were standing in front of Flagler College, you discovered a switch inside your head that permits you to push fear away. Can you now find and make use of that switch like you did unconsciously when the teenager yelled an insult at you?"

After he spoke, I felt a rush of energy quickly rise from my stomach up through my chest, and into my head. It was as if a flow deep within me rapidly ate at the fear until it became much smaller. Not gone, but smaller. I could actually feel my muscles relaxing. Up until that point, I hadn't noticed how tight and tense my body had become.

Not waiting for me to say anything, Lobo nodded again, his eyes flashing. "Very few people in this world could make such a quick turnaround facing the difficulties you have in your path. The energy you sensed just now, and how quickly you turned down the dial of fear within you, just shows how skilled you can be."

What the man said made me feel even better, but I was still worried. "With you coaching me like that," I began, "maybe I'll be OK."

"The coaching and energy I can give," Lobo replied, "will only go as far as the cemetery. Once you are in contact with the Lieutenant, you'll be on your own. I won't be able follow you as you link with him."

"But—"

"There are no *buts*," Lobo said. "You will be on your own after a certain point. Remember though, that you are as prepared as you can possibly be and, as of right now, you have five minutes before we leave."

29

Dead Kid Walking

Headlights from the few cars on the road made the moisture in the air in front of them look like fuzzy bright ghosts quickly appearing and disappearing. What can I say? I had spirits on my mind. Fog. I couldn't seem to get away from it. Tell you what, walking out to Lobo's truck into the stuff on that dark morning creeped me out even more than I already was. I kept thinking about being lost in it like I was after stepping off Lobo's porch—that and looking inside his house through the clear oval around the stained glass hanging there all by itself in the swirling mist.

After Lobo and I picked Carla up, we drove in silence. There wasn't much for any of us to say, I guess, so we just listened to Lobo's windshield wipers slapping back and forth. Carla sat between Lobo and me and leaned her head against my shoulder. That felt nice, but her silence also told me she had to be deeply worried. That made two of us. Lobo? He just seemed intent on driving.

By the time we got to the Castillo, the dull light of dawn had disappeared. The stupid fog had thickened so much that those big old floodlights around the place made it look like a giant bunch of softly glowing cotton. Out on Matanzas Bay, you couldn't even see the Bridge of Lions no less any lights over on Anastasia Island. At the plaza, the city had turned off all the Christmas lights. No more Nights of Lights at that time of the morning. The old-time streetlights they have near the sidewalks crisscrossing that area were still on but the real brightness and warmth I felt the night before didn't … well, exist anymore. Nope. No happy people. No little kids trying to open the fake presents or sitting on the cannons. Instead, clumps of dull light floated in cold, dark wet. To me, it looked as if daylight would never come to the city of St. Augustine again.

As we got closer to the cemetery, I kept thinking about movies I had seen where somebody gets executed. Most of all, an old prison film kept popping back into my mind. In that movie, when the condemned man heads down the hallway under guard to his doom, people yell out, "Dead man walking!" Well, that's how I felt. In my head, I could hear some guy yelling, *"Dead Kid Walking."*

Sure Lobo's talk back at his house about fear and all helped, and to be honest, he was kind of nice about it. Instead of being critical like he had been when we first met, the guy really appeared to be trying to save my life. The things the man had taught me about how my mind worked definitely helped reduce my fear during the truck ride over to the cemetery. Believe me, I kept focusing on my breath and telling myself to not fight the problem. But no matter how hard I tried not to be afraid, I still had this heavy, sick feeling in my stomach. It was a good thing I didn't have any breakfast. I remembered what happened the last time I touched one of those pyramids.

I kept my eyes shut during the rest of that short trip, trying to focus on staying calm. Only after feeling Lobo's truck slow down to a full stop, did I open them again. A tall streetlight in front of us made the fog in that area light orange in color. Other little islands of fuzzy orange here and there showed where more streetlights barely broke through the darkness. Porch lights from some of the nearby houses added to the scene creating their own little glowing bundles of mist.

In all the murkiness, I could barely see the dark bars of a gate on our right a short distance away. We had arrived at our destination, but we seemed to be parked wrong somehow. Deep inside the cemetery to our right, the floodlight I saw there the evening before lit up a large patch of hanging wetness.

"Where are we exactly?" I asked.

"On the opposite side of the cemetery from where you and I were last night," Carla replied.

"Come on," Lobo said, opening his door, "let's go."

I tell you what. When Carla and I got out of the truck and into that orange wetness, I noticed the temperature had dropped from when we left Lobo's place. The stupid, super cold moisture coated every inch of bare skin, making me shiver. I jammed my hands into my jeans pockets and worked hard not to think about what I was about to do. Lobo and Carla both pulled the collars of their jackets up around their necks. Mine didn't have a collar, but oh man, I wished it did.

Instead of immediately moving towards the gate, Lobo reached into the back of his truck and pulled out a couple of plastic tarps.

"What are those for?" Carla asked before I could, her voice muffled by the fog.

"These tarps," Lobo replied, "are to keep our butts from getting soaked and cold." I couldn't figure out what he was planning, but he kept on talking. "Now listen you two. As we go in there, stay close to me and follow every instruction I give you to the letter. Got that?"

As soon as we both swore we would follow his directions completely, he led us over to the gate. When he got there, Lobo looked all around, like he was trying to figure something out, or like something was wrong. The idea of Lobo hesitating didn't help my nervousness. He wasn't a hesitating kind of person, but finally he said, "OK, Carla, open it up." I breathed a little easier after that.

Without saying a word, Carla bent down, and unlocked the thing just like she had done before but on the other side of the cemetery. In seconds, she had it open and we all walked through. I reached out and touched the gate as we went by it. Man, that metal was really cold. Ahead of us, up the driveway, the big floodlight really lit up the fog, tombstones and trees nearby with its light blue color. I couldn't find the flag I remembered seeing there even though the light was tilted up at an angle. The flagpole only went up about ten feet before it got lost in the dense wet air.

Partway into the cemetery, I felt a change of some kind. I couldn't put my finger on it, but something was definitely different. I looked over at Lobo just as he turned his head towards me. Both of us stopped dead in our tracks, and somehow I knew he felt that same something, whatever it was.

"What's going on?" Carla asked.

"Lieutenant Walton isn't the only one watching us," Lobo said.

"What?" I asked in a harsh whisper. "What are you talking about?"

"I'm not exactly sure," he replied. That wasn't what I wanted to hear. "You felt it as I did. It's as if there are others who are focused on you as well."

"Oh great," I moaned. "What others?"

Lobo moved forward slowly and said, "Let's find out."

Let's find out? Are you kidding me? I wanted to say but didn't. Instead, I followed Carla and Lobo until they came to a stop a short distance away. All around us, that dense, light blue fog swirled from our movements through it. Slowly, Lobo turned to the right so he was facing the central sidewalk leading to the pyramids. The floodlight on the ground between two bushes glared at us, and the air felt even colder than before. My nose and ears felt like they might freeze solid.

You couldn't see very far down the walkway because of the floodlight's intensity. It made me think about how dark the ocean gets the farther you get away from shore at the beach—deeper water maybe containing unknown things. *It's all in the mind*, I kept saying to myself over and over again, using Lobo's words trying to ease my rising nervousness. As we waited for him to say or do something, I noticed a shift in the fog between the floodlight and us. It didn't just hang in the air anymore. The stuff actually seemed to be silently coming towards us, as if pushed by a breeze coming from where the pyramids stood down at the end of the walkway in darkness. I could really feel that cold dampness slide over my eyes and face.

"What's happening?" Carla asked. As she spoke, I watched her breath cloud the cold, already dense blue colored air even darker, and get pushed back behind her. How can you see breath in fog? I wondered.

Lobo shook his head and said, "This isn't going to work. We need to leave." Great puffs of blue came out of his mouth with each word and they quickly slid away.

"Hold on now. Wait just a minute," I protested, seeing my own breath, looking like exhaust from an old fashioned steam engine. "You told me my best chance was to come here and now you want to leave?"

"If we continue to stay here for long," Lobo growled, "your situation becomes extremely complicated, and because of that, it will also put Carla in danger."

"Me?" Carla asked. "Why me?"

"Listen closely, both of you," Lobo said. "I can now see that the 'others' I spoke about are many other soldiers from the Dade battle who are also buried here. They too have locked themselves into similar after death dream worlds of anger, fear and regret like Lieutenant Walton has for all these years.

"When we entered the cemetery," Lobo said to Carla, "those other soldiers sensed the deep connection your friend here has to his ancestor as well as his newly awakened abilities. It's apparent to them that in saving himself he might also release Walton from his agony. What is also apparent to them, however, is your connection to Luis Pacheco and your own paranormal capabilities."

Looking back at me, he said, "They see both you and Carla

together as a source of hope—a possible way of releasing them all from their pain as well as Walton. That adds to the severe danger you're in, yes, but what it also does," he said pointing at Carla, "is to make her a target for all the danger you're facing. The closer she gets to the pyramids, the more attached all of those soldiers, including your ancestor, get to Carla, and the more potential exists for her to share whatever fate may await you.

"It's even possible for their dream worlds to connect to that of your ancestor's. They could actually become part of Lieutenant Walton's self-imposed spiritual nightmare making it even more intense. Instead of resisting just his energy, you and Carla might well be facing the combined energy of many other deceased people. However, you really do need Carla's help, and the only way we can use her personal power, and not put her in danger, is for us to get away from the pyramids. We need to go back to my house and make our stand there."

You know, when it was only me at risk, I could deal with it, but with Carla in danger, that changed the picture entirely. I was not going to take any chances with her life. "You're right," I said. "Let's go." As I turned to walk back towards the gate though, Carla stepped around Lobo, reached over, grabbed me by the arm, and spun me around to face her.

Backing up a few feet, with that icy blue floodlight behind her, she said in her fog muffled voice, "Now, Jeffrey Golden, you listen to me! And you too Lobo!" Old Lobo stood next to me, waiting. Here it comes, I thought, and it did.

"Since when do the two of you make my decisions for me, huh?" She barked, with her hands on her hips, her head going from side to side and puffing great, icy blue clouds in our direction as she spoke. Then to Lobo she said, "You told us Jeff's best chance is here in the cemetery, didn't you?"

Big old Lobo nodded without saying anything.

"And even with the possible added energy of all those *others*, because of me, isn't it still better for Jeff to stay here?"

For a moment, Lobo said nothing but after a few seconds, he simply said, "Yes."

"Well, gentlemen," Carla said in a calm voice, but one that told me she had made her mind up completely, "we stay here. It's my choice and not yours to make. You need me to make this whole thing work no matter what, as I understand it, and I'm not going anywhere."

30

Icy Coquina

Carla stood there like some kind of determined little tree with roots sunk down deep into the concrete driveway. Behind her, the floodlight showed that nasty fog coming at us in slow, rippling, light blue waves from the direction of the pyramids.

"Carla, please," I said, trying again. "I admire your bravery, and I can't tell you how much I appreciate your—"

"Jeff," she said, shivering, but with a sharp edge to her voice and folding her arms, "You need me *here* and not at Lobo's. I am not leaving until you are out of danger. That's it. End of story. You are wasting v-v-valuable t-t-time arguing with me." The cold was really starting to get to her, but that didn't change her determination the least bit.

"Oh man," I said, looking over at Lobo. "Help me out here." I didn't want to admit it, but I knew Carla had us in a box unless the old guy could find a way out.

Well, Mr. R. Lobo shook his head, heaved a big sigh of blue out in front of him and said to me in a low voice, "Women! Sometimes you simply can't win even if it's for their own good." With the man's face in shadow like Carla's, I couldn't see his expression, but knew a deep frown had to be part of it. As serious as the entire situation was though, I had to smile. For the first time, I felt, well, connected to big old Lobo, you know? I mean, it was like we were just two guys complaining about being outsmarted by one small but very strong-minded female.

"Yeah, women!" I agreed with a nervous chuckle. "You got that right."

Lobo didn't laugh, of course, but in the darkness covering his face, I saw a slight sparkling where each of his eyes should have been—an eerie, impossible thing to witness. That's when I realized it had been there ever since we left the old guy's house. By then, I guess, those fiery eyes of his just seemed a part of him that I took for granted.

"You two going to grumble all m-morning," Carla asked, "or can we move along to the p-pyramids?"

"You are one crazy lady," I replied, tearing my attention away from Lobo's face. But as I spoke, I noticed a weird sensation flow over the entire surface of my body. It didn't hurt or anything but felt like ants crawling over every inch my skin.

"Listen to me carefully," Lobo said, loudly, "things are happen-ing that—"

Before he could finish his sentence, something exploded with a loud bang and a flash behind Carla. Everything went dark. Man, I jumped like I had been shot and Carla screeched. That's when I realized the bulb in the floodlight must have shattered somehow.

In the near total darkness, Lobo said, "Don't move." I couldn't see him, Carla or anything except for one little ball of orange light high up over the cemetery entrance where Lobo parked his truck. The fog had thickened even though that didn't seem possible. No longer could I see the streetlights on the other side of the cemetery. It wasn't exactly like being lost in the darkness on Lobo's porch but close enough. *At least you have company this time*, I told myself. Even so, I could feel the panic starting to rise from way down deep inside me and I swear, the air got colder by the second.

"The bad news," Lobo said to me into the silent wetness all around us, "is that the bulb exploded back there behind Carla because of your ancestor and all the other soldiers." He then turned on a flashlight he must have had stashed in his jacket pocket. Its beam didn't go very far in all the dense moisture, but at least we could see each other. "The good news is that they didn't intend for that to happen."

"I don't understand," I said and after I spoke, Carla moved close to me and slid a hand around my right arm. Whether she was doing it for me or to try and keep herself warm, I wasn't sure, and I didn't care. All I knew was that feeling her touch helped calm me down. "I don't understand either," she said to Lobo.

"The closer we get to the pyramids," Lobo replied, his voice a deep, muffled whisper, "the more Lieutenant Walton and the others will affect the atmosphere in this place. They are pulling energy from everything around here. That's why it's getting colder and the fog continues to thicken. On the other hand, Lieutenant Walton and those other soldiers just sent out a blast of their own energy in a botched attempt to communicate. That surge caused the crawling sensation we all felt and the floodlight explosion." Carla hadn't said anything about feeling ants, but she didn't object either.

Before I could really digest what the man had said, he grabbed me roughly by my left arm and started talking again. "Carla, Jeff and I have linked arms over here. You keep a tight lock on that other arm." When she agreed, I felt her grip increase as Lobo gave some more instruction. "All three of us absolutely must stay connected like this until I say otherwise, understood?" When we both agreed, he shifted us around on the driveway until we were facing the sidewalk heading to the pyramids. I couldn't see the sidewalk, but I knew he must be positioning us to head in that direction. The single orange streetlight hanging in the fog behind us was where we had entered the cemetery, and the fog pressing against my face told me he probably had it right.

Lobo let go of my arm for a few seconds as he adjusted the flashlight and his load of tarps. When he grabbed my arm again, he had the flashlight in his left hand pointed down at the driveway and slightly angled to the left. "OK you two," he said, "Move forward slowly now until we get to the curb." As powerful as that flashlight was, it barely penetrated the blowing waves of fog creating only a small pocket of brightness. I could hardly see the driveway as we began walking. In seconds, sure enough, there was the curb.

Once we stepped up onto the sidewalk, Lobo pulled us to the left. There the beam of his flashlight showed us the sidewalk's edge with either grass or bushes on the other side. That I liked, a way to keep us going straight, but it also made me think of my favorite book when I was a little kid called, *Where the Sidewalk Ends.* I shivered even more as I thought how when we finally got to the actual end of that sidewalk, my life and maybe even Carla's, could … well, end.

Surprisingly, everything went OK for about fifty feet or so, and then things began changing again. It was the fog. As it blew on my face, little solid things started hitting me. They felt like little grains of cold sand. The stuff really hurt my eyes, so I put my head down. When I did, I lifted my right hand as much as I could with Carla holding onto my elbow and rubbed my eyes. That's when I discovered my eyelashes and eyebrows had ice in them. Yeah, ice! The stupid fog was turning into tiny ice crystals. Talk about draining the energy out of the atmosphere. I shivered and really wished I had on a heavier jacket with a collar and some gloves. Energy had to be draining from us as well as everything else.

Just as I made my ice crystal fog discovery, Lobo's flashlight dimmed and within about ten seconds, the beam disappeared. *Oh crap!*

"I hope you have another f-flashlight, Lobo," Carla said to my right.

"Don't worry about it," he replied.

Don't worry about it? Hell, we didn't stop or slow down. In fact, the man got us walking even faster. I just knew we were going to smash into the bushes, some tombstones or even that tall war monument in front of the pyramids. All I could do was trust Lobo had radar eyes or something. I'm telling you, the man about dragged Carla and me down that sidewalk. There we were, all locked together plunging into total darkness while getting more and more bombarded by little ice pellets. I put my head down and shut my eyes against the stinging grit again and hoped Lobo really knew where he was going. Some of that stuff kept going down the back of my neck, making me shiver even more.

Suddenly he stopped dead, jerking Carla and me backwards because we kept going. That's when I heard Carla gasp and say, "Oh L-lord, w-what is this?"

When I opened my eyes and looked up, it was like ... like we had stepped into a glowing bubble of fogless, frigid air. I know, I know. That probably doesn't make any sense to you. It's so hard to find the words to explain what I saw so I'll try again. Maybe half a bubble would be a better description. No ... a dome ... yeah, that's it. We had walked into this glowing dome of perfectly clear air with the fog, or ice fog, or whatever, on the outside.

This dome had to have been forty or so feet in diameter and maybe twelve or fourteen feet high. On the ground at its center stood the pyramids and they were ... well, glowing with a white light so much you could clearly see everything inside the dome— tombstones, sidewalks and grass. The light coming out of them though, had a tinge of green that touched everything in my line of sight. Yeah, I know. Sounds like a bad horror movie, but I have to tell you exactly how it was.

If that wasn't weird enough, all over the pyramids and the historical marker was a thick coating of white frost covered with little green veins. All over the pyramids only, what appeared to be spiky, icicle type things stuck out of the surrounding frost at different angles. The frost itself extended outward on the ground from the pyramids and historical marker for maybe six feet in all directions—

over the grass, the sidewalk and even onto other tombstones. Little zigzag fingers of it stretched out everywhere. It looked like white lightning with a green core, and I remembered how the pyramids first appeared to me out of a thunderstorm.

For some reason, no frost covered the tall Seminole War monument in front of us. Instead, it had a thick coating of very clear ice. I'm telling you, the place really did look like something out of the weirdest movie you've ever seen.

Don't fight the problem, I kept telling myself the more I shivered. *Don't fight the problem.* When I also tried concentrating on my breathing to calm down, it didn't work very well. My lungs burned with every in breath, and when I exhaled, the air came out in a big, greenish cloud that almost immediately dropped to the ground and then disappeared. It made me wonder if the moisture from breathing out was actually freezing and falling onto the sidewalk as more tiny ice particles.

31

A Big, Cold Drop of Water

There isn't much time," Lobo barked, dragging both of us through the frosty grass to the right of the tall war monument and across the opposite sidewalk. As we walked, our feet made crunching sounds, and I felt ice crystals crumble beneath my shoes. By that time, my feet were getting so cold I was surprised they could feel anything.

When he finally got us between the middle pyramid and the one on the right, Lobo said, "Now, we can let go of each other, but don't either one of you touch a pyramid." He released my arm and Carla did the same on the other side of me.

"Here," he said, shoving his tarps into my half-numb hands. Moving quickly, he went over to the pyramid on the right, walked down towards the back of the thing to where two of the four sides came together. Kneeling, on the frosty ground as we joined him, he put a hand on each flat surface near the base. I winced when he touched the thing, sure something would happen to him like it had to me the evening before, but it didn't. He used his hands to clear away the frost and icicles on either side of the pyramid, each spot about a foot across. That's when I realized the spiky things on the pyramids were really odd build-ups of frost instead of actual icicles. When Lobo touched them, they just crumbled.

"Throw me a tarp," he ordered and when I did, he spread it out on the ground in front of where he had rubbed the frost away. After throwing him the other tarp, he worked to spread it out next to, and partially overlapping, the first one. All the while, he blew out big clouds of greenish breath.

"You first," he said to me after he finished. "You are to sit right in the middle of those two merged tarps, cross-legged in front of where the pyramid's sides come together. Whatever you do, do not touch that thing with your hands, arms, legs, feet, hair or clothes even. You sit there until I tell you otherwise. Got it?"

"Uh … yeah, sure," I replied, blowing my own green breath on my shaking hands to warm them up. I didn't really want to get anywhere near that pyramid, but I knew I had to. "You want me to sit down now?" My words came out kind of ragged and whiney sounding, almost as if I was hoping he would say no.

"Yes, go!" He said.

I quickly took my seat on the tarp and crossed my legs in front of where the two sides of the pyramid met at a sharp angle. In front of me, the icy, glowing coquina stared me in the face looking like a big bomb about to explode. *Dead kid walking!* I heard this stupid voice in my head calling. *Dead kid walking!*

After watching me do as he asked, Lobo sat very close to me on my right with his legs also crossed. "Carla," he said, looking up at her, "sit on the other side of him exactly as I'm doing." When Lobo got through instructing Carla, both of them had a knee touching one of my legs.

"Where our knees touch you," he said to me, "are secondary contact points. Now, I am going to establish the primary contact points with you like so." Next, he put his left hand flat on my back and his right hand on my right shoulder. Just as happened when Lobo helped with my headaches, I felt the same soothing warmth pulse gently through my body. It really helped me to relax.

"Carla," Lobo said, "you do the same on your side."

She did as she was told and I felt her hands press against me.

The warming sensation from where Lobo continued to touch my shoulder and back radiated across the upper part my body directly it seemed, to Carla's fingers.

"This positioning," Lobo said, speaking to me and squeezing my shoulder, "completes the circuit so to speak. In this way, Carla, and I will be able to supply you with all the energy we have to offer. All you will have to do when I tell you, is to put one hand on each side of the pyramid, close your eyes and think of your ancestor."

"Easy for you to say," I replied, my voice still sounding shaky. Memories of everything that happened when I touched a pyramid the first time kept blasting into the front of my mind. I even wondered if our tarps covered where I puked the evening before. I breathed easier when I remembered I had left my barf near a different pyramid.

Ignoring my comment, Lobo went on with his instructions: "As I said, before, your job once you contact Lieutenant Walton, is to convince him he's dead and he doesn't have to continue living in his dream world. Use whatever words come to mind. You will know what to say."

"I will?" Just the thought of dealing with Lieutenant Walton all alone gave me a tight, hard feeling in the middle of my chest.

"Yes, you will."

"But—"

"Do yourself a favor and *don't fight this problem*. You don't have the time."

I started to say something back to him but didn't. The warmth flowing into my body from both his hands helped calm me down, and I took a deep, relaxing breath.

Lobo squeezed my shoulder once again and said, "Should you by some chance get sucked into Walton's dream battle, you must remember that such an experience will be as real to you as what you sense right now. In the event that happens, and the shooting starts, you must take cover. Those rifle balls, without a doubt, could damage your spirit body enough to lock your consciousness into your ancestor's unending private battle hell. As you've heard me say before, your body here would then either die or go into a coma. You do understand all this?"

I had understood it when he told me before, but now that the time had come, his words rang like a fire alarm through my head. "Yeah, I do," I replied. Still, I wondered if maybe I had only taken the bus to Orlando like I thought about doing, things might have turned out better for everyone somehow.

"Carla," Lobo said, "above all, while this is going on, think only of your friend here and that you are giving him something like a transfusion of blood. In this way, you should be able to share as much energy with him as possible. If you do exactly what I have asked of you and concentrate on nothing else, you should stay safe and perhaps save your friend's life. If you don't follow those instructions completely, you could well find yourself involved in whatever difficulties and dangers he might encounter. Is that clear?"

Right after Carla said "Yes," Lobo told her to begin concentrating.

"W-wait a minute," Carla said through a great puff of green breath, squeezing my shoulder like Lobo had. "Jeff …" she hesitated, "good luck, huh. I'm p-praying for you."

"Yeah," I replied with a shiver, "thanks. But you do just what Lobo said, OK?" The thought of Carla sharing any danger I could face made me shiver even more. Sure, I was afraid for myself, but that feeling of being helpless to protect Carla really got to me.

"I will," Carla replied.

"It's time," Lobo said on my right and patted me on the back. Big, bad old Lobo had patted me on the back, like he really cared. His voice was the softest I had heard him use. I don't know, it was the strangest thing. With both Carla and Lobo sitting so close and supporting me, I felt more connected to the world than I had ever felt before in my entire life. Sounds crazy maybe, but besides all the fear, that's how I felt. It wasn't only the physical contact from both of them. It was almost like the three of us had become a little family or something. Anyway, as good as all that felt, it made me really, sad. Why? Because I knew the moment my hands touched the pyramid, I might never see Carla or Lobo again.

"Let's get this over with," I announced, trying to sound brave. After taking a couple of deep breaths, closing my eyes, and thinking about the portrait of Lieutenant Walton, I pressed a hand on each side of the glowing pyramid where Lobo had cleaned away the frost. Man, that thing was *cold*, but nothing happened—no shock or blinding light like before. No nothing! I couldn't believe it. Seconds later, a tremendous sound and a feeling of incredible pressure hit my head on all sides—really forceful vibrations like at a concert when you feel the music pulse deep inside from your toes to your brain, and you think your eardrums are going to pop.

It was so weird! After what happened with the portrait, maybe I should have expected it, but I didn't. At a concert, you're aware it's coming—there with Carla and Lobo, it startled and terrified me. I tried to let go of the pyramid, open my eyes and scream all at the same time, but I couldn't move in any way. Then into all that vibrating chaos came, well, separate voices, men's voices, yelling, crying and shouting—some even screaming. There were so many of them, and they got louder and louder, some even calling my name. They were desperate men, men in pain and agony, and men begging for help.

As quickly as it began, all those voices and noise just … stopped. The only sound right then was my own ragged breathing. When I sucked in a deep breath of relief, I noticed my butt felt wet and cold. Embarrassment pushed its way into my mind since I was sure by being so scared, my bladder had let loose. *Oh great.* Just what I needed to have happen with Carla sitting right next to me. While I kept my eyes shut wondering what to do, I noticed my hands no longer held the pyramid, or anything, really, even though they still stuck out in front of me as if they did.

When I opened my eyes, I'm not sure what I expected to see, really. I mean the idea was for me to contact Lieutenant Walton, so I guess I half expected to meet him face-to-face in some sort of bright and beautiful place like you see in the movies. You know, like they show when people die and go to heaven, and everyone walks around on clouds in knee-deep mist?

Well, to say the least, I didn't meet up with my ancestor. Instead, I found myself sitting in the middle of that same road cut through pines and palmetto bushes I found the first time I touched a pyramid. As I looked around, it became clear to me my butt was getting wet because of moisture coming up from the ground, and not from lack of bladder control. At least I found something positive, right? And there was no nasty smell. Not yet anyway.

Of course, no pyramids stood on the road. My hands sticking out in front of me as if I was holding one looked ridiculous, so I rested them in my lap. Closing my eyes again, I breathed deeply, focused on that breathing and hoped the pines and palmettos would go away. When I opened my eyes a few seconds later, nothing had changed.

"Oh man," I moaned as I slowly put my hands on my knees and looked around. I couldn't be sure if where I sat was the exact same place as before, but it could have been. All those trees and palmettos looked the same. I shuddered knowing that I was again no longer in my own world. A vision of Lobo's Ball of Realities floated into my mind.

Water dripped from the trees as if it had just stopped raining. I could hear the drops as they occasionally hit the ground and plants all around me. Except for the dripping, everything was very still, no wind, no other sounds. The air felt humid, of course, and chilly, but definitely much warmer than it had been in the cemetery—no condensed breaths coming out of me, green, light blue or otherwise. Heavy, grey clouds covered the sky, and in the distance, a blue jay squawked. On the ground to my right, a little grey spider walked a zigzag path over pine needles and around tall weeds.

It all looked so normal, in a way, not like some fuzzy dream. Without thinking, I reached out and touched wet dirt, sand and pine needles. It all felt, well, cold and wet, but as real as anything I had ever touched in my life. The smell of dampness and pine trees filled the air.

I sat there for a minute or two with my heart pounding, still finding it hard to believe I could be back in the same place and again, all by myself. That's when a big, cold drop of water hit the top of my head and ran down my neck behind my collar and down my back. God, talk about something feeling real! When that happened, Lobo's last words to me about the danger of entering into Lieutenant Walton's dream world came rushing back into my mind, as well as his explanation of the Dade battle. Quickly, my mind raced through every detail of that event, especially how the Seminoles lay hidden in a semicircle around a road hacked through the wilderness, waiting for the soldiers to arrive.

"Seminoles," I whispered to myself as I stared into the pines and palmettos on the other side of the road. *No don't look*, I said to myself, and quickly shifted my gaze back to the ground in front of me. Only then did the idea that an actual battle might soon take place somewhere on that road become a reality for me. Real pine trees, real pine needles, *and real Seminoles*, I explained to myself knowing I had to adapt to the situation if I was going to survive.

I tell you what, I was not about to look into those pines and palmettos if I could help it. If those Indians are actually there, dream world or not, I told myself, and they think you know they are there, then you could quickly end up one dead white boy. It didn't matter at all that I sympathized with the Seminoles and their black allies. Obviously it didn't take me long to accept that reality. I guess when your life and future depend on something no matter how crazy it is, you end up taking it very seriously.

"Oh God," I mumbled as my heart pounded and my hands started shaking again, "what do I do now?" I had these visions of jumping up and running down the road trying to find Lieutenant Walton and the other soldiers to warn them or something. The thing is, I had no idea which way to run. In that sunless sky I couldn't tell where north and south were. That meant the Seminoles could also just as easily be on the other side of the road behind me. I almost turned around but stopped myself in time. As I did, I felt pressure on my left leg, my back and my left shoulder. I swear, it felt just like when Carla was sitting next to me near the pyramid, but I couldn't see a thing.

When the pressure kept up, I slowly moved my right hand to where I felt it on my left shoulder and nearly had a heart attack. I could feel a hand there, but I couldn't see anything. That's when Carla flickered into view, on and off for a few seconds, until she appeared right by my side with her eyes closed. At first, I was overjoyed to see her, but my heart sank knowing the danger she would now be facing. As I wondered if the Seminoles had seen either one of us appear, or what they might do, if anything, my stomach did a flip-flop.

While I fumbled with my thoughts, Carla opened her eyes, and man did they get wide. I mean she was almost bug-eyed. It isn't often she's speechless, but that was one of those times. Her mouth hung open and I could feel her grip tighten on my shoulder. After taking a quick glance around, she swiveled her head so she was looking directly at me. Her grip on my shoulder tightened. In her eyes, I could read the same awe, disbelief and fear that had run through my mind in the dark on Lobo's porch, and on the same road where I stood the first time I arrived at that place. Never before had I seen Carla so afraid. It took a lot to scare her.

"Take it easy," I said in a soft voice, but even so, her fingers gripped my left shoulder like a vice. "I'm with you and it's OK," I told her. Of course that was a bunch of crap, but what else was I going to say?

"You … weren't k-kidding, were you Golden Boy?" Carla finally managed to say, her voice really shaky and not just from being cold. Again, she looked all around, but her grip on my shoulder hadn't let up one bit.

"Nope, I wasn't kidding," I replied taking a deep breath. "Welcome to my weird world."

"Dear Lord, Jeff, you described it to me … but seeing it for real is … unbelievable."

"Tell me about it," I replied. I stood up then, making sure I kept my eyes on the road. I had to stop sitting on that wet ground. Carla did the same, but as she rose, she kept staring at something behind me. "What?" I asked, turning to look for myself.

"This is it," Carla said, her voice barely a whisper. "This is where the battle is going to take place."

With a chill of recognition, I had to agree with her. Lobo's description of the battle site included a pond with tall grass— exactly what was in front of us. I felt as if eyes were watching me from behind, on the other side of the road where I now knew the Seminoles hid. My breath caught in my throat as I again tried to figure out what to do.

From far down the road to our left, way beyond where we could see, a dog barked. Lobo hadn't said anything about dogs. Carla's eyes widened even more than they were before. I'm sure mine must done the same thing. At that point though, I had no doubt over 100 soldiers would soon be coming up the road from the direction of the dog bark—right into the ambush.

Dream world or not, this was our reality and our lives depended on what we did or didn't do.

"Jeff!" Carla whispered in a harsh, serious voice as she grabbed my arm again, this time with both hands. I figured she was worried about the 180 Seminoles strung out on the other side of the road, but her eyes had this wild look I didn't understand. She wasn't just scared, she looked petrified and she shook my arm hard.

"What?" I asked when she didn't explain right away. "Come on Carla, what? We don't have much time!"

After taking a deep shuddering breath, she stared at me with the most pitiful expression I had ever seen on a person, and she said, "The soldiers will be … here … with those dogs."

"O.K, we'll deal with it somehow," I said, trying to sound a lot more confident than I really felt.

"No, Jeff, you don't understand. To these people in this time, they'll see me as … as a slave, maybe even a runaway. I don't have any documents to prove I'm not. Besides, they use dogs to track down runaways."

Carla's words and the horror in her eyes sliced me like a knife. Only then, did I understand how real the idea of slavery must be to her. She was scared to death and I had no idea what to do or say to make her feel better. The only words that came out of my mouth were, "Oh man." Pretty lame, huh? My worries from before about what to say to Lieutenant Walton and anybody else on that road had just doubled. *How can I explain Carla?* I wondered, but I remembered what Lobo told me about talking to my ancestor. *"Use whatever words come to mind,"* he had said.

Slowly, it dawned on me that I needed to put into action my ability to manipulate adults. It worked a lot of the time on parents, teachers and even cops, so I figured maybe somehow it might work in that situation. You see, I can make myself sound very logical and use that good memory of mine to confuse adults when I need to. Well, adults other than Lobo that is. I think it works because they don't want to admit that what I'm saying makes no sense, or that I've outsmarted them. Weird but true. Mom says it's my "gift for gab" and I should take up a career in sales.

"Carla!" I said, with the biggest grin I could create as I grabbed both of her hands. "I can handle this but you've got to play along, OK? It won't be easy but you've got to trust me. I can do it."

When her eyes brightened a bit and she said, "OK," I knew we were on our way.

"Great," I replied as that dog barked even closer than before. When a second dog barked, Carla winced. We both kept staring down the road as we talked.

"Now listen," I told her, "if they think of you as a slave, they'll expect me as the white guy to do the talking, right? I'll ah, act as if I'm, er, ah, well, your owner, and you play your part. OK?"

"What?" She screeched, looking at me as if I had lost my mind. "You want me to actually *pretend* I'm a slave?"

"You got a better idea?"

"I ... uh, guess not," she said, right as those two dogs started barking more rapidly and at a higher pitch. In seconds, some of their yapping turned into these long howls, kind of like they had found something.

"Dear God!" Carla whispered, squeezing my arm hard as she stood on her tip toes to see farther down the road.

That's when I saw them—the dogs—big, both kind of light brown in color and coming our way, fast!

32

Contact

We couldn't have been more than a 100 yards away from those dogs, but there was no doubt about it, they had seen us, heard us, smelled us, or whatever. Directly behind them, I saw a white officer on horseback and a black man on foot. In that moment, all of the talk with Carla and Lobo about Captain Dade and his men had become very, very real.

"Jeff!" Carla released my arm, and looked all around like she wanted to run but couldn't figure out where.

My mind whirled trying to think of what to do. There were no trees with low branches to climb and we couldn't run fast enough to get away. Dealing with the men was one thing but dealing with those dogs was another no matter what I said to Carla before. What a switch. Back at Lobo's place his BAD DOGS sign spooked me and now Carla was the one afraid—well, the one most afraid. This time though, we hadn't just walked in front of a motion detector starting a harmless recording.

Knowing I had to do something, but without really thinking, I started jumping up and down and waving my arms. "Call off your damned dogs!" I screamed as loud as I could over and over again. "Call them off!" That's when I heard it. One of the men from down the road shouted a sharp command. It was only a single word I didn't understand, but the dogs sure did. They stopped in their tracks about half way to us and looked back to where the shout had come from.

I tell you what, I stood there panting from yelling and just stared at those dogs, the two men, and the horse. You gotta realize something here. Ever since Carla and I had arrived in that place, we hadn't actually seen any of Major Dade's soldiers. Seeing the dead ones before was bad, yeah, but there in front of us were, well, live ... human beings, you know? Or at least they looked like it.

Living? Alive? Dead? Those three words bounced around in my head like pool balls after somebody breaks, getting me really confused. I mean for a few seconds, they lost their meaning. Have you ever done that? Said a word or wrote it so many times that after a while it didn't sound or look real—like you made it up or something? Well, that's what happened.

According to Lobo's viewpoint, Carla and I being there in my ancestor's dream world had happened because we split off somehow from our physical selves. Our bodies were back in the cemetery with Lobo, which made us ... our doubles or spirit selves, or whatever, but we were still us it seemed, in every way possible. So, did that make us less real than our actual bodies? I wondered. Were the two men and their animals down the road less real because their bodies had already died long ago and their what? spirits? were now appearing in this dream world too? Do you understand how I could get so confused? It's amazing how so much can go through your mind in so short a time, especially when you're under such terrible pressure.

Again, the same shouted word from one of the men down the road to the dogs echoed through the pines and palmettos. It shook me out of my confusion, and I wondered if it had any effect on the Seminoles. I still didn't dare look anywhere except down the road. Finally, the dogs turned around and trotted back to where they had come from with their heads hanging. As Carla and I breathed sighs of relief, the two men appeared to stare at us for a few seconds while they had a conversation. They were too far away for us to hear their voices, but as I watched, I noticed movement far behind them. When I saw that movement had lot of sky blue color in it, I whispered to Carla, "The rest of Dade's men are down there."

"I see them," she whispered back, just as the soldier on horseback started riding quickly towards us with the two dogs right behind him. The black man moved in our direction as well but jogging slowly. The soldier wore a familiar tall black leather hat, a long, dark blue coat and light blue pants. His outfit made me think of vultures, finding dead men in uniforms on that same road, and my ancestor appearing to me more than once. The guy coming towards us was definitely an officer.

Oh crap, here we go. The muffled sound of the man's horse trotting on sand and pine needles got closer and closer. Taking a deep breath, I looked at Carla and said, "You ready for this, I mean like we talked about?" Really, I asked the question of myself even more than Carla. I was definitely not ready. This wasn't like skipping school. I couldn't just sneak away when I didn't like the upcoming class.

"As ready as I'll ever be," Carla replied, staring at the approaching rider. "Oh my God!" she said with this wild look on her face. As fast as she could, she took off her watch, rings, bracelets and earrings. Stuffing them quickly into her coat pocket she said, "Slaves don't wear jewelry like this. And one more thing Jeff, don't get too used to this master and slave business or I'll kick your butt when it's all over."

"I know you will," I said, forcing a smile. As tough as she was trying to be, I saw such deep fear, anger and even embarrassment in Carla's eyes that it made me wince. I wanted to do something to make her feel better, but I knew all I had to give her was confidence in my ability to deal with whatever came up.

As the officer quickly closed the distance between us, I tried to remember everything I had ever read or heard about how people talked in the past. I needed to at least sound like I might belong to this time in history, but I had no real idea how to pull it off. Sure I could try talking in a more formal and flowery way, use bigger words than I usually did, and say sir and ma'am a lot. In the short time left to me, I finally decided to listen to the speech patterns I heard from the approaching officer, copy what I could, and then speak as fast as possible to confuse things. I figured also that with what I already knew about the Dade battle and its participants, I had enough understanding of the situation to make what I said at least sound somewhat convincing.

Seconds later, the officer rode up to us and reigned in his horse. The animal was dark brown in color, and it snorted while lifting its head high, looking in our direction. Behind the officer and his horse, the two dogs also came to a stop and sat down. If all those Seminoles were actually out there in the pines and palmettos, I wondered, why the dogs didn't sniff them out?

Farther back on the road, the black man was getting closer, and by then, I could clearly see some soldiers not too far behind him, one of them carrying an American flag.

Living? Alive? Still, my mind couldn't wrap around the fact I was actually somehow looking at people from so far back in the past. It wasn't only that, but seeing men who would soon be killed, or killed again, or whatever, made me stare at the officer in front of me instead of saying anything at all. He had a long, thin face that for some reason made me think of pictures I had seen of Abraham Lincoln—in the days he didn't have a beard. This man's mouth was small, but he had large dark eyes with heavy dark eyebrows. Part of me desperately wanted to tell him about the Seminoles, but my job was to find Lieutenant Walton and talk to him.

When I looked at the guy's leather hat, I saw a gold eagle and crisscrossed gold cannons on the front. His coat was almost exactly like my ancestor's with a very high, stiff collar and a row of gold buttons down the front. Across the end of each shoulder from back to front, I noticed a gold edged strip of material. I figured that's where his rank was displayed, but I couldn't really tell for sure. He had a white belt wrapped around his waist and from it hung a sword. Hanging from his other hip, I saw a pistol in a holster.

"Young man, who are you," he demanded, his voice high pitched, but full of authority, "and what are you doing on this road?" He didn't say a word to Carla. On his face was this very suspicious look, and before I could answer the man's first question, he asked another. "Did you encounter the advance guard?" *Advance guard? Advance guard?* The words spun around my brain until I remembered Lobo telling me the advance guard was a group of soldiers out ahead of the main force.

That's when I realized we must be standing between the main force coming up the road behind the black man and that other group of soldiers up ahead somewhere. It seemed logical the advance guard would normally stop anybody they found on the road, but there we were, just strolling around looking like Carla and I had never seen them, which we hadn't. I knew I should say something, so I started talking while putting my mind in high gear. "Ah … good morning sir. My name is Jeffery Golden and I ah … am greatly relieved to see you and your … soldiers. We did indeed encounter the advance guard," I lied, giving myself a chance to think, "and Lieutenant Mudge said I should speak with the officer on horseback."

Oh man, I was so thankful for having such a good memory. Being able to remember Lieutenant Mudge of the advance guard from Lobo's history lesson had given me the perfect thing to make my dumb story sound possible.

"He what?" The officer roared, looking down the road past us towards his unseen advance guard like he wanted to shoot somebody.

Good, he believes me. That's when I knew I had to keep talking and quickly create a reason Carla and I were out on the road with no weapons or supplies.

"You see ... ah, sir, when your men up the road found us," I babbled, so making it up as I went along, "we were just about to return to ... ah, Fort King. We had been on our way south to Fort Brooke when a bear frightened my horse." *A bear?* Even as that word came out of my mouth, I wondered where such an idea had come from, but I went on talking anyway. "Unfortunately, the horse ran off carrying all of my supplies as well as my musket." I hoped that all made some kind of sense. I talked about only one horse, because I figured that as a slave, Carla might be walking instead of riding.

"Fort King?" The officer asked anxiously, sounding like he was now more interested in something other than how Carla and I had gotten through his advance guard. "What news have you of the fort?"

Great! Talking about Fort King sidetracked the guy so he didn't ask about my crazy-ass bear, horse and supplies story. But as my thoughts continued to bounce around in my head, that's when I noticed a strong smell, sweaty or something—not bad, but not pleasant either. I figured it had to be the horse. I wondered if Carla was getting a whiff.

"Ah ... well sir," I said, fumbling around in my mind, trying to come up with something to say about Fort King. Then I remembered this officer and the other soldiers were on their way to help defend Fort King from any Seminole attacks. That gave me what I needed to tell him what he wanted to hear. "Uh, all the people at the fort were well when we left three days ago, and there have been no attacks by the Indians." Where the three days came from, I had no idea. It just sounded like the right thing to say.

"I see," he replied, "that is indeed good news." But, as he spoke, he was looking both Carla and me up and down. Not a good sign. "You are both dressed very strangely."

Of course, I knew our clothes would be out of place, but as

I glanced at Carla, I realized just how much. Think about it. I'm standing there in my orange and blue University of Florida Gator jacket, and Carla has on her black leather coat. Both of us wore jeans and sneakers. Jeans and sneakers! Not exactly 1835 clothes, right?

Oh crap! Carla was actually better dressed than me. "Yes, well," I laughed, trying to think quickly, "these clothes I … ah … had specially made in New York City when I was there a few months ago. They are the latest in outdoor fashion, and as you can see, I believe in treating my slaves well." After saying what I did, I kept that fake smile plastered on my face and held my breath hoping the guy would accept such a dumb story. I also hoped Carla wouldn't lose her cool and turn around and smack me.

"The latest in outdoor fashion from New York, and you are traveling all the way to Fort Brooke through hostile Seminole territory, with only a female slave dressed as a man as an escort?" As the officer asked his question, he frowned and shook his head. "In all my years with the United States Army, I have never encountered such absolute foolishness."

Before the guy could go on, I jumped back into the conversation. "Your judgment is understandable, my good sir," I said, trying to think of all the old movies I had seen for ideas of how to really get more deeply into my role as a person from the past. "However, I … ah … am an adventurous fellow and I could not wait to meet my long lost cousin who is stationed at Fort Brooke. Perhaps you have heard of him? Lieutenant Walton?"

I hoped Walton's name would move the guy's attention away from our clothes and walking through Seminole territory alone. I was right.

"Walton?" He asked. "You're Robert Walton's relative?"

"Ah, so you know him?"

"Know him? Young man, it will please you to hear your cousin follows with the main column." He turned in his saddle and pointed down the road to where I could now see two long lines of light blue uniforms, several officers on horseback and what looked like a covered wagon pulled by what had to be oxen. Seeing them dragged the memory of a burned wagon, and what I thought were dead cows in front of it, into my mind.

"What luck!" I laughed, tearing my attention away from the doomed soldiers on the way towards us. "I have never met the man, but his mother in New York told me where I could find him."

"Well, young sir, your opportunity to do so will arrive presently. You may then accompany us in safety back to Fort King. I am Captain Fraser. Captain Gardiner commands the main column you see coming up the road, and we are under the overall authority of Major Francis Langhorne Dade."

"Pleased to make your acquaintance sir, and this is Carla," I said, looking at her. I just couldn't leave her out of the conversation anymore. Besides, according to Lobo, Captain Fraser was, like my ancestor, against slavery.

"Carla," Captain Fraser said, nodding in her direction.

"How … how do you do Captain," Carla replied with a little hesitation in her voice and looking down.

"Very well thank you," Fraser replied but with a tilt of his head that said more than his words, as if the man sensed something wasn't quite right. Finally, he looked directly at me and said, "Now, please wait here. I will inform your cousin and the other officers of your presence. When they arrive, you will join them in the march to Fort King. Do you understand?"

"Of course," I replied with the most confident smile I could create. Captain Fraser then turned his horse around and with the two dogs behind him, quickly rode the short distance back to where the black man still jogged in our direction.

Both men were still close enough that we could hear Fraser's words when he arrived. "Luis, those two will be joining the main column. You run ahead to the advance party. I will be there presently."

"Luis?" Carla whispered with excitement as the Captain rode away once again. "Jeff, that's Luis Pacheco."

"Pacheco? Oh, yeah," I whispered back as the man trotted in our direction. "He's the guy you're related to, your ancestor, the interpreter and scout for the army who survives the battle." I had been focusing so much on Lieutenant Walton, that Carla's family connection to the Dade battle completely slipped my mind.

At first, Carla didn't say anything back to me, but she did nod slowly as she stared at the man coming towards us. I swear, the girl looked hypnotized, her eyes wide and this little half smile on her face. When I followed her gaze, I noticed Luis Pacheco carried something in his left hand covered by a blanket. It looked like it might be a rifle or musket. On his head, a straw hat.

"I know this is all like a dream, Jeff," Carla replied, never taking her eyes off her ancestor, "but no matter what, I've got to meet that man."

"OK," I said, again careful not to look into the pines and palmettos, "but make it quick. We're surrounded by Seminoles and we've got to find Lieutenant Walton."

I guess Carla's fear of being seen as a slave, and her excitement of running into her ancestor, had blocked the Indians out of her mind until I mentioned them. The next thing I knew she was looking all around, her face a picture of pure fear.

"Don't look!" I whispered harshly. "You don't know what they'll do if they think we're aware of them."

Carla lowered her gaze to the ground. "I forgot," she replied whispering back, but this time I could barely hear her. Luis Pacheco had gotten within about ten feet of us then, and Carla couldn't help but look up.

She stared at the man as he went from jogging to walking in our direction. When he got close, she took a deep breath and said, "Hello Mr. Pacheco." Well, the poor guy stopped dead and stared at her with this surprised expression on his face. Then he looked at me, and back at Carla again, checking out our clothes as well.

He was a little shorter than me but built big, a lot like Lobo, all muscle. The guy had a wide, open face and very dark skin, much darker than Carla's. Besides the straw hat, his clothes were simple, a light brown, long-sleeved shirt, dark brown pants held up by a wide leather belt but no coat or jacket. What really surprised me were his bare feet. I thought even a slave out in the wilderness like that would at least be wearing shoes, especially during that cold weather. The soles of his feet must have been like leather.

"Do I know you?" Pacheco asked in a deep rich voice while still looking at Carla.

Shaking her head, Carla took a few steps towards him, or at least whatever part of Luis Pacheco that still existed after death in this dream world of Lieutenant Walton. Anyway, Carla took a few more steps until she stood directly in front of the man.

"No, sir," she replied as I walked up to be with her, "you don't know me, but my name is Carla and this is Jeff."

"Pleased to meet you," he replied, taking off his hat, his eyes flickering back and forth between us very suspicious like. The man had a slight accent, one I couldn't identify.

"Hello Mr. Pacheco," I said and held out my hand to him. Well, the guy just stared at me like I had punched him between the eyes or something. While I tried to figure out what I had done, I watched him quickly look over his shoulder and move sideways enough so I could no longer see the soldiers in the distance coming our way. Only then did he reach out and shake my hand.

He had a strong grip and his hand felt rough, like he had a lot of calluses. "Mr. Jeff," he said, nodding. *Mr. Jeff?* You know, it took all that time for me to understand the man really and truly was a slave. No wonder he reacted to me the way he did, right? Probably, I figured, no white person had ever called him *Mister* before or offered to shake hands. That's why he moved, so the soldiers behind him couldn't see what he was doing when he took my hand.

Oh God, I thought looking at Carla. Of course. Besides me just being white, Pacheco thinks I'm a slave owner just like we planned. Playacting that role with Captain Fraser was hard enough, but knowing Carla's slave ancestor might think such a thing really embarrassed me.

Again, he seemed surprised when Carla also reached out and shook his hand. Looking at his reaction to her, I wondered if females in those days offered to shake hands with men. "Mr. Pacheco," Carla said, speaking quickly, "even though we have never met ... I know about you."

I swear, the poor guy looked like he thought we were both crazy. With tears streaming down her face, Carla spoke again, her voice cracking. "I ... I can't ... tell you how ... but I do know ... that you are a full blooded African ... and you tried to escape many times. I know ... you have no choice but to do this work for the army. And most of all," by then she was openly crying, "I ... I am truly honored to meet you."

Never before had I seen Carla so overwhelmed with emotion, and I wondered what her grandmother would think if she could see what was happening. *Hope we live to tell her about it*, I said to myself.

Now that I think about it, I'm not sure who was more startled with her quick burst of words and feelings, Pacheco or me. The man shot me a quick, questioning glance, and shaking his head ever so slightly, he looked back at Carla. That's when I noticed tears in his eyes. Tears! Both of them! I didn't think it was possible, but our weird, unreal situation had gotten even stranger.

"Ma'am," Pacheco said, after quickly glancing over his shoulder and flashing her a smile of brilliant white, "I don't understand how you know about me, but I think you must be sent from God to bring light into my world on this difficult journey of mine. For that I thank you, but I must go." After speaking, he put his old straw hat back on his head, held the front edge of it with his fingertips as he bobbed his head in a slight nod.

As the man turned to walk past us, Carla stopped him once more and said, "Be careful up there with the advance party. This is, ah, a … dangerous time."

Pacheco nodded, gave her a grim, tightlipped smile and walked off up that chilly road in his tough, bare feet.

33

Face-to-Face

"You OK?" I asked as Carla watched Luis Pacheco walk away. Somewhere in the distance, a woodpecker made rapid-fire banging noises against a tree. It sounded so strange, like it didn't belong in that dream world.

For a few seconds, Carla continued to stare up the road. "Yup," she replied in a determined voice. When she turned back around, she used her fingers to wipe her eyes and face. "I talked to him, Jeff." She said this with the smile and sound of a little girl who had just gotten the best present ever.

"Yeah, you did," I told her. "But now we gotta move fast. No matter what Captain Fraser told us, we need to start walking towards all those soldiers. If we don't get to Lieutenant Walton before he and all Dade's troops arrive anywhere around this area, we could find ourselves caught in the middle of the battle."

"Right," she replied with a nervous edge to her voice. The sound of hoof beats came our way again right after she spoke. It was Captain Fraser, riding at a faster pace than before with the soldiers a couple of hundred feet behind him walking in our direction. In-between Fraser and all those men, an officer on foot also headed towards us, walking very quickly.

"Major Dade sends his regards," Captain Fraser said when he

arrived. "The Major has sent Lieutenant Walton ahead to greet you. However, the time for a lengthy family reunion must wait until we arrive at Fort King. You will join the main column when it arrives and your cousin will return to his duties. You are not to distract him in any way when he does so. Is that understood?"

"Yes sir," I replied trying to sound totally respectful and obedient—not an easy task, but I did it.

"Very good," Captain Fraser replied. "Your cousin will be here shortly." Without pausing for questions or any further discussion, the man spurred his horse and galloped rapidly up the road towards where Luis Pacheco had just gone.

I tell you what, as soon as he rode away, both Carla and I looked back at the other officer walking towards us, maybe fifty feet away. "Here he comes," I whispered, finding it almost impossible to believe I was soon going to actually meet my ancestor face-to-face in his own world. After what the man had done to Lobo's window, down deep, I wasn't sure I really wanted to meet him. Besides, I had no idea what to say to the guy. Whatever words I chose had to be quick and very convincing. Not too far behind Lieutenant Walton, the soldiers kept coming, led by a very heavy looking officer on horseback. He has to be Captain Gardiner, I thought remembering Lobo's description of the man.

By that time, it was too late for us to stop my ancestor before he got to the pond and tall grass area near where Carla and I stood. No matter what we did, all three of us were still going to be in the middle of the Seminole warriors' ambush semicircle. I'm telling you, I really wanted to look into the pines and palmettos on the other side of the road but didn't.

"You going to let him come to us?" Carla whispered.

"Yeah," I replied as quietly as I could. "We don't have much choice now. This time I need you to help me do the talking. No more master and slave stuff. It worked to get us to Walton, but we don't have any more time to act out roles. Now's the time for you to be your normal, twenty-first century self. Maybe that will shake him up enough to really listen to us. Remember, the guy hates slavery anyway, so he might not react as badly as other people in this time."

"I'm not sure how you mean that about my 'twenty-first century self,' Jeff Golden, but I'm more than ready to be me," Carla said with a tight little smile on her face.

"Good," I replied, smiling back at her. We were about to become a real team.

The closer Walton got to us, the more familiar he seemed. With each of his steps, he looked increasingly like the man I had come to know as my ancestor. From what I could tell he was dressed pretty much as I remembered. This time, the man wore one of those tall, black leather hats with the same gold eagle and crossed cannons like the ones on Captain Fraser's hat. From that distance, he looked about my height or maybe a bit shorter.

My mind whirled as I tried to accept the reality of what my eyes were telling me. I mean to me, The Ancestor, the man from the portrait at home, was coming alive. You see what I'm saying? A chill ran down my spine as I thought about meeting my grandfather with five "greats" in front of that word. Very soon, I would find out a little of how Carla felt when she met Luis Pacheco, but I was also about to confront the spirit that might accidentally cause my death and Carla's. Time for me to sort out my thoughts ran out though, when Lieutenant Robert Walton walked up to me and put out his hand.

"Cousin Jeffrey Golden, I understand," he said.

My reaction? I froze—physically and mentally. My mind went blank. All I could do was stare at the man, the spirit, or whatever you want to call him. The person in front of me was the one who caused my bayonet dream, had scared the hell out of me on more than one occasion, and who was currently putting both Carla and me in danger. The thought of touching his hand immediately reminded me what happened each time I touched one of the pyramids.

His eyes. Yeah. I think that's what really did it—those dark brown eyes, identical to the ones staring at me out of Lobo's picture window all by themselves. Freaky! Totally freaky to see those eyes ... come alive even more than they had seemed to when my ancestor pushed part way through solid glass toward Lobo's dining room table.

On that familiar square face with the long sideburns, I noticed expressions that to me looked like curiosity, suspicion and, and maybe even a little embarrassment. Seeing those very human emotions flicker across his face jumpstarted my mind into working again, and I wondered if having a very odd relative show up in a danger zone might not be good for his military career or something.

What I didn't see was any understanding that he lived in a never-ending dream world he had created himself—or with help from other soldiers. The man obviously didn't have a clue that a part of him had reached into my world and pulled Carla and me into his. Suddenly, instead of fearing the man, I felt a deep sorrow for what he and any others had been enduring all those years.

Behind Walton, the two columns of soldiers kept moving towards us. I had to do something quick. Anything. *You're fighting the problem*, I said to myself. *Stupid!* Taking a single, deep breath, I finally made myself shake the man's hand—which was softer than Luis Pacheco's. Nothing happened. Thank God! "Uh, I'm glad to meet you," I said, my voice just a tiny bit shaky. As I held his hand, my life in St. Augustine somehow seemed like a distant dream world. What felt real at that point was the world of Lieutenant Robert Walton.

"You look familiar to me," my ancestor replied as he tried to release my hand, but I held firmly onto his. There wasn't time for politeness, so I figured a more direct approach might work. It didn't take long for a very uncomfortable look to come over his face when

I didn't release his hand.

"You bet I look familiar," I said, feeling a surge of definite purpose. "You've been chasing me all around in your dreams, so take a good look. Here I am." Did I plan what I said to the man? No way! Believe me when I tell you I was really surprised what came out of my mouth. Lobo told me I would know what to say, but I realized my words had to sound crazy to Lieutenant Walton.

"What?" Walton shouted, jerking his hand away from mine, and backing away from me a few steps. "You make no sense. You must be deranged." For whatever reason, I noticed how badly discolored the man's teeth were. I don't know, I guess it was the contrast with Luis Pacheco's brilliant smile that startled me.

"There's no time, Lieutenant!" I said, louder than I meant to. Lowering my voice, but talking as quickly and forcefully as I could, I said, "Please, listen to me. The Seminoles are about to attack and you have to get away." I thought talking to him about the Indians and the coming battle might work better than trying to convince him he was no longer living.

"Don't be ridiculous," he replied loudly. "They would never attack without more cover. Surely our dogs would have sounded an alarm."

"That's where you're wrong," I said, my voice raised as much as I dared, looking nervously at the two lines of approaching soldiers in sky blue uniforms and black leather hats. On the hats, metal glinted as the sun broke through the clouds for a few seconds. I couldn't really tell, but the metal looked like it might be letters or numbers. A few of the soldiers wore a different kind of hat—blue, cloth caps, flat like pancakes. Captain Gardiner was still in front of the soldiers on horseback.

"Lieutenant, you and all your men are about to be slaughtered," I said, "exactly as you were over 170 years ago. This is a dream world you and other soldiers recreate every year on the anniversary of the battle you are about to experience again." Just as I finished saying the last few words, I saw Captain Gardiner heading directly for us at a gallop. *Oh crap!*

"Listen to him," Carla said firmly before Walton could react to my words, really startling the guy. "We know you don't like slavery and you don't believe in removing Indians from their lands—"

Before she could finish, Captain Gardiner nearly rammed his horse into all three of us but stopped short. He had this really round, red face with big jowls. Besides the white belt that held his sword around his huge stomach was something like a long red scarf. His uniform looked like Walton's in a way, but the coat didn't quite seem the same for some reason. "Is there a problem, Lieutenant?" the man said, his voice a deep rumble reminding me of Lobo.

"Sir," Walton replied, snapping to attention, "these two claim we are about to be attacked by Seminoles."

Before Captain Gardiner could say anything, Carla jumped into the conversation with both feet. Speaking only to my ancestor, she said, "You recognize Jeff because he is your descendant and you have been trying to—"

"You speak only when you are spoken to, girl!" Gardiner bellowed, almost standing in his stirrups, making his saddle creak.

"I'll speak anytime and anywhere I so choose," Carla shouted back at him with her hands on her hips.

Oh oh. The real Carla had just emerged. When I heard what she said though, I wasn't sure if that was good or bad. Some of the approaching soldiers must have heard Gardiner and Carla arguing, because they glanced our way in surprise and then quickly looked away.

In seconds, those two long columns of men began walking past us, behind Captain Gardiner, heading up the road to their doom. I say walked because they weren't really marching. Above their footsteps cushioned by the dirt, sand and pine needles, I heard some of the men saying some things but not their exact words. Up and down the double line came rustling sounds and the occasional clink of equipment. Somewhere a whip popped twice, followed by moo-ing that I knew could only come from one of the oxen.

Most of those soldiers wore long, light blue overcoats the same color as their pants. I realized, like Lobo said, they must be keeping their muskets dry under those great big coats. Only a few of the men carried their weapons openly. The ones without overcoats wore the same kind of sky blue, long sleeved shirts or jackets with white belts crisscrossing their chests just like what I had seen on the dead guy I found. Each man had a backpack with a rolled blanket across the top. Some of those guys were so young. I swear, they didn't look much older than me, and they were about to die, no, die again, actually.

With the column of men moving quickly and Carla talking back to Captain Gardiner, I had to do something fast. We couldn't afford any arguments or even a lot more conversation. After Carla said what she did, Gardiner's face got bright red, and his eyes almost bulged out of his head. Things were really getting out of hand.

"I deeply apologize for Carla's bad manners," I said to Captain Gardiner, jumping between the two of them and bowing slightly like I had seen in a movie once. Luckily, some of the red drained from the man's face, and his eyes retreated back into their sockets.

"Please, listen to me," I said to both Captain Gardiner and my ancestor. "The Seminoles are all around here, and they will attack very soon. At any moment now, Major Dade will ride up to the head of the column, tell the troops their long march is nearly over and then promise them a late Christmas holiday at Fort King. Gentlemen, if you should see that happen, please, have your men take cover." It was the only thing I could think of to say, you know? I mean I figured if I could change how things happened, maybe my ancestor would live long enough for Carla and me to convince him he was in a dream world of his own making.

"What rubbish!" Captain Gardiner replied, with a look of com-plete distaste on his face.

Obviously, I was getting nowhere so I said, "Captain, sir, soon after Major Dade talks about Christmas, he will ride up to the advance party where he will be shot dead. Within a short time, over half your soldiers will fall."

"Do you fancy yourself a fortune teller young man?" Captain Gardiner asked, laughing. Lieutenant Walton closed his eyes as if he wanted to be anywhere except next to me, his crazy cousin, and Carla, a back-talking slave. With all that loud conversation, I wondered why the Seminoles didn't go ahead and attack.

"Please," I said to my ancestor, trying desperately to control my frustration, "You were already killed in this same battle over 170 years ago. You and the others here keep repeating it every December 28. Do you really want to go through this year after year, forever?"

"What are you saying, boy?" Captain Gardiner interrupted. "We have no time for—"

He stopped talking as the sound of muffled hoof beats cut through the air. All of us turned as another officer rode quickly up on the other side of the double column of soldiers. Taller and more slender than Gardiner this man had a long black beard, carried a double-barreled shotgun, and attached to a white belt around his waist, I saw a curved sword. Sticking out of his black leather hat was a fluffy white feather. Of all things, he also had on white gloves. Major Dade had finally arrived. It had to be him. *Thank God!*

He brought his horse to a stop near the head of the two columns of soldiers and shouted so they all could hear. "Men, our long march is nearly over. Well done! The danger is behind us. Shortly, we shall arrive at Fort King. There you shall be given three days to have a most happy Christmas." The soldiers cheered and whistled. Some of them even waved their leather hats in the air. God, it was strange to hear the man say those words, so close to the ones Lobo used when telling me about Dade's little speech to his men. Captain Gardiner and Lieutenant Walton watched with surprised looks on their faces as Major Dade then saluted his men and rode off at a trot toward the advance party somewhere ahead.

"See what I mean?" I shouted. "It's exactly like I told you! Do something! Go stop your commander before he gets shot! Tell your men to get down! Now!" Oh yeah, I overdid it. I knew even before Captain Gardiner spoke that I had definitely lost the argument.

"You give no orders here, boy!" he barked at me, his eyes bulging again. To Walton, he issued his own order. "Leave these two here to cower in the undergrowth if they wish, Lieutenant, but you will now accompany me as we move forward."

"No!" I pleaded, and for a split second, Walton hesitated, his eyes searching mine. As quickly as it arrived, that moment disappeared.

"Yes sir," Lieutenant Walton replied, saluting Captain Gardiner. Returning the salute, Gardiner eyed me for a few seconds and then rode away. As the soldiers continued to walk past us, my ancestor looked at me once more, shook his head as if very puzzled, and jogged after his captain. All of our efforts at stopping the battle, or at least slowing it down, had failed. The attack was going to happen any minute, and I definitely didn't want us to join those poor soldiers who would soon become sitting ducks.

"Come on," I yelled, pulling Carla into a run down the road a short way, opposite the direction the soldiers were going.

"Where are we heading?"

"Here," I said pointing to a pine tree, "this one's yours. Get behind it with your body pointing directly towards the road. Lay down with your head right up against the tree and hands over your head. It's the only protection we'll have when the battle starts."

"But—"

"Carla!" I shouted at her, hating myself for doing it. "That battle is going to take place any second and we've got to take cover. Do you want to get killed? You remember what Lobo said about what rifle balls and axes could do to me here even though this is a dream world? You're not any more immune from all that happening than I am."

Carla's eyes widened, as if for the first time she fully recognized the danger. All she said was, "Oh." With no further argument, she dropped flat on the ground behind her tree.

Breathing a sigh of relief she was at least safe for the moment, I hunkered down behind my tree just like I told her to do. Underneath me, the cold and wet from the ground seeped through my jeans and jacket. The smell of pine needles made me think about the time I stepped off Lobo's porch into the foggy darkness and then eventually came back into the warmth of his house. I tell you what, right then, I really wished Carla and I were back at Lobo's, sitting in front of his fireplace.

As row after row of soldiers walked by us, they looked over and laughed. I guess to them we did look kind of funny, all huddled up behind those two trees. Staring into their faces, all I could think about was how all of them except Ransom Clark and another soldier whose name Lobo never told me, would soon die. Which one is Clark? I wondered.

Just as I turned my head to check on Carla, the sharp sound of a single gunshot echoed through the woods some distance ahead in the direction where Dade, Fraser, Pacheco, Gardiner and Walton had all gone.

34

A Slick Coating of Red

1 80 screaming Seminoles immediately let loose with their rifles at our side of the road, sweeping all that noise over us like a crashing wave. Bullets ripped into trees and palmettos all around, one hitting somewhere right above my head. Splinters of wood and pine bark exploded all over me.

You wouldn't believe how fast my eyes shut and how quick my head ducked when all that happened. I thought I was somewhat ready for the battle but no way. Feeling those splinters and hearing the roar of 180 rifles and men sounding like a thousand made me flatten myself against the ground even more than before. Knowing the rifle ball that hit the tree in front of me could have just as easily have shattered my skull definitely made me keep my head down.— for a few seconds anyway.

Scared as I was, I couldn't resist opening my eyes again and taking a quick look. I tell you what, a lot of soldiers were lying up and down the road as far as I could see. Some didn't move at all while others screamed in pain, grabbing themselves where bullets had hit them.

While trying to find cover, the men still standing struggled to rip their overcoats off and get at their muskets. All that time, the Seminoles reloaded their rifles and continued to fire at the soldiers through the blue grey smoke already starting to obscure my view of the pines and palmettos on the other side of the road. Flashes of light deep inside the haze told me the location of the Indians. A couple of times I saw a blur of movement behind a tree or a head popping up behind a palmetto bush. Some of the Seminoles wore turbans, and I remembered pictures I had seen of Osceola wearing the same type of thing.

In the middle of all that chaos, I heard a man's loud, angry voice above all the shooting. As I looked up the road to my right, I saw Captain Gardiner stomping out of the smoke on foot, waving a sword, and coming in our direction. He cursed his men like I have never heard before and once or twice, he faced the other side of the road and screamed challenges at the Seminoles.

The closer he got to us, I saw how Gardiner's round face had turned super red, almost purple, and his eyes bulged so much I thought he might explode.

I'm not kidding you. That guy was so mad it seemed like he flat didn't care about the almost constant rifle fire from all those Seminoles. I figured a lot of them had to be aiming at him. I mean, he was the guy in charge. In a war, you always want to take out the leaders if you can, right? But soldiers kept getting shot all around Gardiner and the man never got hit. It was like he had this invisible shield protecting him against bullets or something. I'm telling you, to me he looked like the God of War.

Suddenly, he stopped directly in front of the trees where Carla and I hid. He stood there in the open, yelling instructions up and down the road to any of his men still able to fight. In the back of my mind, I wondered what Carla thought of the Captain's choice of swear words he used to get his soldiers organized.

"Carla!" I said, realizing I hadn't checked on her since the battle started. I looked over to find her still flat on the ground, up against her tree, arms covering her head. When I didn't see any blood, I heaved a sigh of relief. That's when sounds on my left made me look in that direction. A skinny soldier without a hat or an overcoat now stood behind a pine tree maybe five feet away. He was one of the young ones, probably not more than seventeen-years-old. His brown hair stuck out at all angles and he had pretty bad acne.

The sounds I had heard were from him locking a bayonet onto the end of his musket. When I saw that sharp thing, I had these flashbacks of holding one exactly like it at Lobo's place and something like it sticking up through my mattress. Captain Gardner hadn't ordered his men to attach their bayonets and I wondered why the guy was doing it. The poor kid's hands shook as he pulled back the hammer of his musket and then opened a black leather box hooked to the white belt around his waist. Even with all the noise going on around us, I could clearly hear his ragged, panicky breathing.

From the box, he pulled out a small white cylinder made of what looked like paper, twisted at the end. That twisted part he stuck in his mouth, between his teeth. With a jerk of his hand, he tore that part off and spit it onto the ground. A trickle of sweat dripped down the side of his face as he poured gunpowder from the paper cylinder near the musket's hammer and then down its barrel. Just as he finished doing all that, he happened to look up in my direction. That's when he saw me. Our eyes met and for a few seconds as he stood there staring at me with his mouth partly open. Oh man, those eyes of his—grey eyes. They were so wide with fear I could feel it deep in my gut.

When he looked back down at his weapon, the kid shoved the rest of the paper cylinder into the barrel with his ramrod. He had trouble putting the ramrod into the musket because of his bayonet being in the way. I didn't see the musket ball go in but figured it had to be mixed with the powder somehow. Making a determined yank with his thumb, he then pulled the hammer back another notch, took aim and fired towards the other side of the road. Sparks flew from where he had poured powder near the hammer, and a loud explosion erupted from the end of the barrel with smoke and more sparks. The poor guy never noticed he forgot to take the ramrod out of his gun. When he fired, I saw it sail off into the smoke.

Firing his musket calmed the kid down a little, because he looked over at me and grinned. Why he did that exactly, I didn't know, but his eyes weren't so wild looking as before. It seemed like he wanted me to know he was going to be OK and could do his job or something. Poor guy didn't even realize he had lost his ramrod. The next thing I knew, he jerked backward and to the side. Crumpling, he fell down right next to me, his head smashing sideways into the ground only a couple of feet from mine.

As his body twitched, blood spurted from a large wound in his left temple soaking his hair and flowing across his forehead. The grey eyes that had looked at me seconds before still stared but at nothing in particular. In no time, they had a horrible slick coating of red. Sickened, I turned my head away to the right, but not in time to avoid the metallic scent of the poor guy's blood from rushing up my nose. I didn't know until then that blood had much of a smell. For a few seconds, I got close to puking, but by closing my eyes and focusing on my breath, the nausea slowly went away. Thanks Lobo, I thought, remembering what he had taught me about controlling my emotions.

In front of us, Captain Gardiner still shouted and cursed. Soldiers kneeling or standing behind trees were firing back at the Seminoles, the sound of their weapons different from the sharp cracking of those the Seminole were using. I remembered Lobo saying the soldiers had the older muskets while the Seminoles were somehow able to get their hands on the more modern rifles. Again, Gardiner's voice boomed over the gunfire. This time, he shouted a very specific command. "Bring up that damn gun! Bring it here now!"

I didn't know what gun he was talking about, but the soldiers did. To my left I heard them repeating the command down the road through the smoke to where I could barely see the covered wagon.

Looking down there though, meant I couldn't help but also see the soldier's bloody head on the ground next to me. So I wouldn't have to look at him, I used my left hand to block that part of my vision.

In front of the wagon in the distance, the three oxen lay on their sides as if they had gone to sleep, but I knew better. Suddenly, behind the wagon, I saw movement of some kind. As I looked, an officer on horseback waving a sword came around the right side of the wagon followed by three horses pulling a cannon on wheels. "Of course," I whispered to myself. Captain Gardiner's "gun" was the cannon Lobo had mentioned. Two soldiers on foot trotted on the right hand side of the horses popping bullwhips to keep the animals moving ahead. Five or six other men ran from tree to tree trying to follow the cannon and not get shot.

The officer on horseback galloped ahead to where Captain Gardiner stood. He quickly dismounted, smacked his horse with the flat of his sword sending it galloping away. That has to be Lieutenant Basinger, I thought, remembering Lobo saying who commanded the cannon. All I could really see of his face was a thick mustache and a small beard. *Basinger!* My mind flashed back to the young soldier who had almost run into Carla and me at the National Guard Headquarters. Again, I wondered if the two men were actually related, and shook my head at the *coincidence* of us going by that building at exactly the right time.

Furiously swinging his sword above his head and then moving it in an arc pointing up the road, Lieutenant Basinger shouted and urged his cannon crew coming towards him to keep moving. This he did over and over again until the horses pulling the cannon came within about twenty feet of him. That's when a huge volley of gunfire erupted from the Seminoles ripping into those poor animals. Screaming, one horse reared up on its hind legs as much as it could with all that harness and showered blood everywhere. Oh, God it was terrible. I've never heard anything like it. I could see its eyes rolling in pain and fear. I had always thought of people screaming but not animals. As the first horse went down, the Seminoles fired at the other two. In minutes, those horses collapsed with hooves thrashing and eyes darting all around. Three beautiful animals lay dying, locked together in bloody, twisted harnesses. The cannon could go no farther.

To my right, I barely heard Carla sobbing through all that noise. I knew she must have seen the attack on the horses, and maybe even the men getting shot. When I looked over, she had her face buried in her hands, but otherwise she seemed to be OK.

Lieutenant Basinger ran to the horses and yelled at his men who had hidden behind trees or were flat on the ground hoping not to become Seminole targets. Man, I didn't blame them a bit, but Basinger made those guys get up, cut the horses loose from the bloody harness and pull the cannon around to face the Seminoles. As one man stood up, a bullet caught him in the back. He pitched forward, smashing his head into a pine tree before going all the way down.

Still, Basinger shouted orders, forcing his frightened men to set the cannon up and then load it. "Fire!" he shouted once those tasks had been completed, and that big piece of metal erupted with a huge roar making my ears ring. With a big burst of flame and smoke, the cannonball, or whatever it was they used, shattered a tree on the Seminole side of the road. The top part of the thing fell into another tree behind it, and slid to the ground.

While rifles and muskets kept firing across the road, the cannon also continued blasting hot metal toward where the Seminoles hid. One-by-one, Lieutenant Basinger's men fell, only to be replaced by soldiers ordered to do so by Captain Gardiner. After a while, smoke from all the weapons fire covered the road like a blue grey fog, and it drifted right over us. Man, the stuff had a stink to it. Maybe it was only my sensitive nose again, but it had a real sharp acidy kind of smell and at times, it even had the scent of rotten eggs. Nasty. I looked all up and down the road but couldn't see my ancestor, probably because of all that smoke.

Any time there was a lull in the noise, I heard soldiers moaning, some even crying. Like listening to the screaming horses, the voices of men and boys in pain cut right through me. Carla no longer sobbed as far as I could tell. Instead, she just lay there with closed eyes and her ears covered by her hands. It looked like she couldn't even stand listening any more. I knew just how she felt.

35

2011?

I'm telling you, the fighting roared on for what seemed like days. OK, hours, anyway. I remembered Lobo telling me the first part of the battle really lasted for only about an hour, but I knew he had to be wrong. Since I don't wear a watch, I couldn't really tell. All the noise, those screams of pain, the stink of gun smoke and blood, and the fact that I couldn't protect Carla, all mixed together in my head until I thought it would burst. Talk about feeling panicky and helpless. In the end, the only thing I could do was to focus on my breath and whisper Lobo's words over and over, "Don't fight the problem. Don't fight the problem."

The more I actually concentrated only on my breathing and nothing else, the calmer I got. Besides, I knew if all I did was lay there afraid of getting shot, worrying about Carla, and focusing on all the suffering going on in front of me, I would go freakin' nuts. There was nothing else to do but try and calm down and wait it out.

Eventually though, the sharp cracking sounds of the Seminole rifles slowed, and then stopped. "Cease Fire!" It was Captain Gardiner's voice shouting above the remaining musket and cannon noise. In seconds, the sounds of battle died out altogether. For a moment after that, all I could hear were men moaning in pain and begging for help. I realized this had to be the time when the

Seminoles retreated for a short while like Lobo said.

I lifted my head and looked over at Carla through the blue-grey haze. That smoke! It hung in the air between us and all over the battlefield. I could almost taste it, and the stuff burned my eyes. "You think it's safe?" she asked, blinking her eyes at me from a very dirty, tearstained face. Pine needles stuck out of her hair and her head lay on her arms. Really thankful that she seemed OK, I started to answer when Captain Gardiner again began shouting at his men, getting them organized into groups and sending them in all kinds of directions. Carla and I both peeked around our trees and watched as the soldiers still standing moved quickly to follow the commands.

Realizing it was as safe as it could be just then, we both stood up, brushed ourselves off a little and looked around. I guess Carla hadn't seen the boy lying next to me die because as soon as she spied him, one hand went to her mouth and the other to her stomach. Sure she was going to puke, I stepped between her and the boy so she couldn't see his body anymore. "Don't look anywhere else but at me," I said to her. "Breathe deeply and it'll pass." I was starting to sound like Lobo. Man did that feel weird when I thought about it.

"OK," she replied in a shaky voice after swallowing hard. "Thanks, but we've got to find your ancestor, Jeff, and make him understand. The Seminoles are going to attack again. That's when Walton gets killed, and so do we if we can't change what's going to happen!"

"All right, tough lady," I said, admiring her even more than ever. I knew she was right, but part of me wanted to hide her in the woods and away from danger.

"You bet I'm tough, and don't you forget it," she said, grabbing me by the arm and urging me towards the road. "Come on, let's go." The thing is, as we started to walk, Carla kept hold of my arm. Her tight grip told me no matter how strong she sounded, she was still scared to death. Well, that made two of us, especially when we saw all the dead, dying and wounded men lying up and down the road. We tried not to look down too much, but we couldn't walk unless we did. In addition to all the men on the ground, there were overcoats, hats, backpacks, muskets, shoes, bayonets, and ammunition boxes all over the place.

When we got close to the dead horses, we started to go around them and not really look, but they were just too large. I mean those huge animals were like magnets pulling our eyes in that direction. Not a good thing. All of those bullet holes in them and tons of blood everywhere were bad enough, but against one horse lay a dead soldier with his head back and his arms outstretched. One of the animal's legs had kept him from falling down completely. The smell of blood in that area was overpowering.

"Oh God, Jeff," Carla moaned as we both stared at him. A rifle ball had smashed its way through the man's right eye and into his skull. Blood covered half of his face and the front of his uniform. My stomach lurched and Carla doubled up puking. The poor kid. Man, I knew how she felt, but for whatever reason I didn't get sick. All I could do was to stroke her back and wait until the spasms stopped, but in that short time, I realized how much my view of war had changed. Never again would I think of a battle as some stupid little fact in a book nobody cared about.

Carla straightened, wiped her lips with the back of her hand with a look on her face somewhere between misery and embarrassment.

"It's OK," I said, "I've been where you are now, remember?"

"Yeah, I do," she said nodding. As we turned away though, I felt something hit my leg. Automatically, I glanced down and found myself looking into the light blue eyes of a man, probably in his forties or so. His hand lay near my leg, so I figured he had tried to grab me. "Please," he begged with what sounded like an Irish accent, "for the love of God, help me." He had taken a rifle ball in the stomach. Blood smeared the front of the man's light blue uniform and the white belts crisscrossing his body.

Part of me wanted to run away from him and the whole stupid battle, but another part wanted to stop and do something, anything. The guy looked a lot like my dad which made it even worse. How do you turn away from your father? I mean, that's how I felt. "I'll see if I can find a doctor," I told him. At that moment, two soldiers came up and dragged the man over by the cannon. Nearby, Captain Gardiner stood there glaring at us.

"You two," he shouted, pointing at us, "come here."

"Oh crap," I whispered and looked at Carla.

"Now!" The man shouted and we walked to where he stood. My God, the guy was short, like Lobo said. On his horse, he looked bigger, or taller anyway. But on the ground, the man didn't stand much higher than Carla. What he lacked in height, he made up for in weight. I'm telling you, the guy was just … really wide.

I figured Gardiner intended to bite our heads off or something, but as I looked down at him, he said in a much softer but still gruff voice, "I should have listened to your warning."

Well that really blew me away.

"How you acquired such foreknowledge of what was to happen here is beyond my comprehension, but your efforts to save us are very much appreciated."

"Ah … you're welcome sir," I stumbled, thinking of how to take advantage of the guy's new attitude. "Believe me, Captain Gardiner, we might be able to prevent a final massacre here if you will only allow us to speak with my cousin once more."

Gardiner eyed me for a few seconds, glanced at Carla and looked back at me again. "Did I hear you correctly?" he said, his voice even softer and with this really sad look on his face. "You asked Walton before the attack if he wished to continue fighting this battle forever?"

"Yes sir," I replied, trying to be totally respectful, but his question really startled me. I couldn't believe the man's sudden shift in attitude.

He nodded at my reply and said, "I have dreamt of this battle it seems every night as far back as I can remember. It is always the same and I struggle to awaken but find I cannot." Impossibly, the God of War almost appeared to be asking for my help. Because of what I said to my ancestor, some part of Captain Gardiner had become conscious. His dreams of the battle, I figured, had to be his constant reliving of it as we was doing at the moment.

"Yes! I know!" I replied, hoping to keep his attention on his dreams. If we could somehow convince him of what was really happening, I figured, he might actually help us get to Walton again. A quick glance at Carla told me she agreed. One raised eyebrow was all it took.

"Sir," I went on, "you, ah, well, dream of fighting that occurred long ago. What we are experiencing now is actually one of those dreams."

"We are here," Carla said excitedly, jumping in to help, "to stop this battle from happening ever again. To do so, we must convince Lieutenant Walton this is all a dream. He is the key."

Captain Gardiner nodded, almost as if he really did understand and said, "Perhaps you both are my salvation." Pointing behind us, he said, "Your opportunity is about to arrive." As I turned to look, a long line of soldiers with axes led by my ancestor approached where we stood, coming from the direction of the wagon with the dead oxen.

"I will tell him to listen to you after he disperses the men," Gardiner said in his unusually soft voice, motioning my ancestor to join us. The man had offered us one final chance.

When Walton arrived, he stopped, stared at Carla and me with a suspicious look on his face and saluted his captain. In that instant, I hoped Captain Gardener would tell my ancestor about his own dreams. "Once you have the men working," Gardiner said to my ancestor in his gruff voice, "your cousin would speak with you." He said nothing about his dreams. *Crap!*

Walton hesitated as if he couldn't believe what Gardiner had just told him, but in a tight voice, he said, "Yes sir." He then did an about face and went back to his men who had gathered a short distance away.

As I looked back at Captain Gardiner I saw his expression had changed, and he said in his God of War voice, "When Lieutenant Walton returns, you shall both be under his command. You will do whatever he requires of you. If you interfere with his duties, you shall be bound and gagged." Without waiting for a response, he turned around and walked away, barking orders to his men. My heart sank as I realized the part of Captain Gardiner that remembered the repeating battle had gone back to sleep. Any hope of getting him to tell Walton about his dreams had completely evaporated.

"Oh damn!" I blurted and realized I was swearing in front of Carla. I guess because of the situation, she didn't react. Besides, I didn't have the time or the energy to play nice.

Not seeming to notice, she sighed heavily and said, "Yeah, for a minute I thought sure he might really be able to help us get through to your ancestor."

About forty feet in front of us, Lieutenant Walton finished giving instructions to his men. Seconds after that, he was back, standing in front of us. "Well?" He asked, staring at me as the thud of axes hitting trees floated into my ears. He had a look in his eyes that was anything but friendly. Even so, I hoped maybe because we had predicted the attack he might be ready to listen.

"Look," I began, again giving up totally on the old-time speech patterns, "what Carla told you is true. I am your descendant and you are in a dream just like I said. You already told me I look familiar, remember? How else can you explain me knowing about Major Dade and this attack?"

"I think young man, to have such knowledge, you both must be in league with the Devil himself."

"The Devil?" I exploded in frustration, feeling the heat of anger welling up inside me. I wanted to grab the man by the front of his stupid military coat with its silly little gold buttons and shake him until he woke up.

"Jeff!" Carla said, putting a hand on my arm. That caused me to remember the little switches in my head, and I found myself watching my breath. As I calmed down, I came up with an idea stolen directly science fiction.

"Sir," I began, fishing in my pocket. "First of all, we don't know anything about the Devil. But we do know about things that are going to happen because ... well ... we're from the future." The man stared at me with this blank look, but I kept talking anyway. "Maybe what I'm saying sounds insane, but it's still true. You see, we have this machine we use to travel through time. It's hidden way back in the woods, miles from here." I figured talking about a machine might push the Devil out of the guy's mind long enough to catch his attention. Watching all that science fiction on TV had to be worth something.

"Here," I said pulling a quarter out of my pocket and holding it out to him. "Please, look at it." I almost showed him my cell phone, but since it didn't work in that world, a modern quarter was the only other thing I had. It seemed to me a dead cell phone would look weird, but a coin he could understand.

At first, Walton didn't seem to want to touch it, or even get too close to me, but he finally reached out and took the quarter in-between two fingers like it had germs or something. When he looked at the thing, his eyes narrowed. Then he turned it over and looked on the other side. "2011?" he asked, his eyes wide.

"Yes," I replied. "We live in the twenty-first century. This battle of yours is history to us. That's how we know what will happen."

As he handed the coin back to me, I could see a slight change in his face so I continued talking. "The Seminoles will return and overrun your little fort you're building and kill everyone except

Ransom Clark and one other soldier. Luis Pacheco has probably already been captured." I was never so thankful for my good memory in my life. I hoped by saying the names of the two battle survivors I knew, Walton might really start to wonder. I was right.

"Clark? Pacheco?" he asked with the sounds of chopping continuing in the background. "How do you know those names?"

"As I told you, this battle to us is history."

"Tell me sir," Carla interrupted in a strong, clear voice, "do I look or sound like any slave you have ever known?" Whoa, I thought, go get him Carla!

Walton just stared at her for the longest time as if he couldn't believe what she had said to him.

"Of course I don't," Carla said, answering her own question. "Slavery was outlawed by the 13th amendment to the United States Constitution in 1865. In my time, black people have been free citizens for well over a century and a half."

"Please," I said, not wanting to give Walton any time to come up with objections. "Please, you must—"

"Enough!" he shouted, looking wildly confused, and I knew we had lost him. A tree crashed into palmettos in front of us and another fell farther back in the woods. "Sit!" He commanded, pointing to the ground in front of us. When both Carla and I didn't do as ordered he yelled, "Now, damn you!" We did as we were told.

"You will not move," Walton ordered in a stern voice, "and you will not say a word to any of these men." In an oddly softer tone, he said, "If we all survive this day, perhaps we can then discuss the strange things of which you speak."

"There won't be any later," I hissed up at him, but Walton just pressed his lips together, turned around and walked to where his men were cutting branches from a fallen pine. For some reason the smell of fresh cut wood right then really pissed me off.

"Jeff," Carla whispered next to me, her voice all urgent like. "If he dies at the start of the next attack like history says ..." She didn't finish the sentence. She didn't have to. Visions of Carla and me dying and returning to that battle over and over again sliced through my mind.

36

Elizabeth

God that was frustrating. I mean Carla and I had to just sit there and do nothing or get "bound and gagged" like Captain Gardiner told us would happen.

"Jeff, we've got to do something," Carla said as another pine tree crashed through palmettos to the ground with a huge thud.

"I'm open to suggestions," I replied as I watched a group of my ancestor's men strip away branches from a fallen tree.

"Showing him your quarter was cool."

"Yeah, fat lot of good it did though."

"No," Carla said with encouragement in her voice. "When you did that, it made the man stop and think for a minute. You almost had him."

"Almost won't save our lives and get him out of this ... this never ending world of his."

As I spoke, two groups of Lieutenant Walton's men, about twelve each, started picking up the stripped pines and hauling them into position to the left of the cannon. Those trees had to be close to eight inches thick and fifty or sixty feet long, a lot to carry even for that many people. It took me a minute to realize there was no more chopping and stripping of branches going on. I thought for sure my ancestor needed lots of logs to make his fort, but I counted only nine tree stumps. Nine! That was it! Nine logs to make a freakin' fort. No wonder the thing didn't do them any good in the end.

Placing the logs one on top of each other, the soldiers used the trees to create a triangle just like Lobo had explained the night before. They put three logs to a side with the base of the triangle facing where most of the Seminole fire had come from. The other two sides made the triangle by interlocking the remaining trees with the base.

It looked exactly what I had seen when I visited the road after touching the pyramid the first time. Each of the two sides faced the road in opposite directions, and they angled back directly towards Carla and me almost to a point. That open tip of the unfinished triangle is what they used for an entrance. The skinny ends of those trees came close together on the ground, making the walls at the opening really low to the ground. Inside the fort stood several large, living pine trees.

I swear, that little place didn't seem like it could protect anybody or anything. It looked more like an old-time split rail fence than a fort. For God's sake, the tallest part was at the base of the triangle, but even there, a man would have to crouch or kneel to get any kind of protection at all. In between each of those logs, I could see enough wide-open space where rifle balls could easily come through and find a human target.

As the soldiers brought the wounded into the fort through the opening, Captain Gardiner and my ancestor walked inside with them. They stood there talking and looking our way as an idea finally popped into my constipated brain. "Carla," I whispered, "there's one thing we haven't tried."

Carla's weary, dirty face looked up at me and she said. "Golden boy, it had better be a good one because time is running out."

"This could work!" I said, getting excited. "We haven't talked to Walton about his wife and daughter. If anything can get to him that just might be it. Between us, we know enough from reading about his background in those old letters and things, right?"

Slowly Carla's beautiful sunshine smile spread across her dirty face. You should have seen it. Man, that about made everything OK all by itself. "Absolutely," she replied and we quickly reviewed what we knew about my ancestor's family.

While Carla and I talked, the soldiers took muskets, pistols, cartridge boxes and other supplies into the fort. It didn't take long, and when they were done, most of them stayed inside their little crappy triangle along with Captain Gardiner and my ancestor. It made me shudder to think about the final slaughter that was on the way and knowing we might be part of it. As much as I sympathized with the Seminoles and the free blacks, I sure didn't want to be around for the rest of that battle.

"Are they going to leave us outside?" Carla asked in a nervous whisper, but soon after she spoke, Lieutenant Walton turned around inside the entrance to the fort, picked up a musket and motioned us to join him.

"It's now or never," I whispered back to Carla. My voice didn't sound very steady.

"At least we have an invitation," she replied, as we both stood, "so let's make the most of it."

As we entered the fort, all the soldiers in there looked up at us. There must have been thirty of forty of them. Except for the wounded, the ones loading their muskets or stacking supplies stopped and stared. Obviously, they didn't know what to make of Carla and me. Captain Gardiner stood next to one of the living pine trees with his arms folded, back in his God of War personality. Lieutenant Walton walked behind us so that he blocked the opening. We had to turn around to face him. "You are now in the United States Army," he said, shoving the musket into my arms.

Oh man, that thing was a lot heavier than I thought, and the metal felt really cold. "What?" I yelled, but Walton went right on talking.

"You and your … companion are welcome here, but you, sir, will be expected to fight like any other soldier."

"Wait," I shouted, "you still don't understand. We have to—"

Before I could finish my sentence, shots rang out from somewhere in the pines and palmettos behind us. Walton lurched backwards with this startled look on his face. Without thinking, I turned around to see where the shots had come from. A split second later, it felt like somebody had hit the left side of my body with the full swing of a baseball bat. Vaguely, I heard Carla scream.

The next thing I knew, I found myself lying face up on the ground looking at the tops of some pines trees. Pain like you wouldn't believe ripped through my upper left arm and shoulder. I tried to say something, but nothing came out of my mouth except a hoarse croak.

Gunfire erupted all around me. Right outside the fort, the cannon roared so close it actually made my teeth rattle. New clouds of that terrible smelling smoke drifted over me as rifle balls thudded into the wood fort. Instead of being outside of the battle like we were before, we had walked right into the middle of it. Through all of the noise I could hear Carla calling my name, but I had no idea where she was. I didn't know what happened to the musket my ancestor had given me, but I really didn't care.

Gritting my teeth against the pain, I grabbed my left arm with my right hand. What I felt was warm stickiness. When I lifted my hand to look at it, the glistening dark red moisture on my palm and fingers told me I had been shot. "Oh crap," I whispered, trying to focus on my breathing instead of the pain. This time when the smell of blood hit my nose, I knew without a doubt it was mine. Directly over my head during a slight lull in the fighting, I heard a sharp hiss and figured it must have been a rifle ball slicing through the air. I had no idea you could hear a bullet, rifle ball or whatever, coming your way.

"Jeff," Carla yelled above the noise. I turned my head to the left and there she was, lying next to me, dirty but still beautiful. "Oh good Lord," she said, for the first time seeing my bloody hand and arm. Instantly, her eyes filled with tears.

In that world of hurt, my mind blurred for a few seconds, but then I thought about Lobo and his lessons. I guess it worked, because my brain suddenly speeded up, little switches flipped in there and somehow, the pain lessened. I can't tell you exactly how it happened, but it did.

A few feet above us, a dragonfly flitted back and forth as if asking what we crazy humans below him were doing. Its dark yellow body and delicate, blue-green wings looked just like the dragonfly on Lobo's blue Tiffany lamp. I wondered why it was flying around in that chilly weather. I thought they only came out when it was warm.

"Carla?" I finally said, barely over the battle noise. Her head popped up again, this time with tears streaming down her face. I guess she figured I was dying or something. "Are you hit?" I asked.

"No but you—"

"I'll be OK, but you keep get your head down," I barked. "There's more blood on me than there is damage to my arm," I lied, knowing there was much more to my wound than that.

Carla's head disappeared from view, but I felt her gently grasp my left hand. As she did that, a pleasant, gentle warmth rippled up my damaged arm and into my shoulder. The sensation reminded me of how I felt when Lobo eased my headaches, and the pain in my arm lessened. From Carla's touch also came an understanding about what to do next as clear as anything I have ever experienced.

"Walton is down, right?" I asked, shouting over the gunfire in a surprisingly strong voice.

"Yes," she said getting close to my ear. "It looked to me like he got shot just before you did. He's on the ground right behind us. His head's near the entrance. "We're pretty well—"

Again, the cannon thundered, making us both jump. "We're

pretty well protected by the bottom logs of the fort all around," Carla shouted over the gunfire coming from inside and outside the fort.

"Good. Now listen. I have this strong feeling Walton's still alive, and if he is, we have a chance. The thing is, you have to trust me on what I'm going to tell you."

"Sure," she agreed. "but let me check your arm first."

"No time!" I shouted back at her. "Trust me, I'm OK. If we don't help Walton and he dies, you and I are stuck here, remember?"

When I heard what I thought was a muffled agreement, I said to her, "First of all, I need you to keep low and crawl up to see if Walton is living."

"But Jeff—"

"Please, Carla, check him out and let me know. And keep your head down."

After hesitating for a few seconds, she yelled, "I'm on my way," and she released my hand. As she crawled towards Walton, I reached out with my bloody right hand, grabbed a fresh cut tree stump with it, dug the heel of my left foot into the ground and turned myself onto my stomach.

Well, when my body flipped, my wounded left arm did too, of course, but like a floppy doll's arm. I had no control over it, and the thing slammed into the ground. I howled in pain, started shaking and then must have passed out for a few seconds. When my head cleared, I heard Carla calling my name, and the cannon exploded again. Once I took a few panting breaths and worked on not fighting the problem for a moment, I stopped shaking and looked up. To the right of the tree stump I used to pull myself over, I saw Carla flat on the ground next to Walton on his left, near the fort entrance. She had this look of horror on her face.

Whether that look came from seeing Walton's condition or seeing me in so much pain, I didn't know. I couldn't see Walton's face, just his bloody chin and nose. "I'm OK, really," I called to her. "Now, what about Walton?" I could tell by the expression on her face she didn't believe me. "Carla," I yelled, again, "What about Walton?"

Lifting her head up slightly, she looked at my ancestor for a few seconds and shook her head. "Jeff, it's not good. He ... he got hit in the chest. He's coughing up blood, and it's all over the front of his uniform. I think the bullet pierced a lung." The memory of seeing Lyle change into Lieutenant Walton in the plaza flashed across my mind.

"All right," I yelled, "here's where the trust comes in and I know you can do this. Think about how you crushed that Coke can at Lobo's place."

"What? Why that?" She shouted back.

"Believe me when I say you have so much more power than you know. I felt it when you held my hand a minute or two ago." After saying that, the pain in my arm actually lessened even more.

For a few seconds Carla was silent. "OK, so?" she yelled back above the gunfire.

"So, you've got to use that same power to keep Walton alive at least for a little while." Man it was strange, asking Carla to help my ancestor right in the middle of his dream world battle, but I had this gut feeling she could do it. Besides, I didn't want to think any more about what would happen if the man died.

"What? Keep him alive? I can't do that."

"Yes, you can. Reach over, put one hand on his chest and the other on his head, exactly like Lobo does to get rid of my headaches. Then ... well ... close your eyes, pray or whatever, and imagine the blood flow stopping while fresh air goes into his damaged lung. You can do it."

I had no real idea what I was saying. It seemed like the words flowed out of my mouth all on their own.

As I watched through the drifting smoke, Carla hesitantly put her hand on Walton's bloody chest. That had to be difficult I knew, but she did it and then laid the other hand on his head. I nodded to encourage her to keep going. She nodded back at me and closed her eyes.

Quickly, I used my right arm and both feet to pull myself around the tree stump. Slowly, I crawled up on Walton's right side, dragging my useless left arm along for the ride. God, it hurt, but I didn't have any other choice. I had to get up to where Walton lay. *Focus on your breath*, I kept telling myself as I continued to move forward. *Focus on your breath*. Behind us in the fort, soldiers fired their weapons and outside the fort, the cannon boomed once more, shaking the ground.

When I finally did get to Walton, I lifted my head and saw that his eyes were open and blinking. Wet blood stained his lips, chin and neck, but he appeared to be breathing pretty well. Badly splattered with blood, Carla's left hand and arm rested on the man's stomach and chest. I figured he must have coughed up some more while I crawled up to him. Deep in her concentration or prayer, Carla probably hadn't noticed. *You are really something else*, I said to her in my mind, admiring her ability to cope with everything that had happened so far.

Walton's eyes suddenly shifted and he looked right at me. The tiniest of smiles barely curled his lips, and ever so slightly, he nodded. Carla's efforts at keeping him alive, if you can call them that, were working. I was about to smile back, when a large black bird swooped down to the ground behind Walton's head. The thing's arrival startled me. I mean who would expect a bird to fly into all that wild chaos, right? In the next instant, I realized I was staring into the dark, glittering eyes of a one-legged crow. "No way," I barely whispered.

"Caaa," the thing screeched above the noise of battle, making Carla open her eyes and look up.

"Edgar?" she asked, her eyes wide with disbelief.

"Caaaa." The bird hopped over to her on his single leg. When he got to Carla, he tipped his head towards hers, grabbed several strands of hair in his beak, pulled them a little and let go. How he did that on one freakin' leg I will never know.

"Edgar, it is you!" Carla shouted with a smile, and looked at me as if asking how Edgar could be in my ancestor's crazy dream. I just shrugged in confusion, but somehow knowing Edgar was there made me feel better. That's when Carla's gaze shifted to Lieutenant Walton for the first time since trying to heal him.

"He's doing better," she shouted over the gunfire with obvious disbelief. Walton's eyes shifted back and forth between us.

"You bet!" I replied. "Keep it up."

Again, the feeling of knowing what I needed to do filled my mind and I edged as close to my ancestor as I could get. "You have to live for your family," I said into his ear, "especially for your daughter, for Elizabeth." At the mention of his daughter's name, Walton's eyes went really wide. "Yes, Elizabeth, I have seen a picture of her as an adult with her two fine sons. She grew up in St. Augustine where she married and had a happy life. Remember, we came from the future so we know these things."

When I finished talking, Walton shook violently for a few seconds and coughed up a lot of blood, spraying it all over the front of his uniform, as well as Carla's hand and arm. I thought the guy was dying, but then he pulled in this deep breath of air. Again and again, he breathed easily with no trouble at all. Carla grinned as she watched him breathe so much easier.

I don't know how to explain exactly what happened next except to say that everything just ... well ... stopped. Instead of the battle sounds being deafening, the *silence* became deafening, and the air thickened somehow like it had when I first started talking to Lobo in his house. In this case though, I'm talking about no sound whatsoever and absolutely no movement. Well, that's not totally true. It was as if everything and everybody froze inside some sort of soundproofed but unseen material—all except for me, Carla, Walton and good old Edgar.

I'm telling you, I glanced back at the men behind us in the fort and they looked like stop action players on a TV football game. One soldier was doubled over, caught in a fall on his way towards the ground. Flashes from the muskets in men's hands glowed at a constant rate and the puffs of smoke coming from their weapons looked like you could almost reach out and grab them. Behind one of the pine trees in the fort, Captain Gardiner aimed his pistol in the direction of the Seminoles but didn't fire.

Like watching a stone drop into a perfectly still pond of water, Carla's voice blossomed into the silence. "Jeff, what is this?" Next to her, Lieutenant Walton's looked all around as if he also wondered what was happening. His deep breathing sounded very loud in the weird silence.

"Caaa," Edgar said and he flew up to perch on top of a small pine tree right outside the entrance to the fort.

"I don't know what's going on," I said, looking up in time to see my friend the dragonfly swoop down to Walton, hover over him for a few seconds and then land on the ground next to him. My ancestor looked at me as if to say, "What the hell?"

"Father?" A child's voice came from somewhere down the road to our right. As soon as he heard it, Walton struggled to get up, forcing Carla to remove her hand and arm from his chest. Just as he came to a full sitting position, my ancestor coughed some more and looked around. I've never seen such a change in a person in my life. Through all of that, neither Edgar nor the dragonfly moved.

"Father?" The voice called again, closer this time, and both Carla and I also sat up. All three of us looked over the skinny ends of the fort resting on the ground. There, coming up the road, walked a little girl, maybe five-years-old or so. As she made her way through the smoke hanging in the air, I noticed my left arm didn't hurt any more.

"Oh Heavenly God, Elizabeth," Walton croaked. Slowly, he struggled to his feet, walked outside the fort and took a few steps down the road towards the child.

I watched as the little girl stepped delicately around the bodies of men and horses, heading in Walton's direction. When she got to him, she reached up and took her father's hand.

That's when I noticed a tunnel of clear air going back through the smoke behind her, exactly where she had made her way through the battlefield. The child's black hair had these springy little curls hanging down on either side of the cutest little pudgy face. How she looked made me think of those little Valentine's Day angels—cherubs. Her dress was long and dark red with a ruffled collar.

As Walton stared at the child in what looked like total disbelief, she said to him, "Come father. You have been away much too long. Mother and grandmother are waiting for you."

For maybe five or ten seconds, Walton didn't say anything. Instead, he stared at his little visitor while holding her hand. Finally, he nodded, and said to her, "Yes dear girl, I have been away far too long." In the next instant, both Walton and his daughter looked right at Carla and me. Tears streamed down Walton's face and he smiled. The girl smiled too, a cute little kid smile, but as I looked at her I had this overpowering feeling somehow her age could only be measured in centuries, or even more, but definitely not only in years. That made no real sense to me, but it was what went through my mind all the same.

Elizabeth shifted her ancient gaze back to her father and tugged on his hand as little kids will do when they want to go somewhere. My ancestor, my five times over great grandfather, Lieutenant Robert Walton, allowed his daughter to guide him through the clearing she had made in the motionless smoke and down the road. Carla and I watched in the frozen silence all around us until they … well … just … vanished.

"Caaaa," Edgar said again from on top of his little pine tree near the fort entrance.

37

Crow Eyes

Edgar's dark eyes glistened in the sunlight as a stiff breeze ruffled his feathers and the trees behind him. Somehow, those trees didn't quite look right, but I couldn't figure out why. Only one thing was certain; the sound and feel of that wind were so different from the total stillness of before.

Guess my brain wasn't functioning very well. I was partially lost in a mental numbness, the fuzziness of mind you feel when you first start waking up in the morning. I did notice my breath came in little gasps, as if I had been exercising hard. Drips of sweat ran down my face, or was it tears? Could be both, I thought without much real interest.

A jagged hardness dug into my palms. What it was, I couldn't imagine, but it hurt. Took me a few seconds until I realized I was pressing with both hands against what looked like a huge triangular rock sitting directly in front of me. As I pulled my hands away from the roughness and rubbed them together, old Edgar fluttered his wings and did a little one-legged dance on the top of the triangle. From his glistening eyes, I got this immediate but strange sense of incredible intelligence and authority.

"Welcome back Mr. Golden."

The rumbling voice from behind splashed over me like a bucket of ice-cold water. *Lobo!* Slowly, the triangular rock in front of me became a familiar coquina pyramid. Oh man, I tell you what. I sat there for a few seconds staring at the pyramid's sides not sure what to believe. Then in a rush, it all came blasting back into my weary mind, everything that had happened since the day before when Carla and I stood talking at Lobo's gate. I mean it was like having scenes on giant movie screens firing one after the other right at me from different angles but freakin' fast. Even so, on every screen I could watch myself living through each event one at a time.

Seconds later, I found myself fully and completely reliving one of those experiences. I was back on the battlefield with Carla as she used her abilities and prayed, desperately trying to save Lieutenant Walton. Horrible pain again shot through my arm. Smells of pine needles, blood and gun smoke forced their ways into my nostrils. The explosive sounds of cannon, musket and rifle fire pounded my ears.

"Snap out of it!" Lobo said from somewhere above me but very close. At that exact moment, my whole body convulsed slightly and my mind started to clear.

I looked up and there he was, old Lobo standing right next to the pyramid and shaking my shoulder, hard. As I stared up at him, the last visions, smells and sounds of the Dade battle drifted away. The intensity of the man's fiery eyes made me wince. *Crow eyes.* I shifted my gaze to Edgar standing on top of the pyramid using his single leg. I swear, both man and bird eyes looked exactly the same to me at that moment—dark, probing and sparkling with a tremendous power I flat did not understand.

Finally, Lobo released my shoulder from his iron grip and as he did, I slowly became more aware of the world around me. It was chilly sitting there in the wind, but not the deep cold like when we entered the icy dome of clear air around the pyramids in near total darkness. *No more fog and ice.* A shaft of early morning sunlight bathed the tombstones in my line of sight with a yellowish-orange glow. The huge flag on its tall pole at the other end of the cemetery snapped and popped in the breeze. A big truck rumbled by some-where behind me. Occasionally I got a whiff of bacon. Somebody around there was cooking breakfast and it smelled awfully good.

"You going to make it, Jeff?" Lobo asked, still standing above me and breaking in on my slowly awakening mind. The old guy had a frown that could freeze water, but it hit me he had used my first name. No more *Mr.* Golden. The man had said, "Jeff." I can't really explain how the sound of my first name coming from him hit me except to say I felt like I had graduated or something. Wild, huh? Anyway, that did it. The rest of the fuzzy headedness cleared and I blinked my eyes as I looked around, expecting the cemetery to disappear again. Didn't happen though, no matter how many times I blinked. I still made sure not to touch the pyramid.

"Your ancestor's dream world has collapsed," Lobo said as he stood next to me. "He and the others are free as are you. These pyramids no longer pose a danger to anyone."

"So he's OK? Walton?" I asked, still not sure I heard the man right.

"He is, and grateful, as are all of his associates for the help you and Carla gave so generously."

Only when the man finished talking, and he walked behind me again, did I really believe I was back in my own world. Thankful I had survived, and thankful my ancestor and the other soldiers were at peace, I closed my eyes, took a deep breath, and let it out slowly. Carla did it, I thought. She saved us all. "Carla?" I shouted as a hor-rible thought hammered my brain. I had returned to my body, but I didn't know if Carla had done the same. Neither one of us was sup-posed to be in the Lieutenant's freakin' dream but most of all her.

"I'm here," said a small, muffled voice, slightly behind me and to my left.

As fast as I could, I untangled my legs and spun around on my butt. There Carla sat on one side of a sky blue tarp, legs pulled up towards her chest. Elbows on her knees and hands covering her face, she looked all scrunched up. That's when I saw blood, sand and dirt all over her arms, hands and jeans. Pine needles still stuck out of her hair at all kinds of wild angles as it had on the battlefield.

Oh man, what a relief to see her sitting there. "Thank God," I whispered, but it slowly dawned on me that she had brought back with her evidence of Lieutenant Walton's dream world. *Not possible.* Carla's real body hadn't actually been on that battlefield, or had it? Besides, the place was a creation by Walton and the others. Then I remembered the pine sap on my hands and moisture on my clothes left over from being in the dark fog outside Lobo's house that even he hadn't been able to explain. For just an instant, my mind shifted rapidly back and forth between being in the cemetery and reliving memories of being on the battlefield.

As Carla separated her hands, I could only see her eyes and her nose. "Hi," she said in a tired, groggy sounding voice while she took her arms off her knees and sat up straight. Blood stained one hand and arm, her face, shirt and coat. Tracks from tears streaked her cheeks. Seeing her like that gave me chills as I recalled how close we both came to never coming back to our own world again. Slowly the fogginess I saw in her eyes seconds before seemed to evaporate.

"Jeff!" she yelled, staring at me. "What about your wound?"

Following her gaze, I looked down at my left arm and saw my jacket, torn, still wet with blood and caked with darkened sand and dirt. In fact, my whole left side looked like the same way, even the top part of my jeans. The nasty memory of getting shot pushed its way back into my brain, and I made a quick grab for the wounded arm with my other bloodstained hand. After feeling it all over, I couldn't find any injury at all. How that could be with all the blood on me just didn't make sense.

"It's fine," I smiled at Carla in surprise, lifting my arm and wiggling my left hand. "I'm … all right, I think. You?" I asked, pointing to her arms and clothes.

Carla closed her eyes for a few seconds, took a couple of deep breaths and said, "I'm OK" But, when she glanced down at herself, she whispered, "Oh Lord." As she looked at me, I could read in her expression the same questions I had about all the blood, sand and dirt.

"How ..." she started to ask but stopped, looking very confused. I shook my head in silence and put my hands out palms up to show I had no answer.

"You two done jabbering yet?" Lobo barked, startling us both. He had been standing next to Carla, but I wasn't thinking about him at all. Well, I was focusing on Carla, right? When Lobo had our attention, he did something I never thought I would see him do. He smiled. Oh, it wasn't much of a smile, I gotta admit. A corner of his mouth turned upward, just a bit. But during those few seconds, the constant frown vanished, and the tiniest touch of warmth and approval radiated outward from those flashing eyes.

With a jerk of surprise, I realized Lobo somehow knew everything that happened in Lieutenant Walton's dream world. Don't ask me how I knew, I just did.

In the next instant, that hint of a smile on the old guy's face was replaced by an all too familiar frown. "Come on you two," he said, waving for us to follow him as he turned to head back to his truck. As if in a daze, Carla and I sat there and watched him walk around the tall war monument and up the sidewalk we had blindly stumbled arm-in-arm with him on in that horrible freezing fog. Not wanting to be left behind, Edgar exploded into flight from his one-legged perch on the pyramid, zoomed past Lobo, and then veered off to the right on his own path home. As I watched him, I wondered how that crazy bird had somehow appeared in Lieutenant Walton's dream world.

Before following Lobo back to the truck, I gave Carla a big hug. It startled the poor girl at first, but then I felt her arms wrap tightly around me. Couldn't help it, you know? Thoughts about what might have happened to her during that battle, and the possibility she might not have come back with me to our own world flooded my mind. God it was so good having her close to me. As I held her though, I thought I felt her trembling. It took me a few seconds to finally realize it was me, shaking all over, ever so slightly.

38

The Invitation

On that drive back through downtown St. Augustine, I felt like I had been running a marathon for three days without rest. Tired doesn't begin to describe it. Part of me wanted to sleep so badly, but another part couldn't stop looking at every little thing outside Lobo's truck. The city seemed brighter, fresher somehow, as if for the first time I saw it fully in focus.

As she did on the trip out to the cemetery, Carla sat between Lobo and me. This time though, we held hands as if both of us never wanted to let go. We didn't speak much. Didn't need to, I guess. Lobo? Not a peep out of him. No questions. Nothing.

Most of the people I saw at that early hour of the morning looked like locals going on errands or to work. A few tourists had already hit the sidewalks but not many. I kind of grinned each time I saw some, surprising myself. Yeah, me the tourist hater. Why? I think seeing them helped me more completely accept being back in St. Augustine with no strings still attached to me from my ancestor's dream world. I mean, up until then the memories of Lieutenant Walton's never-ending battlefield occasionally swamped my mind so much I feared getting sucked back into it no matter what Lobo had said about it being gone. Score one for the tourists, right?

When Lobo stopped his truck for a red light in front of the Bridge of Lions and the plaza, everything all around me instantly slowed up. I mean, at that moment, the cars and people were all moving in *extremely* slow motion. In that small amount of time before the light changed, I was able to study everything and everybody outside the truck as if I had hours to do it. I didn't even think about Carla and Lobo. Why, I don't know.

Right in front of us, a little kid about four years old seemed to take forever to drag his parents across the street. He had on a cardboard pirate hat and he was walking backwards, pulling each parent by a hand. Watching him made me think of Elizabeth, Lieutenant Walton's daughter. In my mind, I could still see that little girl leading her father down the military road through the clear tunnel she had made in the gun smoke.

My eyes shifted to the Castillo directly in front of us in the distance, and from there, over to the big old cannons in the plaza. And you know what? As I studied those things, and the little family in front of us, I felt a sort of … wave, I guess you would say, of understanding. For the first time, I looked at St. Augustine as tourists see it, I guess, and I understood why they wanted to visit our city. Yeah, me! It was as if the history of the place stood out in my mind like big, flashing neon lights. For the guy who used to hate history, the past had become a living thing instead of just dates out of a history book or words from the lips of a teacher. For the first time I began to see how Carla felt about such things.

When the world around me finally went back to its normal speed, Carla looked over, gave me a little smile and squeezed my hand. I smiled back and glanced down at our fingers locked tightly together—one set stark white and the other light brown, but both still covered with dirt and dried blood. To me, the contrast of the two skin tones added to the physical evidence of what we had just been through and presented me with the most fascinating combination I could ever imagine. I also wondered what Luis Pacheco would have thought if he could have seen us holding hands while riding in an old, rusty truck driven by an Indian through modern

St. Augustine.

As we neared the Castillo, one of those ghost tour trams passed us going the other way. It was empty except for the driver, probably heading to gas up before starting the day. I wondered what the tourists who would soon fill those seats might think if they could hear the very real story of a long dead soldier from 1835, two teenagers and a dream world battle. No, I decided, they might accept some of the tour guide's other ghost stories, but probably not the one about Carla and me barely surviving Lt. Walton's reality. It was too fantastic for most of those people to believe and only the day before, I would have been one of them.

Lobo didn't stop at my house or at Carla's. Instead, he pulled up to his big old aluminum gate. I figured he planned on getting us both cleaned up, and that's what he finally told us. Good idea, really. I was so tired and my mind so overloaded it hadn't occurred to me. We sure couldn't let Carla's grandma see us looking so wildly messed up. How could we explain the blood and dirt? No way. My mom would have gone straight to work from her boyfriend's house, so I didn't have to worry about her.

On the gate, Lobo's BAD DOGS sign reminded me of being with Carla on the Fort King Road. One more time, I could hear those two dogs barking and see them coming right at us with Captain Fraser and Luis Pacheco in the distance.

"Here," Lobo said to me. Between two fingers, he held a single key attached to a key ring that had one side squeezed together in an odd but familiar way. From it dangled a shiny oval. Both were an exact duplicate of Carla's all silver key ring. "Open up the gate." It was an order not a request. Typical Lobo.

"Lobo, have you ever in your life thought about asking somebody to do something nicely?" Carla said, but he didn't even look at her. Instead, he gave me that fiery stare of his.

I tell you what, I was so exhausted by then, I wanted to tell him where he could put his stupid freakin' key. That would have been my usual way of dealing with things, but this time, I definitely did things differently.

Instead of putting my mouth in gear before thinking, I thought about Lieutenant Walton and the other soldiers recreating all that killing over-and-over for so long just because of their thinking and emotions. I didn't understand how it all worked and by then I really didn't care. But when I put that together with what Lobo had told me about not fighting my problems, I figured, OK, Lobo old boy, I'm going to use your advice against you. Today I'll play along with your dumb ass little power game instead of getting all pissed off. Little switches clicked in my head thrown by me this time, and it felt good—really good.

When I started to reach across Carla for the key ring without arguing, Lobo smiled, briefly, a tiny smile like the one I had seen on his face in the cemetery. I'm telling you, to see Lobo smile once was weird, but twice was downright freaky. The next thing I knew, he had flipped the key ring at me without warning so quickly I barely saw his hand move. Really, we were so close it should have hit me in the face, but it didn't. Instead, I watched the thing slowly turn end-over-end once and stop right in mid air where it stayed, directly in front of Carla. That's when I noticed everything else around me no longer moved as well, exactly like when Lieutenant Walton's daughter showed up to retrieve her father. Exactly as it had on the battlefield, the air seemed to thicken.

Outside the truck, leaves on the trees that had been blowing in the wind no longer moved. A car that had been coming fast down Water Street towards us on my left was at a complete stop. When I glanced at Carla, she was still looking in the direction of where Lobo's hand once held the key ring. The only things actually moving were Lobo's eyes, watching me.

When everything froze on the battlefield like that, it freaked me out but not there in Lobo's truck. It almost seemed normal somehow. Don't ask me why. I don't have an answer for that question.

But because it all felt so natural, I reached out, gently grabbed the key, and pulled my hand back. Under my closed fist, the silver oval swung back and forth, hanging from its ring.

Carla's head whipped around and she stared wide-eyed at that little piece of silver for the longest time and then looked at me. "How ... did you ... do that," she stammered.

"Uh, beats me." I shrugged my shoulders and laid the key, its ring and silver oval on my leg. OK, I realized all Carla probably saw of my movements was a blur, the same way I saw Lobo's actions a few seconds before. But to explain what I had just done? No way. I didn't understand it myself. Instead of saying anything else, I looked to Lobo for some kind of hint as to what had just happened. His response wasn't what I expected.

"After you lock the gate behind us," he said to me, his fiery old crow eyes blazing even more than usual, "keep that key ring. Once Carla teaches you how to fish, come over and wet a line whenever you like. You never know what might be sliding beneath the surface of the waters down there off my dock. One thing is for sure though, whatever you catch will always be interesting." A slight twitch of a smile pulled one side of his lips upward for a second and then disappeared.

Author's Notes

1. The battle where Major Francis Dade and his soldiers died fighting Seminole Warriors, as described in this book, actually happened on December 28, 1835. That event took place in an area now known as the Dade Battlefield Historic Park, located in the present day city of Bushnell, Florida.

    The following Internet web site from the Florida Online Park Guide gives details about the battlefield's location, facilities and hours of operation:
    www.floridastateparks.org/dadebattlefield/default.cfm

2. Just as in Lieutenant Walton's dream world, the ambush of soldiers in sky blue uniforms by the Seminoles takes place every year at the Dade Battlefield Historic Park. On the first full weekend every January, reenactors in period costumes thrill visitors by recreating the battle.

    Although Lieutenant Walton is a fictional character, Major Dade, Captain Fraser, Captain Gardiner, Lieutenant Basinger, Luis Pacheco and Ransom Clark live again, if only for a short while, during this reenactment. Muskets and rifles fire, a cannon roars, smoke drifts through pine trees and palmettos, and Seminole war whoops fill the air.

    To find information about this recreated historical event,

go to the Internet web site below for the Dade Battlefield Society:

www.dadebattlefield.com

3. In the St. Augustine National Cemetery, the three coquina pyramids mentioned in this story do indeed cover the remains of 1,468 soldiers killed during the Second Seminole War (1835 -1842), including those of Dade's command. Before the remains arrived in the city for final burial in 1842, officers and soldiers of the United States Army then stationed in Florida volunteered one day's pay to finance those monuments.

   The Website for the U.S. Department of Veterans' Affairs below explains the Dade battle, describes the pyramids, and offers information about the cemetery's location and hours of operation.

   www.cem.va.gov/cem/cems/nchp/staugustine.asp

   To see photographs of the cemetery, the pyramids, and St. Augustine, please see the photo gallery on my website below:

   www.dougdillon.com

4. The pen and ink drawing used on each cover page of the book's four parts shows the city gate in St. Augustine as it appeared in the nineteenth century. The artist was a Mr. Ernest Meyers who first came to the city as a boy in 1875. Even though he and his family moved away in the 1880s, Meyers eventually came back as an adult and created enough of his drawings for them to appear in a booklet. That booklet and the original drawings are in the care of the St. Augustine Historical Society's Research Library. One of those pictures, below, showed the St. Augustine National Cemetery and the pyramids marking the burial place of the soldiers killed in the Second Seminole War.

5. The Seminoles eventually freed the slave, Luis Fatio Pacheco, but the United States government sent him to live out west with Seminoles who surrendered after the war. He lived there until 1882, when at age eighty-two, he returned to Florida.

Because he survived the Dade battle, many people in white society believed at the time that he was actually an ally of the Seminoles and had given them information leading to their victory. For the rest of his life, Pacheco fought against such claims. He even gave an interview for an 1892 Jacksonville, Florida newspaper article explaining exactly what happened and how he had barely escaped the battle with his life. The historical record backs his story.

Also interviewed in that Florida Times Union article was Susan Philippa Fatio L'Engle, daughter of Pacheco's first master, Francis Philip Fatio, Sr. Mrs. L'Engle apparently helped Luis when he arrived back in Florida in 1882. Most likely because of her support of Pacheco, at the time of his death in 1895, he had a white doctor and many white people from Jacksonville's old families attended his funeral. For more interesting details about Luis Pacheco, see the booklet titled, The Life of Luis Fatio Pacheco: Last Survivor of Dade's Battle, available from the Seminole Wars Foundation. Here is their website address:

www.seminolewars.us

6. If you ever go to south Florida, consider visiting the Ah-Tah-Thi-Ki Museum at the Big Cypress Seminole Indian Reservation. Here the Seminole Tribe of Florida uses exhibits and artifacts to show how their ancestors lived. The museum also, "Collects, preserves, protects and interprets Seminole culture and history inspiring appreciation and understanding of the Seminole people." In an introductory film, visitors come to understand the dramatic struggle over the years for Seminoles to remain in Florida.

    Listed below first is the museum's website address and second address is the website for the Seminole Tribe of Florida:

    www.ahtathiki.com
    www.semtribe.com

7. One final thing. A monument to Major Dade and his men also stands in the cemetery of the United States Military Academy at West Point, New York. Also in that cemetery is a joint gravesite where both of my parents rest—Walter Walton Dillon and Muriel Dillon Brewer. Dad was a proud graduate of West Point, class of 1942, and flew thirty bombing missions as a B-24 pilot during WWII.

Acknowledgments

This is my unique chance to thank those wonderful people who helped make this book and **The St. Augustine Trilogy** possible. Contrary to usual form, I am listing those people, or groups, separately in order to more fully honor their contributions in a very direct way.

To:
All of the teens I've either taught or worked with over the years
It was from my contact with all of you that the characters Jeff Golden and Carla Rodriguez were born. Thanks guys.

My beautiful wife Barbara Dillon
Without your love and support, this book and the trilogy would never have been published.
You were the first fan and one of the toughest editors.
What a great combination.

My adult children, Nicole Dillon, Greg Dillon and Fred Steeves
Your constant encouragement was worth its weight in gold.
Nicole, reviewing the book as you did from so many angles helped me hone some of those details to a much finer degree than would have otherwise occurred. **Greg**, I take special pride in

your brilliant photography that helped bring the forefront objects on the cover of each trilogy book into such exquisite focal points. See Greg's professional work on his website at
www.gregsgallery.net

Chuck Dowling, novelist
www.chuckdowling.com/author.htm
Chuck, you were the first to fully read and then offer your purple pen edits of this book's manuscript. That went a long way, buddy, in making *Sliding Beneath the Surface* at least somewhat readable in the early stages. Your final proofreading sure did smooth the remaining rough edges.

Sandi Thomas
As one of the early readers of this book, the excitement you expressed, and asking when you could read Book II, told me I was on the right path.

Mary Ann de Stefano, editor, book coach and more
www.madaboutwords.com
Your full editing of my manuscript not only helped to make the book fit to print, it also helped me to hone my skills as a writer to a much higher degree. I am in your debt.

Frank Laumer, author of
Dade's Last Command and *Nobody's Hero*
Frank, your two books played a key role in my understanding of the 1835 Dade battle and the people who fought it. Thanks so much for allowing me to call you asking all kinds of detailed questions. Your patient and knowledgeable responses provided me with very solid footing.

Gary Stehli, high school friend, St. Augustine resident, and artist

You, your delightfully tree shrouded property and our walk past the St. Augustine National Cemetery set the stage for key pieces of the book's content. Your graciousness in allowing me to stay with you and write parts of the trilogy to my heart's content will never be forgotten. The pen and ink drawing you did for me of the Castillo is now the logo for all my books and is truly a gorgeous piece of art.

Charles Tingley, Senior Research Librarian for the St. Augustine Historical Society's Research Library
www.staugustinehistoricalsociety.org/library.html

The richness and accuracy of historical detail about St. Augustine depicted in the trilogy is due in no small part to your efforts. What a joy it has been to sit in your library so many times surrounded by the books, maps, articles, and photographs you provided.

Tiffany McIntyre, design specialist of many talents
www.signaturedesignsolutions.com/index.html

Those digital enhancements you did of the book cover logos and the internal pen and ink art came out just perfect.

The Dade Battlefield Society Reenactors
www.dadebattlefield.com

Your excellent recreation of the Dade battle gave me the feeling I had actually been there back in 1835. Writing about that event then became so much easier. I applaud you all for keeping such an important part of Florida history alive.

Rob and Amy Siders, the book formatting team
www.52novels.com
You two not only put this book in awesome shape, you also guided me expertly in areas where I had no knowledge whatsoever.

Michael Lynch, book cover designer
www.bookcoverdesign.com/bookcoverdesign_about.html
The trilogy book covers are a tribute to your technological and artistic skill. You were the perfect person to capture the essence of each volume and display the needed information. The personal interest you showed in my efforts was an unexpected dividend.

CPSIA information can be obtained at www.ICGtesting.com
Printed in the USA
LVOW10s1326130616

492385LV00001B/37/P